THE WHITE ROOM

CB editions

The White Room

Erik Houston

CB editions

For Kirsten

First published in 2007
by CB editions
146 Percy Road, London W12 9QL

Printed in England
by Primary Colours Print & Design, London W3

The moral rights of the author have been asserted

ISBN 978–0–9557285–1–8

§ 1 *Time stops, and Bjørn remembers a parrot, amongst other things*

IT WAS THE END OF A YEAR NEAR THE END OF A CENTURY, BUT in London, as in so many other places, life was moving ever onwards. In the West End traffic roared harshly, and the usual December cold had been joined by a dampness that, had it a colour at all, was grey. On the north side of Piccadilly stood Bjørn Olsen, who was waiting at the lights, having had the idea that he might be able to pick up a magazine in a shop opposite. Crossing the road he raised an eye to the street's Christmas decorations, dodging people as he went, before walking a few yards along and into a bookshop.

Coming from the other direction towards the same shop was a lady in a beige coat – a neutral tone, yet she never blended with the crowds as she walked through them. Had this lady any idea who she was about to meet she would surely have turned back before passing the Ritz; instead she carried on, perhaps even quickening her step as she crossed St James's.

Once he was inside the bookshop, Bjørn consulted the store directory before walking downstairs. There he scanned the well-filled shelves whilst mumbling to himself through straightened lips. Then, having been unable to find a copy of *European Shoe Salesman*, and whilst cursing himself for having forgotten his copy on the plane, he began looking around for a member of staff, but instead he saw the lady in a beige coat. She was leafing through lifestyle magazines, as if this was just any other normal day thrown in amongst a heap of similar days. Bjørn stood motionless, looking at her. He watched as a heron might watch the water – out of time, transfixed – so that it may have been a second or minute before he came back from the past and almost smiled.

In that second or minute, as Bjørn stood heronesque, a tear formed at the edge of his eye, and in that tear lay a thousand memories. No one in the shop moved, no one breathed; as the present stopped, the past lived again.

Eva had owned a beautiful grey parrot. Beautiful to her, that is. Others found it a bit scruffy, her mother said that it smelled – but none had disliked it as much as Bjørn. Eva thought that this might be because she so obviously loved it. Perhaps Bjørn felt threatened by this parrot. So, every time that Bjørn was due to visit, she would cover up the parrot's cage and put him in the kitchen, where he was less likely to be found and abused. The parrot was quite sensitive to insults, although most visitors thought him to be simply an arrogant villain.

Haakon the parrot had been a seafaring bird. Years before he had belonged to a ship's captain, who had picked him up from a peasant boy in Brazil. The boy told him that if he was to eat the parrot's brain he was sure to develop a much-improved memory, which would probably be of use to a ship's captain. Indeed the boy had only kept the scrawny bird alive this long to ensure that all the goodness remained in the head, and for a little extra the boy would perform the necessary butchery, thus saving the captain a messy task and the need to carry around the bird, which, between the two of them, didn't smell too good. The parrot looked dejected. There was a pause whilst the captain seemed to think about it. Then he took some coins out of his pocket and, having counted them, held them in his fist right up next to the boy's eyes. The parrot strained for a better look. 'I'm going to give you the money for the bird,' he said, 'but if I ever catch you threatening such a noble animal again, I'll beat you to a bloody pulp,' and he produced a small but adequately heavy club to demonstrate his seriousness. The boy fled, counting the coins as he did so, whilst the parrot strutted.

'You smell,' said the captain, '. . . of lilies.'

The bird was taken to the ship, where he was given free run of the place. He would sit on the rails and shit onto the deck as the sailors mopped it. At lunch he stole biscuits from their plates. Yet none dared strike the bird, or even swear at it, as it was well known that the captain was prone to the most fearsome rages and that he regarded the bird as the true first mate of the ship, the official holder of that office being, in his eyes, neither as honourable nor as wise as the parrot, but, quite frankly, a bit of a poof.

The captain and the bird continued thus for a dozen years before they undertook their final voyage together. They were due to deliver a cargo of Spanish dolls to Sweden and all was much as usual until they arrived off the southern coast of Norway. Then an electrical fire broke out in the engine room. The alarm was sounded and the sailors, having abandoned hope of putting it out, headed for the lifeboats. The last man up from the lower quarters was Uri, the electrician. He was followed by the parrot, which looked sooty and quite heroic, and carried a piece of flex in his beak.

'Lord, thank you!' cried the captain, weak with relief, as he saw Haakon emerge.

'It was that fucking parrot that started the fire!' shouted Uri. 'He's vermin, and we should have eaten him a long time ago.'

Uri looked around to the other sailors for support; but everyone sat silently in the readied lifeboat, so that all that could be heard was the slapping of the waves against the hull, and the hunger of the fire below.

'Vermin, is he?' asked the captain, saying the first word quietly so that Haakon would not hear it. The captain got up off his knees, from where he had been saluting God's mercy, and approached Uri. As he did so his hand went to the inside of his coat. Out came the club. Uri stepped backwards.

'Are you mad? The ship's on fire.'

'You're going to wish you'd stayed downstairs,' said the captain.

'Bravo!' said the parrot.

The electrician put up his hands, but it was no use. The captain beat him without mercy. Then, quite unseen by the captain, the first mate approached them. In a matter-of-fact way he produced a pistol, and taking scant time to aim he shot the captain twice. Haakon threw himself at the first mate, but it was too late. The captain lay dead in the soupy mess of his own head.

3

Uri looked at the first mate, stunned. (Shit, you've killed him.)

The first mate shrugged. (These sorts of things happen all the time at sea. Don't they?)

The last two of the crew joined their comrades in the lifeboat and abandoned the ship as the fire raged, leaving the grief-stricken bird to pull uselessly at the dead captain's sleeve.

Some time later, after the Norwegian rescuers had already picked up the Ukrainian crew, a bird was seen flapping above the burning wreck. Using a loudhailer, the Norwegians tried, in several languages, to persuade the bird to be saved. When eventually the parrot flopped, exhausted and singed, onto their deck, out of his beak fell a shiny metal button.

The Norwegian coastguards were hugely pleased with their new pet parrot. Thinking him to be a girl they named him Mimi, and thinking her to be good luck they made him their mascot. The Mayor of Birkesand came to the lifeboat station to be photographed with the bird and to name a new boat after her. Daily, plates of the parrot's favourite ginger biscuits were left out, for all knew that looking after your mascot could save your life. But this bird had lost his love of sailors, and once he had recovered sufficient strength he flew off through an open window, heading inland. The lifeboat men saw this desertion as a black omen. In 1894, when the dog who was living at the station in Unbliksund was run over by a horse, not only did the entire crew perish at sea the very next week, but the church that was due to hold their memorial service burnt to the ground, leaving only the bell uncremated. (This bell survives today in the town's new church, built on the same site.) The lifeboat men of Birkesand had their boat re-blessed by the Bishop. Their wives knitted furiously.

Good luck, rather than any innate sense of direction, took Haakon to town rather than to the west, where lay only vast areas of nothingness. He was soon noticed by the residents, who tried to entice him close enough to grab. Nets and cages were employed; trails of nuts led to lobster pots – but it was only when he flew into the baker's shop one morning, looking for biscuits, that he was apprehended and taken, screaming in protest, to the animal refuge.

Haakon was horribly unhappy here, and between bouts of grief for his master he would find solace in thoughts of rows of Ukrainian sailors being cruelly tortured by an army of forest birds.

Then he met Eva. She cleaned out the cages during the school holidays, talking to each animal in turn. When this parrot turned up, Eva became immediately fond of him, and spent extra time petting him and telling him stories about her friends. Soon Haakon had formed such an attachment to her that each day when it was time for her to go home, he would throw himself on the floor of his cage and feign violent illness – coughing and muttering in Portuguese: 'Mother Mary help me, it's the plague,' or 'My legs, my legs – they are shot to ribbons!'

No one at the Birkesand animal sanctuary knew Portuguese, but Eva understood that she would have to try to convince her father that keeping a parrot at home was a good idea.

Unusually, Eva Thorsen had known Bjørn since before either of them was born. Their expectant mothers literally bumped into each other in a queue at Kristen's Coffee House.

'My God, you're almost as big as me!' cried Mrs Thorsen, wiping tea from her blouse.

'Much bigger, and much less neat – must be a boy,' said Mrs Olsen, struggling to pick a fish-paste sandwich up from the floor.

Thus a friendship was born, and, soon after, a boy and a girl. The girl grew up not thinking much of her little friend who lived close by, and would turn up to play at all the wrong moments. She much preferred his bigger brother Karl, who went out on Friday nights to the cinema on his moped. There was something disturbing about having a friend who wanted to come round the whole time – especially a boy.

One day, when Eva and Bjørn were walking home together from school, despite Eva having dawdled long enough to make sure that Bjørn couldn't possibly still be hanging around the gates waiting for her, Bjørn stopped to watch a brown dog that had been shut out of its house. The dog sat sadly on the porch and stared at a door, whilst Bjørn stood at the gate and stared at the dog.

'I'm not waiting for you, spot-head,' said Eva from a few paces ahead, and Bjørn had begun to cry – very quietly, but without hiding it. In fact, without moving at all. He just stood there sniffing as tears fell softly into his jumper. Other children from their class were coming down the road. Desperately hoping that somehow they hadn't seen her with this idiot who just happened to live near her, she ran, not looking back once, all the way home – but having got there she could think of nothing else but the small pillar of sadness that she had left standing alone in Roseveien. Thereafter, Eva kept her distance from Bjørn, but never called him spot-head again, instead referring to him as 'the short boy'.

In the autumn Bjørn went to a different school, this one a boarding school in England, and Eva had seen him only now and then until, on one such occasion, when they were fifteen and Bjørn was home for the summer, they met on the path by the swimming lake. The path was burnt dry; warm dust clung to Bjørn's still-wet legs. He looked different now and not at all local.

'I didn't see you down there,' said Eva, pointing to the rocks with her nose.

Bjørn didn't answer, which he thought was fair enough, since it wasn't a question. He seemed happy with the silence, but Eva broke it with an awkward, 'But it's good to see you now.' She turned away quickly as Bjørn smiled.

Bjørn was quiet compared to the other boys in Eva's class. He seemed to know something important that no one else did. Whatever it was, he was not letting on. As a result, Eva found herself thinking about Bjørn more often. The less he said the more interested she became. Living abroad had obviously taught him something more about life than staying in Birkesand would have done. What did he know? What could he tell her?

When they were nineteen years old Bjørn and Eva became engaged. Thinking about it later, Eva was always unsure how this had happened. She had said yes, it was true, but exactly why remained forever unclear. Love perhaps, of a sort. As a child, she had imagined meeting someone extraordinary, maybe through her work at the animal rescue centre. There, she should have met a man who turned her giddy. He would have been gentle, despite his commanding height, and he would have fallen in love with her only slowly; then, perhaps on safari in Mozambique, there would have been a ring. This is what she had imagined. Reality lived as a cruel contrast. It changed her, making a stone where there had been a flower.

The first time Bjørn hit her, Eva was so shocked that she ended up doing nothing. The next time, she was paralysed by the shame of having done nothing the first time. Now, she just tried to avoid doing anything that might provoke him. She had never thought of herself as this type of person. She had imagined that she was the sort of girl who would drive a skewer through the ears of any man laying an unwanted hand on her.

'Ha! I can see that you don't need me to look after you,' her imaginary husband would say upon hearing the story, and as they sat holding hands in the evening sunshine they would talk of botany, or how his sisters were getting on running their mission in Peru.

Now, aged nineteen, and back in the real world of un-held hands and bruised arms, Eva was pregnant. At school she had learned that a black hole was about the size of a pea but weighed as much as a planet. She had not believed it until now.

Snow fell. It was New Year's Eve and Eva had been due to go to a fancy-dress party – but her milkmaid's costume still hung in the wardrobe. Bjørn would arrive soon and she would have to pretend that sudden illness had struck. She would have loved to go, but it was now of course impossible. Food poisoning, perhaps? Leftover udder that she just knew she shouldn't have lightly warmed through for lunch.

Outside it was long-since dark. Cold sat in the alleys and street-lamps lit up only passing snowflakes. A naval officer crossed the courtyard with a chicken. They rang the doorbell and were let in.

'Oh, hello Marianne,' said Eva, not looking at Bjørn. The chicken smiled.

'We're going to be late,' said Bjørn, without moving his mouth. He was looking at Eva's dressing gown.

'I'm not coming. I'm ill.'

Silence.

She put her hand to her belly to indicate sickness. 'Udder.'

In the kitchen, Haakon the parrot sat in his cage and looked ahead into the darkness. Somewhere out there he heard a door close.

When Bjørn and Marianne had gone, Eva took Haakon from the kitchen into the living room. There, she let him sit on her knee, whilst she stroked his feathers. Softly sobbing, she began telling him the story of when her great aunt Margaretta had travelled by rail to China, encountering so many bizarre examples of humanity on her way that, upon coming home, she had made an alphabetical list, lest she ever forget. Eva fell asleep where she sat, leaving her great aunt stranded in Irkutsk, in a waiting room peopled by bandits, bishops, and a rather lovely bellboy. In the background the radio mumbled quietly, eventually bringing in the New Year on its own.

Suddenly there was a thumping at the door. 'Open up, lady, I'm a naval officer!' A man on the radio was reading the shipping forecast. A clock said 2.30 and Eva was scared.

'I'm in bed, I'm ill. I'll see you tomorrow.'

'But we've had reports of milkmaids pretending to have eaten dodgy udder. I must come in and check for *nasty lying little milkmaids*!'

He was screaming now, but, from somewhere, Eva found strength. She feigned firmness.

'I will speak to you tomorrow, and then only on the phone. Goodnight.' And she felt surprised at the ease of it all. A large door separated her from harm. If she had realised that this was all there was to it she would have had more fitted when she moved in. After some thunderous bellowing and door kicking there was calm in the corridor. Nervously, she looked through the peephole. Bjørn was folding up a piece of paper and laying it down on the floor. He did so with a flourish.

'I'm sorry,' he said quietly, as if he knew that she was close. Then, in a louder voice, he said, 'I've written it all down. Just do me the courtesy of reading it and we'll talk tomorrow.' And with that he disappeared.

Haakon was standing on the back of a chair, ready to attack, but Eva said, 'It's all right, baby, he's gone.' Even so, she waited for more than half an hour to make sure, before opening the door to read the letter. The letter lay in the middle of the corridor under the only light, as if it was the star in a show that was about to begin. Eva went over to it and bent down. She was surprised to find that it was not a letter but a receipt:

> *17 vodka cocktails*
> *24 pints of lager*
> *1 Singapore sling*

A shadow fell over the concrete floor. 'I've just won a bet,' said Bjørn. 'I bet myself that you were as fucking stupid as you look.'

And there began a horrible grating noise as Bjørn ground Eva's face into the floor. But before he could really get stuck in Haakon was upon them. Like the angel of death, his furious wings were silhouetted against the light, whilst his claws shredded Bjørn's cheek. Haakon was not surprised that Bjørn had turned out to be a sailor. It explained many things. This would be his revenge on all men who would float around the world being wantonly violent. 'Die, vermin, die!' he screeched in Portuguese. But Haakon's many fantasies upon the theme of killing sailors had never included what happened next. Bjørn, hardly able to see through the blood, had drawn his sword and, aiming a wild blow at the winged demon, had sliced him in half. There was quiet as Bjørn stared disbelievingly at the bloody sword.

'Who would have thought that they'd give me the real thing?' he asked.

There was no answer. Moving as if from the scene of a car accident, Eva got up, took both pieces of Haakon, and turned to go back inside. The remains of love dripped from her hands as she stopped to close the door with a foot.

IT WAS LATE WHEN THE BOYS CAME IN, ALREADY ROWDY FROM their reunion drinks. A waitress let them find their own table as they loudly shared their conversation with the bar.

'Do you like ribs, Paul?' asked the square-headed one. 'Horglund, we are having ribs.' Horglund was looking for the bathroom, eventually walking off to check downstairs.

'Ribs,' said square-head to Paul, who was smiling broadly.

Paul sat down and studied the drinks menu. Not much of it made sense. Still, he took his time pondering who knows what? His eyes had already become vacant.

'Lars, will you order me a drink? A Coke or juice or something.'

'Excellent!' shouted square-head. 'We shall all drink Norwegian juice.' Slapping Paul hard on the back, he called for aquavit.

Horglund returned from the bathroom moments before the ribs arrived; they were brought by the same pretty waitress who had left the boys to find their own table.

'Won't you join us?' Lars asked her. 'There seem to be enough for four.' But the waitress had already turned to leave.

'Don't you just love quiet women?' asked Lars.

'Especially ones who bring you food?' added Horglund.

Paul was watching her legs swing in and out of focus, and seemed not to disagree. In fact, he was thinking more about her black eye than her figure, but the bizarre smell of the ribs kicked his thoughts towards more immediate troubles.

'Wow, what are these?'

'These are mutton ribs, Paul,' said Horglund. 'One of our most especialist dishes.'

Paul looked at his more closely. 'They smell strong.'

'That is because they are buried for three months,' said squarehead. 'Then they are soaked in water for two days to removing the salt and making them tasting so delicious.'

Suddenly Horglund got up. 'To the chef who thought of this!' he shouted, downing his glass.

During the ceremony of the ribs, which his friends assured him was a tradition dating back to Viking times, Paul felt increasingly unwell. There were toasts to Paul's mother, the Norwegian royal family, and to Paul, their much-loved arty friend from England who, upon celebrity, would remember those Norwegians who had looked after him so well in the past. The young artist was looking unhappy. Tables and chairs had become less solid. The plate of sheep's bones looked back at him. He wasn't even sure if he was sitting down. His chair, which he may not have been sitting on, was moving around like a small boat on the fjord.

'I'm going to be sick.'

'Paul, you're an animal,' said Lars. 'I thought this was going to be civilised.'

Horglund was searching for a suitable container. 'Do you mind if we borrow your ashtray?' he asked their neighbours.

Resolutely, Paul got up and made an effort to salvage some dignity. Simply realising that he was now standing, now walking, now heading towards the bathroom, seemed to help. He clung to these thoughts as he slowly approached the stairs.

As all this was going on upstairs, Eva was downstairs in the bathroom. She had finished her shift early, having been told by her boss, Ole, to go home.

'You shouldn't have come in, having been mugged yesterday,' he said, with parent-like sternness.

'Yes, I know, but I need the money.'

Ole often wished that he had more tact. 'Of course,' he said, after some thought. 'We all need cash, bugger it. Thieves really need something horrible doing to them . . .'

He was about to speak again when Eva jumped in. 'It's fine, Ole, I'm OK. I haven't been feeling great anyway.'

This was true, she had been sick on and off for some days. She thanked her boss for his concern and hurried downstairs, low heels clicking on stone steps.

It was darker down here, and colder. Eva opened the bathroom door and went in, standing still in the blackness for some time after

11

the door had shut behind her. When she switched on the light, she stood in front of the partially cracked, slightly grubby mirror. Her hands leant on the basin. Looking first only at the mirror's edge, which had lost its silvered coat and reflected nothing, then at the harshly bright strip-light above it, she saw everything too clearly: the dirt on the poorly fitted tiles, the flecks of mould. Then, facing straight ahead, she saw herself. She didn't move and didn't look away, so that it was only as her eyes filled with tears that her image softened, sparkled and disappeared.

Some minutes later Eva emerged and began up the stairs. She paused almost immediately, as if she had forgotten the way out. As she looked up into the smoky light of the bar, and heard the muffled noise of the late-night crowd, the figure of Paul appeared above her. He moved strangely and seemed to shimmer mystically in the light, so that Eva wondered if she was about to have a vision. The hazy figure wobbled before stepping theatrically aside. Whilst gesturing *ladies first* with one hand, he reached for the banister with the other – but the banister wasn't there. Frowning, Paul tumbled down the stairs.

Watching from the bar, two regulars smiled. 'That man's studied classical ballet,' said one, without looking away from the now empty top stair. The other finished his drink – but the sound of shoe on wall and bone on stone was sobering to all and brought a concerned group quickly to the scene.

Paul's head had been smacked like a just-caught trout. Multi-coloured stars were sucked into nothingness. Now there was a feeling of tumbling, as if he was in a washing machine. Then, somewhere, a light came on and the pain started. People were arguing unnecessarily. Opening his eyes, Paul eventually focused on two strangers' faces. This pair seemed friendly, helping him to sit up. There were other people there too, including an older man, who began shouting at them. He was very ugly, so the three left as quickly as possible, the two larger carrying the smaller. As they lurched up the stairs, Paul looked briefly back, and saw the waitress below them.

Paul thought he had escaped with only the smallest chip in his tooth, but awoke the next morning having had the first dream, in what would turn out to be a series of recurring dreams, about a pantomime horse.

Eva woke up with a freshly bandaged ankle; an eye that had begun to go yellow; and, for the first time since school, the absolute belief that she knew what to do next. Sitting in a shallow but scalding hot bath, her bad leg held uncomfortably at an angle, she scrubbed her body furiously with a nailbrush. She imagined her visit to the doctor. He would be able to flush out what she could not.

'Ooo, how did you do that?' he would ask, as she entered his room on crutches. As she came closer he would gaze at her face and ask, 'And this?'

There would be a silence.

'I'm not here about that,' she would say eventually, and the doctor would put down his pen.

Before this, she took Haakon from the fridge, where he was lying in a shoebox, and dropped him over the side of the ferry that sailed twice hourly to the other side of the fjord. She wore her hooded coat. Outside, the day was as brisk as a winter fox.

After waking from his dream, Paul dressed quickly and went to the kitchen. Here, his friends' father was already boiling eggs. So, whilst Lars and Horglund slept on, he breakfasted with their dad.

The kitchen was a mess, with the evidence of the last days' meals spread over most of the worktops, making Paul glad that he would be gone before the boys' mother returned from her dental conference in Scotland: there would be a price to be paid for letting the house fall into this sort of state.

Paul, knowing his duties as a guest, had made more than one attempt to clean things up, but each time he had been heckled and abused by his hosts. Horglund had thrown socks at him when he began to fill the sink with water, whilst Mr Nordveit had shouted, 'Paul, no! Am I not entitled, just occasionally, to live in peace?' and 'Step away from the sink. Step away from the sink, I am armed and dangerous!' whilst waving his hands in the air. Little could be done in the face of this resistance, so Paul breakfasted amongst unwashed cups and bean-veneered pans.

Mr Nordveit offered Paul a coffee. 'You look awful. Was it a rough night?'

'I don't think I'm quite used to your drinks yet . . . I fell into a waitress.'

Mr Nordveit smiled. 'Was she at least pretty?'

Paul held his head. 'I think I broke her ankle.'

'Seriously?' Mr Nordveit's eyes were wide. 'Paul, you are obviously as careless with women as Horglund is.'

There followed a story that may have involved a trip to the zoo and a girl that Horglund had taken to bed; but Paul had stopped listening. In his mind he had already gone, retracing his steps to Eva.

After breakfast, and having borrowed a map, Paul went to the bathroom. As he brushed his teeth he followed the roads back to the bar that he had been in last night. Later he would pass Avedals Gate and Kirkeveien, lifting his collar against the wind, hurrying to get out of the cold.

Standing at the bar holding a small bunch of freesias, Paul was talking to the barman. He spoke in English, which made the barman respect him even less.

'But I only want to say how sorry I am.'

The barman was drying a glass with his back partly turned.

Paul continued. 'Maybe she's coming in later?'

'You broke her foot. I imagine she'll be off awhile.'

'I could send these to her, if I had her address.' Paul realised that he was becoming pathetic. The barman turned fully away to clean a tap. Paul was leaving when a young woman in an apron came up to him. 'I'm seeing her later,' she said, taking the flowers.

Outside, ice lay in patches like lichen on rock. Having nowhere else to wait, Paul went across the street and sat on a bench. It was a bitter morning. He closed his eyes against the wind, lest they freeze. After a while, during which time he was very uncomfortable, Paul found that the best way to be was still. Then, calmness replaced cold. The seconds slowed. Time drifted. He had begun to forget where he was when a girl carrying flowers came out of the bar and hurried off down the street. Paul fell from the bench. Now awake, he stumbled after her, once more cursing with cold.

They walked across much of town, this strangely disjointed couple, until the girl approached an apartment building and then a door. She was about to ring a bell marked '4A' when Paul, who was now right next to her, said, 'I think I'll give them to her myself after all.'

'Shit,' said the girl.

From the other side of the courtyard, and unnoticed by Paul, Bjørn was watching as patiently as a stone. He had been thinking how great it would be to kill both Eva and himself, then awaken together with her in another time and place, where the past was gone. Now, he would also have liked to kill this unknown flower-boy who was already inside, making his way upstairs towards Eva's flat.

That night Paul dreamed of his waitress. He was walking through London, following her, never catching her up, until after they had passed Westminster for the third time. Now she slowed down and waited, without turning, so that Paul could come quietly up behind her and tell her that he loved her.

She had fine blond hair which, now that he looked more closely, began to seem a bit thin – and she had bad dandruff. When she turned round and grabbed him, it wasn't her at all, but a foul old man who coughed and spat as he gasped for air. Paul tried desperately to remove those bony hands from his lapels, but the fiend not only hung on, he pulled himself closer. 'Help me,' he hissed.

§ 3

BACK AT THE BOOKSHOP, TIME WAS READY TO STIR ONCE
more. People were beginning to blink and stretch. Bjørn was coming back to reality too. He was feeling fuzzy, though, and needed a
push. A woman wearing a badge, who was always quick to wake,
approached him.

'Can I help you?' she said, concerned that any customer should
look so lost; and his world began moving again. Shoppers nipped
into queues and girls danced up stairs. All around was the noise of
today.

Bjørn, shaking a little, looked beyond to where Eva was still
standing. He had thought about her often in the time since he had
last seen her, and here she stood only yards from him, the one who
could finally cut him from his past, looking well, and still so young.
She seemed to have fully moved on; he could have simply walked
away.

'Can I help you?' repeated the shop assistant. Bjørn pushed her
aside as if she was driftwood and walked towards Eva, who was
moving off to pay. Catching her up as she waited at the till, he said,
'Hello, I'm sure that . . .' But she didn't notice him as she flicked
through her magazine – she wasn't even looking. So he said, this
time in Norwegian, 'Eva, I . . .', and now she was. She stood, unable
to move, not yet sure that this was happening.

'Will you come outside and talk for a few minutes?' asked Bjørn.

Flushed with anger, Eva met his eyes. 'No,' she said, speaking
English, as if to distance herself from a distasteful past. Then she
pushed her magazine into his middle and started to leave, moving
with surprising grace, considering her speed. Suddenly desperate,
Bjørn shouted after her, 'For God's sake, help me! That was all in

the past!' This outburst only made her walk faster. Bjørn, once more linked to the past by the strength of his fear, roared, 'You know that I loved you!' After a few slowing steps, Eva stopped and turned round. Everyone in the shop who had been staring now looked away, and Bjørn approached Eva, unwatched by his captivated audience.

'Will you have lunch with me?' he asked.

Hush.

She said, 'Yes,' and someone smiled. She added, 'But I only have half an hour,' with enough harshness to leave some shoppers wincing. A few shook their heads.

The strange foreign man left with the cold thin lady, and a banker holding newspapers turned to a housewife with envelopes and said, 'The pretty ones are always bitches' – and then regretted it.

They were out in the street when Bjørn said, 'My hotel is just round the corner.' He added, as Eva stared disbelievingly at him, 'Very quick lunches.' And so it happened that Eva Thorsen sat opposite Bjørn Olsen, ready to have lunch at a less than first-class hotel near Piccadilly. They ordered omelettes and Bjørn talked, whilst Eva wished that she could leave. She wasn't listening carefully to what he was saying, but could see that Bjørn was obviously agitated. His monologue rambled across many confused subjects. Exchange rates, marriage, the people that they had known at school; why China and the USA were bad for business; travel by rail, car, aeroplane; the breakfast habits of different European peoples: his conversation was seemingly random. He eventually ended with a question.

'How are you?'

Eva got up. Had he dragged her here to ask this? She was wasting her time.

'I can't go on listening. I left a country because of you, and I can certainly leave a lunch table.'

'But are you happy now?' he asked quickly.

She couldn't see why Bjørn thought he had the right to expect anything from her, no matter how simple. Nor could she understand why she had come here. It had taken only a very few minutes for her to realise that she felt no sympathy for Bjørn at all. So she didn't answer his question and didn't even change her expression.

'I need to know,' he whined.

She reached for her handbag, ready to leave.

'Just tell me something about your life now.'

Nothing.

'Are you still with Paul? Someone said that you lived with him. For a time.'

She pushed her chair in, and part turned.

'I'm sorry for the past.'

'And you can never change it,' she said, already walking out.

These were the last words that she ever said to Bjørn, and she spoke without a glance back.

After she had gone, Bjørn finished both omelettes. A waitress, who had understood nothing of their conversation, busied herself with a place setting.

'Can I have a Scotch?' Bjørn asked her. 'No ice.'

When she brought it she looked sadly at him. This concerned Bjørn.

'Don't worry about me, sweetheart,' he told her. 'It's over. Thank God.'

And that would very much have been that if, upon entering the hotel, en route to the restaurant, Eva had not remembered her fax. 'Oh Lord,' she had said. 'I have to fax Moscow before they close.' Thinking that this might be an honourable way out of lunch, she produced the letter as evidence.

'Oh, you have it here?' said Bjørn, and he took the piece of paper to the hotel desk. 'Could you send this straight away?' he asked the too-young clerk.

Seeing the vacant look that answered him, he added, 'You *have* sent the one I gave you this morning?' The clerk began looking through the post. Bjørn, desperately trying to control himself, was pointing. 'There! Over there! It's exactly where you put it this morning.'

Snatching both faxes, Bjørn wrote two numbers on separate Post-it notes in large, uncompromising digits. Sticking them on the relevant faxes, he held one up after the other:

'Moscow, Norway. Moscow, Norway.'

The clerk took them nervously. Peeling the numbers off the faxes, he began to dial. Bjørn turned to Eva and tried to look unrattled. He did a bad job of it. Meanwhile, the clerk was wondering which of the peeled-off numbers went with which fax. Bjørn was still looking furious, so the clerk smiled as he ran one fax through with one number, then the other. He thought that this would do nicely, because even he could tell that one was a work fax and the other personal. When the odd foreign couple had gone to lunch he would send both faxes to the other number too. Someone might be confused, but everybody would have everything. Job done.

At that moment, an unsigned, handwritten fax, in Norwegian, came out of a machine in an office in Moscow. A secretary looked at it, but didn't understand it. She took it to her boss, who didn't understand it either, but thought that it might be from Bjørn Åsterlund, the legendary Danish banker.

'I think this is about the Ukrainian deal,' he said, nodding to himself encouragingly. 'Look, here's something about a refinery.'

His secretary looked doubtful. 'Surely that says "Dear Marianne" on top?' she said, pointing.

'Yes,' said her boss. 'Marianne de Brink of Unico Oil? Is she Marianne? I can never remember.' His secretary did not know, but thought she might be.

'Someone's screwed up and sent us the wrong fax,' gloated her boss, straightening his tie. 'Get me Igor Kogan on the phone.'

A few minutes later, the hotel clerk in London was watching Eva's fax go through to the second number. In Birkesand, it emerged cautiously to sit on a small telephone table in the cool, dark hallway of a suburban house. This fax was followed, after a longish pause, by the note from Bjørn. No one was home, so, both faxes coiled round on the same piece of paper and waited in the half-light for Bjørn's wife to return. Murderous misunderstanding was less than an hour away.

§ 4

Bjørn still sat in the restaurant at his hotel. He was the last diner to leave. Tablecloths lay ruffled and marked, like still warm bedsheets. The smell of smoke had lingered longer than conversations. Bjørn felt tired. He felt old. So he sat vaguely, as the aged do, thinking about the present only as a door to the past. Having finished his drink, he toyed with his glass; and not sure what to do next, but knowing that part of his life had reached its end, he put on his coat and walked, seemingly calm, through the lobby. Inside his pocket he hid a clenched-white fist.

Bjørn walked down Regent Street with scenes from his life mixed up inside him. The movement of walking only agitated them further. Soon, he was so uncomfortable – due to this bubbling and frothing inside – that he found himself looking around pathetically for somewhere to rest. A bus coughed past in one direction, whilst cars came from the other. Exhaust rose over people, over buildings and into the low clouds. Under this, Bjørn found a café, ordered a drink and sat at a pavement table. Next to him, freezing tourists finished a late lunch. In front, pre-Christmas London busied itself dancing and shouting, yet Bjørn didn't even notice as he sat alone and drifted towards the bruise-coloured sky.

As a little boy, Bjørn had at first been happy. He knew that this must have been true, as he had kept all his memories of this time safe in a lacquered box covered with pictures of river fish.

Darkness had come gradually, but inexorably, as his mother's vague and unspoken discontent became ugly and more obvious. Early one summer the threatened storm broke. It was the day after Bjørn's eleventh birthday and he was in the garden, sitting in his climbing tree. From here he could see as far as the fjord. Although most of it was lost behind ridges of the hillside forest, a silvered arm reached out far enough for him to see. A bird hopped below him. He was invisible.

The back door was open, and the garden wasn't very long, so the shouting coming from the house had little trouble finding him. His excellent hiding spot was no use now. Each word landed like a smack.

'Oh yes? Mmm. Really? Well, let me hand on a few simple truths. They might shed some light on all this crap!'

It was now that Bjørn learned that his mother was furious with his father for being such a weak and unsuccessful shit of a man. Bjørn heard things being thrown and broken. But his father's response remained unclear. Bjørn knew that his father would never shout angrily at anyone. This was one good thing.

One Saturday at the end of June Bjørn was told by his father that, in September, he would be going to school in England. This would be just whilst his parents sorted out their difficulties. His older brother, Karl, would move in with their cousins, who were also almost finished at school. Bjørn inferred from this that he would be going to England on his own, although he didn't ask, in case it was true. He hoped that, by August, this idea would have been forgotten, just like their holiday to Spain had been. But it was not. By the second week in September his cases had been packed and stood in the hallway, ready to leave.

Bjørn's time at boarding school seemed unreal. All things there happened as if at a distance. Part of him hid; part of him survived by repeatedly imagining his escape. He often thought of his mother, who would be frantic at the break-up of her family. On Sunday afternoons he wrote to her, but always as late as possible, so that if she arrived in a taxi to collect him, he could say, 'I didn't write to you today, because I knew you'd come!' and it would be true.

One day, Bjørn's loneliness grew so huge that he no longer felt it and thought it had gone away. It happened whilst he was leaning against a tree, watching some boys kicking around a rugby ball. He closed his eyes and found himself at home. To check if this was for real, he pulled open a drawer of the cupboard in his hallway and breathed in the pinewood scent of childhood. Under his fingers, knitted socks and hats tangled with each other. There was also the smell of coffee, so his mother must be in the kitchen. He counted three seconds of eternity, before opening his eyes to see what sort of magic tree he had been leaning against. A smear of resin marked his blazer's arm.

That dinnertime Bjørn stole a knife from the dining hall. From then on he returned to his tree regularly to cut it open and let it bleed into his handkerchief. The knife was blunt and it always took some vigorous sawing to yield results, so when he was called in to see the headmaster some time later, Bjørn thought that someone must have spotted him gouging away at the tree. Being mistaken for a vandal was not what frightened him – this would only cause some minor trouble – but that anyone should find out that he was covering his handkerchief with resin so he could sleep at night terrified him. He decided not to deny stealing the knife. He would then claim a great interest in bugs, and that he had been searching for the grub of the Giant Wood Wasp, which he hoped to find under the bark of a large pine tree. This story, Bjørn hoped, would highlight both his intellectual curiosity and his boy-like qualities, whilst not offering a hint of the weakness that walked with him everywhere, holding his hand like a blind twin.

The headmaster opened his door and hurried Bjørn in. He sat him in a chair, which was both too large and too soft. Bjørn slid to the edge and had to hold himself up with stiffened legs. It was very tiring. Bjørn looked at the headmaster. Where he had expected to see sternness, he saw none. Nor did he notice concern or understanding.

'How are you getting on, Olsen?'

'Very well,' said Bjørn, wondering when he should mention the bugs.

'Yes, foul weather for rugby, though. Jolly muddy.'

Bjørn was concerned that the headmaster had the wrong boy before him. He was now at his desk arranging papers and pens, as if he had meant to do this before Bjørn came in but had forgotten. Bjørn looked around. This room was less comfortable than it appeared. A clock beat each second.

'We have had word from your family in Norway, Olsen.'

The ticking was really quite oppressive now; there was not much space for anything else. In the gaps his headmaster was speaking. The basics were these: Bjørn's mother had left home and gone to America; his father was finding it hard to cope. It had been suggested that Bjørn would spend the half-term holidays with Edward Thorpe's family. That they had agreed to this showed just what compassionate people they were. The headmaster felt sure that, given time, Bjørn's father would come to terms with his new situation.

'Rugged people, you Norwegians.'

With a paternal smile the headmaster opened the door so that Bjørn could leave.

When he was in the fifth form, Bjørn was known as a survivor. This gave him an air of authority amongst his year group, but left him open to practical jokes. Cruel or embarrassing humiliations were reserved for the weak. Pranks of any kind were avoided near larger boys, such as Jones or Stevens, who were known to be unbalanced and potentially violent. Bjørn, however, was one of the survivors – they didn't kick up too big a fuss when waking to find toothpaste in both ears; perhaps this was their secret.

These bursts of humour were often unplanned. They might come about after a chance discovery, for example, such as the night that the boys were throwing books from one end of the dorm to the other. Bjørn had already fallen asleep. Some nights he would lie awake for an hour or two, but once he had surrendered there was no waking him. Tonight he was out within minutes and soon was unrousable.

A book fell short of its target: Volume One of *Biological Science* slapped into Bjørn's back. 'Shit, sorry Bjørn.'

Not a peep.

'He hasn't just slept through that, has he?'

Several comrades gathered round Bjørn's bed to check.

'Is he well?'

The consensus was that Bjørn was comatose, and that, well or otherwise, this was not an opportunity to be wasted.

It was early June, and unusually warm during the nights. Others had trouble sleeping as a result. Mason took charge. 'Off with the lights, then all his things outside.' The approved route ran downstairs until an extraordinarily large window beside the locked fire door. The window was opened fully – which required Jones, the tallest of them, to stand on the sill and pull with great effort – then Bjørn's side table, bags, books, light, clothes and chair were carried out and placed under a cherry tree. 'A beautiful spot,' said Mason. 'Now for the main event.' Eight boys carried Bjørn in his bed down the stairs, whilst the runt-like Edwards checked outside for signs of discovery. Even with two boys at each corner it took more than half an hour to transport Bjørn to his resting place outside. The window, large though it was, proved to be a tricky obstacle. Many oaths were swallowed before Bjørn lay, soundly sleeping, under the tree. Then it was only a matter of arranging the light and books on the side table, and the clothes on the chair, before everyone ran back upstairs.

Bjørn did not stir until, at six-thirty, his housemaster gently patted him awake and asked, 'Do you notice anything out of the ordinary, Olsen?'

At the age of sixteen Bjørn returned from England to live with his father. There were several reasons for this. Firstly, Bjørn was not keen to stay in England any longer, and considered his education in love-free living to be already thorough enough. Secondly, Bjørn's father had wanted Bjørn to come home quickly ever since he had become strong enough, once more, to wash himself and take solid food. Thirdly, and perhaps most pertinently, Bjørn's maternal grandparents, after five years of paying for Bjørn's schooling, had spent enough money to make them angry that their daughter had ever had children at all.

Consequently, a sixteen-year-old Bjørn returned to Norway, to live in a house of unfathomable mess, with a father whose head had changed shape.

§ 5

IN FACT, IN THE HEAT OF GRIEF, MR OLSEN'S ENTIRE BODY had distorted. As a result of this, and out of a desire not to be constantly humiliated, Mr Olsen had removed every mirror in the house; he also stayed indoors. So, for a while, this metamorphosis went mostly un-noticed – but now that his son had returned there was someone to stare at his mallet head and gawp at his ridiculously narrowed shoulders. None of Mr Olsen's old clothes fitted his new body, and, although his father didn't know it, it was this that embarrassed Bjørn more than any deformity. His father's jackets flapped at the elbows and jutted at the shoulders. His trousers constantly required hitching. He also badly needed a haircut. Furthermore, Mr Olsen's much-thinned fingers were unable to keep hold of his wedding ring. He found safety for it on his middle finger for a while, but in cold weather it fell off this too. Over the span of a year it passed from index finger to thumb, where it clung on, looking quite unusual and even a bit quirky. This made Mr Olsen happier.

Once his son had returned, Mr Olsen knew that he would have to start to speak again too. He thought that this might come about naturally, since his voice had disappeared only after he had seen Bjørn onto the plane and sent his son off to live unhappily with people who, whilst they may have been cold-hearted, at least were pretty sure that they weren't going to kill themselves sometime soon. They didn't spend weeks in silence. They looked normal. Yes, Bjørn had been better off to go – although it hadn't stopped Mr Olsen wishing that he could have his son back. Nor did it help his voice, which squeaked in shame, even when Karl came to visit. Not that Karl ever stayed for long.

Once Bjørn had returned home, Mr Olsen practised his diction every evening. He waited until he was sure that his son was asleep, then began with simple vowels. Next came single syllables and finally longer words. Sentences could wait. The improvement that these exercises brought about in his condition pleased Mr Olsen greatly:

the last years had not been easy. Early on, soon after his wife went west, he thought that, if he was going to make some effort to stay alive, he had better go out into the world and, somehow, carry on. He took three weeks off work, citing personal crisis, and began the task of remembering how to do small things. This positive start may have been due to some residual energy that had stayed in his extremities. More likely, Mr Olsen had yet to admit that he had been left. 'Come on, Harald, time for lunch,' he would squeak to himself. Then, with great theatre, his coat and wallet were found, shoes were donned and off he trotted into town. This bluster seemed to help hide the truth for a little longer. That he couldn't see straight, or form a coherent thought, was ignored. The voice-box problem might well be a virus.

Mr Olsen is seated at a small, round table in a simple café on a sun-blessed autumn day. He has perused the menu and, having decided on a sandwich, is ready to order. The waiter stands, poised.

'Heeep sandwich (please).' The only thing loud enough to understand is the squeak. The 'please' doesn't come out at all and the waiter is confused.

'Sorry?'

'Heeep.' Now he swallows, gathers himself, and, magnificently, forms the word: 'cheese'.

'Just cheese? Nothing with it?' asks the waiter. Mr Olsen nods, unable to go further.

'And anything to drink?'

Mr Olsen is torn. His mouth is moving, but eventually, lacking courage, he just shakes his head. The waiter leaving relaxes him a little, and soon he is eating cheese. Then, as is bound to happen in a town with a small centre, Mr Olsen is spotted by someone he knows. This man enters the café.

'Hi, Harald. I thought it was you. You look terrible, but no surprise there, considering what's happened.'

Harald wants to swear at this man – an acquaintance, no more – but is unable. Even the bird noises are gone. How is it that everyone in Birkesand knows that his wife has left him?

26

'Good for you, coming out to confront the world again!' (This is loud enough to have other diners turn around.) 'I told Laura: after losing his entire family it'll be a miracle if he survives the winter. "No, no," she said. "He'll soon be back in the saddle." And she was right!'

He glances at Mr Olsen's plate, then looks around, ready to order a coffee.

'Odd lunch, Harald.'

So, forced by his vocal deformity and the feeling that, outside his front door, everyone was aware of his shameful position, Harald Olsen stayed inside, thought endlessly about his marriage, and drank the cheapest whisky. His one need – for a continuous supply of alcohol – was met by a mini-supermarket nearby. The shop assistants here did not speak Norwegian, so were delighted with customers who slunk in, looked at their feet, and never queried their change.

Harald Olsen was now totally alone. Job resigned, he could sink without hindrance.

At the end of Bjørn's first term back in Norway, he accompanied his father to the school parents' evening. Bjørn spent the day before worrying that the stress of this might overwhelm his reclusive father, and that he might, as a result, end up having to carry a weeping man home, slumped over his shoulder. Before they left for the school, however, Mr Olsen had showered and washed his too-long hair, in order that he would look, if misshapen, then at least clean; and on the walk to the school, Mr Olsen had been entirely in control of himself, his only worry being his hat, which no longer fitted his oblong head and kept falling off into the snow. Displaying a strength that gave Bjørn further encouragement, Mr Olsen said, 'Sod this!' and threw his hat into the first bin that they walked past. Unfortunately, his hat had left Mr Olsen's still-wet hair moulded into the shape of a breaking wave, and by the time they reached the school this was frozen into an immovable arc. The many white hairs foaming on top of this quiff made it look even more realistic.

Bjørn, on tiptoe, tried and failed to pat the thing down. As the two entered the school, Bjørn began to fall behind.

'Come on, kid,' Mr Olsen called to his son, as the ice-sculpture began to melt. In front of his history teacher, Bjørn watched a puddle grow. Everyone else, it seemed, watched Bjørn.

At home, the Olsens lived in chaotic squalor. Bjørn took every opportunity to escape and spend time elsewhere. Meals, though, he ate at home, having too little money to sit in burger bars, and too much concern for his father's health to leave him to sit alone and starve. One afternoon, Bjørn came in to find his father attempting to repair the cooker.

'You are more likely to burn down the house than fix that thing,' Bjørn told him.

His father put down his screwdriver and, with a droop of his head, admitted defeat.

'Tomorrow, I'll order a new one,' said Mr Olsen, to Bjørn's surprise.

That night they ate directly from tins warmed up in the kettle.

Two days later, a package arrived for Mr Olsen. 'Ahh!' he said, as if a long-awaited gift had arrived. Bjørn looked on as his father unwrapped an electric element.

'Here we go!' exclaimed the delighted Mr Olsen. 'No more instant noodles for us.'

Bjørn was hoping that this was not the replacement cooker. His father confirmed that it was. 'But Dad, are we just going to boil things in one pot from now on?'

Mr Olsen looked confused, as if trying to work out what the alternative might be.

Saturday was Bjørn's turn to cook. In the past, this weekend duty had allowed him to sneak some roasting and baking into his diet. Now, with nothing but boiling on the cards, Bjørn attempted coq-au-vin. In with the chicken, tinned tomatoes, tinned mushrooms. Having found only beer and whisky, he added a little of both in place of wine. In went the element, and cooking was under way.

The element, however, had the drawback of furiously heating the liquid around it, whilst leaving the rest of the pan cold. Regular stirring was required. So, Bjørn, ever resourceful, took the pan with him into the living room, in order to watch a film whilst the dinner bubbled. He put the pan on the television and sat close enough that he could stir the pot without getting up from his knees. This he did for almost two hours.

'Good thinking, Bjørn,' declared Mr Olsen, when he followed the smell of cooking into the living room.

'Yes, won't be long now,' said Bjørn.

But as the two looked on, the pot started to slowly sink through melted plastic and into the middle of the television.

A small fire broke out – Mr Olsen smothered it with his shirt.

'I guess we'll need a new telly too,' said Mr Olsen later, as he ate from his bowl of salvaged stew.

When Eva turned seventeen, she threw a party. Mr Olsen was upset when he found out – not on account of this party, but because of the one he had failed to give Bjørn. There was Eva (who had after all known Bjørn since the womb), having a carefree childhood, followed, now that she was a young woman, by a great, if fragile, string of boyfriends. The feckless cow. Did she not realise that life was not meant to be like this? Had her parents not told her? Probably they were too busy being rich. Mr Olsen saw something of his wife in Eva.

Remarkably, Mr Olsen did not yet think of his wife as an ex-wife. Despite her six-year absence, he did not feel separate. Nor was he free. He thought that this was what it must be like to have an immovable illness – simply wanting to be rid of it was never going to be enough. In the weeks before his wife left he had even managed to convince himself that things were returning to normality. There had been fewer arguments; he had been planning the return of his sons. In leaving when she did – without saying anything, without her things, whilst her husband was at the shops – she left the impression that she had just popped out and might return at any minute. The house may have been empty when he had returned with dinner that day six years ago, but the kettle was still hot and there was newly sprayed perfume in the air. Only his wife's keys, left on the table by the door, suggested that she might not be returning – and they only whispered.

His friend Nils had traced the fled wife as far as America, but in the Prince George Hotel in New York she had disappeared. Most who thought about it at all, imagined that she now lived in the Midwest, surrounded by a new brood and slapping down a second husband, who was, no doubt, earthy and robust, though perhaps none too bright. Mr Olsen, however, had yet to allow himself to think such things.

Bjørn returned from school one afternoon to find his father crying in the hallway. It seemed he was upset about Eva's party. It occurred to both that Bjørn had lost his father too when his mother had gone.

As soon as Bjørn arrived at Eva's party, he was glad he had not been given one of his own. Waiters had been brought in to serve canapés and mini-crêpes, and nothing on those trays required more than one bite. A caviar-topped blini could come before crab, or after a drink. This was real grown-up stuff. And there was alcohol – a year too soon. And everyone appeared to be effortlessly elegant, as if they did this sort of thing all the time, school being merely a welcome chance to escape and catch up with sleep. And there were French doors opening onto a sunny garden. And there was Eva.

Since he had come back from England the year before, Eva had daily overwhelmed him with her already grown beauty. But he had never said anything. In fact, he had found life easier since he had lost the last bit of enthusiasm in him: and smoother still when he had forgotten that he had some to start with. At this point, which had come upon him at least four years ago, he had begun to sit slightly apart in class. He now kept his, often vacant, thoughts to himself. In England, before rising to the status of 'survivor', he had been seen as a sad loner who was not even making an effort. In Norway, however, partly because he had known many of his class from before he had left, he was immediately regarded as a thinker returned from abroad. That no one knew what any of his thoughts were in no way lessened their depth. These compatriots walked through the empty catacombs that had opened inside Bjørn, and marvelled at the space. They enjoyed the echo of their own voices. So it was that Bjørn Olsen arrived at Eva's party feeling totally out of his depth, yet spent the next hours listening to pretty girls talking about not a lot, then watching him for those much admired signs – a series of small nods, a half-raised eyebrow – that told them that he understood.

It was now that Bjørn left his silent fortress and came out, blinking, into the world again. He did this not because he felt it was safe to do so, but because he was lured out by someone who reminded everyone who could remember, of his mother.

Towards the end of her party, Eva came over to him and asked if he would stay a bit. He opened both eyes slightly wider, before she turned away.

Sometime after this, Bjørn felt the need to talk to his father. This was unexpected, but, having been drawn into the open, he now saw things that he had previously been able to ignore. For several days Bjørn avoided conversation with his father, cutting him off mid-sentence by leaving the room, or turning the television louder if his father came in and seemed about to speak. These defensive measures were inadequate. Within a week, Bjørn burst into the kitchen – where his father had finished his dinner and was now on his third can of beer – and demanded to be told everything.

'Everything is a big subject.'

'About Mum.' The word made them both redden.

Mr Olsen drained his can, then left for the bathroom. When he returned, he poured himself a large tumblerful of whisky and drank it neat, in long single mouthfuls, talking about nothing but the price of whisky until he had finished the lot. Then he re-poured, and signalled, with a flop of his hand, that he was now ready.

He began slowly, remembering with shame how his wife had found him defective in almost every husbandly sphere. He drank more, whilst Bjørn regretted what he had begun.

'She came back at night at any old time,' went on Mr Olsen. '"Where the fuck have you been?" I'd ask her. "Careful, or I'll tell you," she'd reply, more often than not.'

Bjørn was hoping to move the conversation on. This was not the sort of stuff he wanted to hear. But his father had not finished, and would not be rushed, so that within a few minutes Bjørn had taken a glass himself and poured some whisky too. This did not have the anaesthetic effect he was hoping for. Mr Olsen, now on autopilot, went on to say more than he ever should; he seemed to have forgotten that there was anyone else there, and spoke as if dictating ideas into a machine.

It emerged that Bjørn's mother had never wanted a family at all. She had been only eighteen at the time of her marriage and twenty when Karl was born – until then at least she had been young enough to control – but she resented every sicked-upon blouse and restless night, and Bjørn's father realised that, in choosing to have a son, he had lost a wife.

If one had been bad enough, imagine her dismay at the next. Having been brought up a Catholic, she felt she had no choice but to have the child. (Who knows what she hated more – her religion or her husband? In this at least, Mr Olsen was glad to be keeping such good company.) Bjørn had, almost certainly, come about as the result of a mostly awful second honeymoon. Why had he thought this might save his marriage? He was a dunce.

Mr Olsen stopped now, seeming to think for the first time. He lost this thought, but gave chase, nodding to himself when he caught it. 'Yes,' he said, still nodding, 'Yes, that is probably what happened.' The only mystery, apparently, was why Bjørn's mother had stayed so long.

Cheered up by this confessional, Mr Olsen slept well. He woke without a hangover and went for a brisk walk. Bjørn, however, was left in pieces. He had emerged from his cloud of nothingness and been foully butchered.

§ 6

AGED NINETEEN, BJØRN UNDERTOOK HIS NATIONAL SERVICE
and was posted to the north. Eva was keen that he write, telephone
calls being very dull and everyday; and so, to her, Bjørn (before he
even left) had become more romantic – a white figure in the distance, often unheard from, but thinking who knew what fond
thoughts of home? Bjørn was to be her soldier-lover. That he was
not daily running the risk of being bayoneted did not matter. Nor
did thoughts of frozen eyelids or shovel-dug toilets enter her stage.
Instead Bjørn floated above the crass and mundane. He might send
her poetry.

By contrast, Bjørn, dizzyingly close to the top of the world, had
his thoughts firmly grasped by the simplest of things. Living was
distorted up here, the year having been comically stretched until it
had become just one enormous day. In summer, there was light;
now, as winter approached, the longest dusk dimmed, and total
darkness took over. They would not see the sun again until March.
Dark, though, was less of a devil than the cold. Cold ate at them,
and it crapped with them. Some became obsessed with it as if it was
their lover.

The first person that Bjørn spoke to when he arrived here was
Berent. Berent was one of those whose reason had been corrupted
as the temperature fell. Even sleep did not rescue him: he dreamed
repeatedly of dying naked up a mountain. He didn't take one step
out and three to the left of the tent, as was normal, but pissed
straight out of the front. This did not go down well with his comrades. Nor did he make himself popular with his habit of sidling up
to people and coming close, in order to get out of the wind; several
accused him of attempting the most unspeakable things. He became
totally desperate, and came up with the fine solution of buying four
batteries and some wire, in order to convert his boots into mini-
heaters. Bjørn was concerned that Berent would electrocute himself, but his friend assured him that any cattle-prod-like shocks
would be worth it for the Mediterranean warmth that his feet

would be holidaying in. On manoeuvres the next morning Berent began with his usual foot problems, and usual scowl. Then the heaters warmed and for thirty minutes he hid a look of smug bliss under his hood. After this came a grimace of despair, as his battery-powered socks hotted up beyond all expectation, leaving him, finally, jumping all about and shouting high-pitched curses like a burning witch. All but Bjørn thought him mad, and for a brief time it looked like he might get a medical discharge – but soon after he was back, more depressed than ever.

Since Bjørn had gone to the north, Eva had written regularly, but after two months had passed, Bjørn had sent nothing back. The problem was not that there were many pressing things to be doing, but that Bjørn had a great fear of writing letters. He had written his last love letter, aged eleven, and posted it the day before being called in to see his headmaster:

> *Lots of good things going on here, what with the holidays coming up. Although, I'm sure I've learned a lot (especially English) I can't wait to come home and play some handball with Karl. They've never heard of it here.*

It would have arrived after his mother had gone, lying on the side table for a while, until his father found the courage to bin it, having admitted to himself that here lay not a letter so much as an obscenity.

Thus, Bjørn, absolutely unable to write, phoned Eva instead. She made it clear that this was no real substitute, but should be only an extra. Even Bjørn would have admitted that these calls were sterile. Since it became dark, he often thought of Eva as a shaft of sunlight; he fell asleep with the picture of her, transfigured by the sun, burning his eyes. Without her he could easily have believed that it would never get light again. But he did not tell her this. Instead, when he phoned, he told her that he had no idea why he didn't write, and that God it was cold.

One night Bjørn failed to sleep and became overwhelmed by the idea that Eva was entertaining someone else back in her soft single

34

bed enclosed by the warm peach-coloured walls of her very own room. How safe she must be feeling, with big lustful hands all over her, knowing that Bjørn was at the exact other end of the country, encoffined by ice.

Still Bjørn did not write, and now that he had imagined her faithlessness, he did not phone either. Nor did he respond to being phoned. Eva wrote to him in increasing fury. Now her letters arrived like bailiffs, come to take what was theirs. Bjørn had learned early on, from watching his father, that the way to deal with debt collectors of any sort is to refuse to open the door.

'Bjørn, you little shit!' the last letter shouted. 'Stay in Kirkenes going pale and thin. It'll do you good. You have no spine, and I don't need you.'

Strangely, as the winter deepened, it was often Bjørn's mother who seemed to spit out these messages. She continued Eva's theme in a similar style, but added a certain spiteful drama that Eva, being younger, as yet only aspired to. The ex-Mrs Olsen was making herself heard more regularly during these post-poisoned days. It appeared that she and Eva were in cahoots. But, unknown to Bjørn, Eva regretted writing such hurtful things as soon as she had posted them. Bjørn's mother, however, was in no mood to regret these words that she had never said, so continued to hide behind her absence, and curse Bjørn in any way she felt fit.

Bjørn returned home for Christmas in a panic. This awful bitch who was constantly hijacking his thoughts, this callous harlot who had made plain her contempt: she might leave him! It was quite impossible to reconcile this absolute need for her with his bitter hate. He was trying, but it was only making him unwell.

On Boxing Day, Bjørn was out of bed by 4 a.m. Sleep was not going to come – which might not have been a bad thing, considering the sorts of dreams he had been suffering recently – but once up on his feet he felt giddy and ill. He began to pace. If anyone else in the house was awake, they were surely wondering what he was up to. Still, they wouldn't check: they were nursing hangovers. So it was Bjørn who shuffled round the house alone, transcribing strange shapes with his muddled steps, until he was attacked again by a nausea that forced him to run to the bathroom and be violently sick. The fourth time that this happened he gagged away ineffectually for at least a minute before shouting 'Enough!' at the mirror – which had been shamelessly gawping at him.

He vowed to put an end to his present misery.

'I must tie her to me,' he croaked, as he hauled himself along the darkened corridor.

He took his coat, all the time mumbling away about the past, and opened the door to the frozen road. He breathed in the smell of his childhood for the last time, before walking out towards the next stage of his life.

§ 7

ON THE HEELS OF THIS BADLY BORN PROPOSAL CAME A YEAR of love and violence; one was always hiding behind the other, and soon Eva feared both equally. The way the two seemed to mingle and blend, when they had no right to, also had the effect of disorientating her. As a result, she often found it difficult to spot what was heading her way. In any event, such an arrangement only ever has a limited lifespan and within a year Eva saw her love slain. Now, into this post-battle scene stumbled Paul, and he brought with him enough new energy to confuse everyone. Eva had been anticipating a lonely time, a period of bereavement; instead she found herself flattened by another hero. Within days she could feel the pull of the new possibilities. She did not try to resist.

It was now, after she had met Paul and decided to leave Bjørn (but whilst she was still stuck in Birkesand), that Eva began to see Norway only as an over-large waiting room – but a life in England was still fantasy, so Eva passed the time by clinging to small things.

Her new lover wrote regularly, and these foreign envelopes seemed as good as brightly wrapped presents. The first letter Paul sent her, however, was an overly sweetened thing. Had it been edible, Eva's mouth would have shrunk inwards in horror – what good luck it was, then, that she had never received letters from abroad before and therefore could make no harsh comparisons; that she read English significantly less well than she spoke it; and that in experiencing the love of an Englishman for the first time, she assumed that this is what the best of them were like. It also helped, that Paul, an art student, could draw well enough to make ladies blush. He included a small flower at the foot of his first letter. Soon after this Eva told him clearly: less words, more drawing.

In the weeks following this order, large-sized envelopes arrived for Eva. She stuck the contents to her walls. Soon there were horses jumping over houses with birds below and cats above: but best of all was a woman's face – yet in front of this beautiful thing, Eva found herself annoyed. Paul had previously sent a drawing of Eva herself: three lines only, but implying more. It had been better than poetry. But now, when Eva received a second face – this time someone else's – she flushed a different colour.

'Who's the lady?' she asked Paul on the phone.

Paul was unsure how to answer and this heightened her rage. Eva was of the type who speak more quietly when cross, and these people can cause trouble; but today, with Paul thinking how he had come upon such a face, the icy words were soft enough to have been missed, and not slipped upon. 'She just came to me,' he said eventually. But Eva now knew that she needed to be more specific in her demands. Events like this, she would let go only once.

So it was that Paul found himself required to draw all manner of subjects. It was as if Eva was testing the quality of his love. If he couldn't find an African bush shrew to draw her (she had seen one on the television), then how could she rely on him when it came to more important things? But Paul was an artist of the old school, he wanted to draw from life, and this provided him with problems. Rising to this challenge, he often found himself paying a visit to the zoo or countryside. A Norwegian red fish, he found at Billingsgate market. 'Trade only, son,' the entryman said – requiring Paul to look askance and become restaurateur for the morning. But there was more: a stall-holder wanted to know why he was taking notes.

The fishmonger was feeling oppressed by it. 'Yes, that's as maybe,' said Paul, who was moments from completion, 'but the ministry must have records.' This seemed to do the trick, until two fish-sellers combined to tackle this intrusion. 'What's this about a ministry? Show us your badge.' Paul added a last downward curve to the unfortunate fish's mouth. 'My supervisor's over there (point), and he's going to be wanting words with you.' With this, Paul departed, weaving through iced fish, leaving an angry pair of fishmongers to stride around in search of unwelcome officials.

Now, this selfish edge to Eva, that had been responsible for imagining all Paul's tasks, was softening – it had already begun to do so on the rocks of her relationship with Bjørn. On which stones it had been sharpened, perhaps only Eva knew. In the new, brighter light that Paul threw around her she had soon seen her awkward angles, and she vowed to round them out. But such changes are not instant; little time had passed since Bjørn. Indeed, for Bjørn, the clock was not yet officially ticking. This was time in transition: Eva was between countries, almost between men. She was in danger of slipping through the gaps. Yet normal life continued, and with it came the unexpected.

Eva still worked in the same bar where she had met Paul, though now only on some evenings and weekends, as the holidays were past. Paul, who was yet to meet Eva's parents, but was aware in a vague way that they were rich, did not understand why she needed to work – but he didn't ask, having an animal's nose for trouble.

One Saturday evening, on the way to work, Eva stopped to buy a pepper. She intended to roast it later, but was distracted from further thoughts of dinner by a man with an enormous cucumber. He seemed to be attempting to shoplift it, but was having trouble, due to its size. In his trolley lay a baguette, which he seemed ready to abandon. Eventually, after much whispered cursing, he resigned himself to paying for his salad. His jacket was inadequate, and a seasoned thief would surely have worn something longer, but this man had not thought of it, or perhaps he had been seized by a sudden impulse upon seeing the magnificent vegetable. In any case, now that he was to pay for it, he demanded a large bag to go with it. He was adamant that the standard carrier would not do. A larger and reusable one was found, but this cost him extra. He left, snorting.

Eva had followed him to the checkout, being keen to take whatever small entertainments came her way. But this theatre was not over, it was merely changing scene.

The bar. Not so full. Smoke not yet thick in the air. A man enters. He walks towards the barman.

'Give me the money. All of it.' It is the salad thief. 'Quick, or you're fucking dead.'

Mostly, people are scared, but Ole is weighing up his chances of jumping the villain.

The salad thief points his bagged weapon at Ole. 'Give me the bloody cash!'

It is now that the headline 'The Ice Queen Triumphs' is born. Eva, immediately recognising the intruder, begins throwing anything that comes to hand: to start with, ice cubes. The gunman is at once found out, as he is unable to respond. He aims a blow at Ole, which breaks the cucumber in half. Mayhem follows, with everyone brawling and throwing things – mostly at the would-be robber. Eventually the police are called, which saves the salad thief from a nastier scene, with both Eva and Ole keen for a more brutal fight.

Later, everyone is laughing and patting each other on the back, as well as rubbing their bruised bodies. Eva, however, stands apart. She is waiting for something; already, she is an outsider.

Bjørn, who was not yet aware that he was in transition, lurked near, and Eva was not always able to simply pull the curtains shut and block him out. He had invaded her, and the scars she had received during his removal still bled in her mind. The blood washed into her dreams. One-winged birds flew in circles, behind every door waited a killer. It was already past the time to leave.

So it was that Eva made plans to begin again in England and only now did she realise that, for the believer, plans are as good as facts. Simply deciding that change was called for brought relief. Sorting through her possible moves gained her a feeling of control. She now made a life-changing choice. She would run to Paul. He did so many things that made her happy and was flexible enough to change those things that did not; he lived across the sea; he loved her, and was even willing to write it down – several times over, on occasion. Yes, Paul was her nominated rescuer, and now that she knew this, nothing seemed to be in a rush. The present was bearable because it was now part of her past.

Paul, once he had been informed of his role as saviour, sold his bicycle and took a ferry to Norway.

The ferry set sail and Paul was upstairs. He was still nervous at the speed with which his relationship had escalated and thought over things whilst drinking schnapps in the bar. Some people only ever drink spirits in transit and Paul was one of them. The increasing swell of the waves did not distract him.

A Danish woman, almost middle-aged, came to sit and drink too. In Paul's troubled stare, she mistook confusion for loss and thus fancied that she had stumbled across a brother in arms. She rose and came to sit next to Paul.

'What are you drinking?'

'Um . . . Schnapps.'

Excellent. To the barman: 'Two more of the same.'

Paul had no taste for liquor, but liked the atmosphere that hovered above the glass. The thought of another drink did not please him. Still, he lived with the comfort of good manners and could not refuse.

'What room are you in?' asked the Dane.

Paul became confused as to how to answer, despite the simplicity of the question.

The woman responded by answering another question herself. 'I'm in 27. Come along later, I'll be there.' And she sunk her drink as if thirsty, before leaving.

Paul, being young, was now in a quandary. Having come to the conclusion that he had been propositioned, he felt guilty at not having declined the offer. Then he worried that a lonely woman would wait all night for him, and he would not come. This saddened Paul, who was wary of lonely women, and he spent an hour considering whether it would be worse to go to the lady's cabin, in order to thank her for the offer, which he was unfortunately unable to accept, or to let the episode slip from his mind. During this time he returned to his cabin and drew himself from the mirror. Then, at dinnertime, Paul decided that if he met the Danish lady again, he would pretend he had a wife who was suffering from sickness in their cabin. Thus armed, he made for the dining room, but the lady was not seen again.

The evening after he arrived in Birkesand, Paul met Mr and Mrs Thorsen for dinner at a restaurant specialising in cold fish. He arrived, with Eva, late. This was not his fault, as he was born forgetful and could do nothing about it – but it was his lapse that prevented their leaving on time. Still, before the forgetfulness had been remembered, there was time for comedy.

They were dressed and ready to leave, when Eva, by force of habit, looked out from her window, as if to check for rain. She spied Bjørn, stage-lit by a streetlamp.

'I can't believe it. He's out there on a Saturday.'

'Who? The loony?'

'Yes. Let's take the fire escape.'

Paul was not keen. He wanted to confront this shadow that hung near Eva, but he would not do so against Eva's wishes, and she forbade it. Just leave him, she said.

So, the couple, dressed for an expensive restaurant, crept along the corridor (as if Bjørn might have spies near) on their way to open the door to the fire escape. This fire door had recently caused heated words at the building's tenants' meetings. Ideally, it should have been locked from the outside, but been openable from inside, with a fire alarm sounding when it was pulled. This was its function. In the past, it had always been unlocked – both for coming in and going out. Eva had recently found its easy opening to be a bonus. It allowed for quick and unseen exiting. But this lax security angered the residents. They despaired of the owner's casual attitude – he seemed destined never to fix it – so they engaged a lawyer to write to him. Unfortunately for Paul and Eva, the landlord had acted to secure this door on that afternoon. Earlier, whilst they were making love on Eva's floor, workmen had been hammering away in the corridor. The couple hadn't noticed. Thus, that evening, Paul firmly pulled the door and held it open for Eva, causing an extraordinarily loud siren to wail into the springtime night. Neighbours fell from their flats. 'Out!!' was the cry.

'No, it's nothing,' said Eva, mortified.

'Never, ever take chances with fire,' scolded her old-man neighbour, grabbing her arm and leading the couple to safety.

Now, this diversion did not delay them, in fact it may have sped them up, Eva being keen to hotfoot it from the scene in case Bjørn appeared – he must surely have been watching with interest. Instead it was simple forgetfulness that slowed them. Getting on the bus northwards, Eva asked Paul for her purse. He looked lost. 'The purse.' Lost.

Now followed an argument in the manner of a long-married couple. The purse, it seemed, was with Paul's wallet, in Eva's other bag. Paul looked contrite.

Late to the restaurant, Paul shook hands with Eva's parents, whilst Eva explained that there had been a fire alarm. Paul sat down awkwardly – he had been strictly briefed on what he could and could not say, and the thought that he must on no account mention Eva's planned escape to England stifled everything he might have said. He must also come across as a platonic friend, Eva warned, with perhaps a hint that things were progressing. In Birkesand, he was staying with other friends.

This fabricated story, coupled with the Thorsens' stilted English, made for a trying night. Still, Paul gave it a go: At least dinner was already cold, he laughed. The Thorsens nodded at the truth of this.

Later, mentally all set to leave, Eva planned to move most of her things to her parents' house. There was not much that she owned, the flat having come furnished, but some books and clothes were packed, ready to go, along with an empty birdcage. There were also plants, some of which had grown beyond a sensible size, and an omelette pan, and the curtains that Eva had made to brighten the place, and a folder of Paul's drawings. Then, too, there were disks of music and a radio with a broken top. In fact, when everything was out, there was rather more than Eva had been expecting, so she called for assistance.

Kati, Eva's friend, drove a tiny car. It was barely able to fit in two small people and a bag of shopping, but both girls thought that willpower and an immaculate sense of tidiness would help them defy logic. 'If everything is packed beautifully, it will all fit,' declared Kati. Eva nodded in like-minded agreement.

Packing commenced. It was followed by rearrangement, then unpacking and rethinking. Hopes dimmed, until it was found that an African violet fitted into the birdcage, along with all Eva's tea towels, and a tablecloth. Also, Kati's spare wheel was already in use, leaving a space under the boot. Once the girls had realised this, they began it all again, with renewed optimism.

And it was done. One full car. There was now little enough space for one driver, let alone a passenger, so Kati said: 'You drive to your parents, I'll wait here and . . . and go for a walk.'

So Eva drove to her parents alone, which relieved Kati, who did not get on well with them. But whilst there was room enough for Eva to make the car function, especially if she crooked her neck far to the left, there was no way of seeing in any direction but straight ahead, which view was itself strictly limited by the way Eva's duvet had slid from its allocated spot. When Eva came to a junction, she was stuck, totally unable to see to her right. So she stopped, got out of the car, looked left and right, then leapt back into her seat and sped off. Her journey was a staccato one: on the way she amused a lorry driver, outraged a schoolmaster and very nearly drove off the side of a hill – regularly stopping to snatch a fuller view, like a swimmer might a breath.

Now, with her life stored or packed into bags, Eva was ready to leave. In Norway only her mother, father and Kati knew that she was going. Her parents were both in shock and did not offer to see their daughter off – so with no fuss, the next Wednesday morning, Eva slid from view.

§ 8

ONCE EVA WAS GONE, BJØRN IMMEDIATELY KNEW HOW MUCH he had lost. Now that it was too late, he would have done anything to prove that he wanted to change; but whatever gestures he thought up were made pointless by her going. On Tuesday, she had been living at her flat on Parkveien; on Wednesday, she was not.

Eva, in fact, had managed this transition – from victim to flown bird – with great skill. She had obviously been working according to a plan: but not one that Bjørn had foreseen. The first week after Haakon's death, she had been uncontactable. Then, there had been six weeks spent half-talking, during which time she awkwardly avoided Bjørn – but as if accepting some contact was inevitable. Next, when Bjørn, who had boundaries to his patience, insisted that they talk properly, she had said: 'Yes, but not now. We must have a pause. I cannot speak to you yet. If we are to get back together it will be on my terms.' After that, she went on a brief holiday. Finally, as Bjørn was reaching the point where he might have sledgehammered her door in, shouting 'I can't go on without you!', she left, silently.

Bjørn had been in the habit of walking home from university via Eva's flat. Before Christmas he went in almost daily, shared a joke with the parrot, and chatted to Eva about not a lot; but recently, things having become so unhappy between them, he just stood in the street and smoked, looking upwards to see if he could catch any sight of her, even if it was only a glimpse as she closed the curtains. Bjørn had found the exact spot that afforded the best views of two sides of the building. This was, unfortunately, at just the point where the streets funnelled the wind into an icy jet. Nightly, Bjørn's neck was frozen at unhealthy angles. Sleep was often impossible as a result, so he would hobble around his unlit flat at night, looking like the ghost of a recently hung man. These sleepless nights gave him the unwished for chance to relive his fights with Eva. He always remembered every word that she shouted at him, and as he counted them out, drops of coldness condensed on each.

Being alone on those haunted nights, Bjørn's anger did not have far to look for vengeance. It came in from the darkness without his noticing, locking the door behind it, then quietly throwing the key from a window. The first Bjørn knew of it was when he felt a draught. But by then it was too late; he had been found – easy prey. Bjørn had only enough time to shriek, before being hit. Now, unable to speak – his words being strangled before they had time to squirm out into the night – he howled and grunted his way around the flat, breaking everything in his path, before finding the knives. Neighbours heard yelps and screams that disturbed them greatly, but were put down to cats or owls.

What? Was he keeping cats and owls in his flat? Unlikely, I would have thought, yet no one said a word, not even to each other; they were silent in their bedrooms. The only reaction came from the birch tree that had been growing with full vigour outside the block since before it was built, but now withered and died.

Bjørn missed his frozen vigil outside Eva's flat on the last evening that she spent in Birkesand. He had an essay on the population fluctuations of jellyfish to complete, and spent the evening at the university library, before going straight home to bed. The next day, Wednesday, Bjørn was on the pavement as usual, but, unlike before, dark windows looked down on him. Although it was, of course, possible that Eva was late home, or simply out for the evening, Bjørn felt uneasy. He called her parents in the morning, but only ever got the machine. Sure that if anyone knew where she was it would be her mother, he went round to her house, his hands trembling. Eva's mother opened the door. She wore the look of someone recently bereaved. It was the first time that Bjørn had seen her look old. She did not say a word, and after a few seconds pushed the door closed. Bjørn, anxiety-weakened, could do no more than knock forlornly and beg through the letterbox, but the door became a wall.

After lunchtime had passed, he gave up hoping that Mrs Thorsen would change her mind, and returned home to consider what to do. Later that afternoon, having failed to come up with a better plan, he went back to the Thorsens' home, intending to put his foot in the door as soon as it was opened. Then, whilst Mrs Thorsen tried to dislodge this foot by repeatedly banging the door onto it, he would declare how much he loved Eva, and that he had to know where she was, so that he could tell her this in person. But the door was not opened at all, which made Bjørn enraged. He attacked the front garden, leaving a currant bush uprooted and two chairs in the hedge. A week later, as soon as he had managed to fully calm himself, and having, by now, gathered from Eva's contacts that she may have moved abroad and probably wouldn't be coming back, Bjørn returned once more to the Thorsens' house. He intended to apologise and give them a letter for Eva. In the tidied-up front garden he was beaten giddy by Eva's shovel-wielding father. The letter went into the bin. Soon afterwards, Eva's parents moved away too. Families had not disappeared this completely since the war.

That year, Mrs Thorsen had seen everything that was important to her vanish before Easter. How different things had looked only months earlier: Eva had been a student at the university – once she had enrolled, one of the primary duties of her parents had been discharged, and anyone might have thought that the worst worries of parenthood were in the past; Eva was engaged to be married; no one yet knew that her fiancé was a violent criminal, and the world seemed to live in permanent springtime.

Eva had only told Mrs Thorsen that she had been expecting to produce a grandchild for her after this child was already dead in a bag at the hospital. This was not something that, assuming it was possible to believe she would have consented to a termination under any circumstances, Mrs Thorsen would ever have upset her own mother with.

Eva had come round, without phoning first, one afternoon.

'Mum, I need to tell you something.'

(Silence, enhanced by a look of confusion: When did we start telling each other things?)

'It's serious.'

These were not words that Mrs Thorsen wished to hear. There were more.

'Sit. Yes, you'll need to.'

46

Eva stared at her mother, who looked all around.

'I've never told anyone about this, no one. But Bjørn's been hitting me.'

All around. All around in circles.

'And there was a baby. That is, I was pregnant at any rate.'

Make this stop.

'And the baby's gone. I went to the hospital.'

You're not my daughter.

'Soon I'll be going, too.'

Her mother focuses on these last words.

Eva explains. 'Abroad. England.'

Her mother has nothing to offer. She can't speak.

Soon after, Eva ran off to England, leaving her mother to turn to God as the only solid thing left in her world.

Now Mrs Thorsen wept acid. She told no one but her husband about Eva's termination, and, as a result, many poisonous thoughts filled her guts. These had only one means of escape – corrosive tears stripped the floor beneath her of varnish, and each poisoned drop cut a line into her face before it fell; the burnt furrows did not appear fully for several more years, but when they did, Eva's mother knew who to blame. She remembered, and cursed, Bjørn's name every time she looked in the mirror. Her husband, though, became more in love with his wife every time a new gouged-out mark became visible on her cheeks. It was only now that she appeared vulnerable, human. He sat up late, so that he could watch her for as long as he liked, as she slept. Nowhere in this world, he thought, were there carvings as beautiful as those on his wife's face.

§ 9

PAUL, WHEN HE WAS TWENTY, ENTERED THE EAST LONDON College of Art. This had seemed, to everyone else, a rare achievement – most of his schoolfriends having gone to university to read subjects such as English or Physics. But a great and fulfilling career in Art (the details which were not clearly defined in the minds of those non-artists who so liked the notion of someone they knew being so very, very arty) did not await the young Paul. Indeed, by the time he was falling down the stairs of his early life, and into the ankle of his adult life, it was clear to everyone in his college class that as an artist he was an arse.

Perhaps it was simply bad timing – which can be held responsible for so many of life's problems – but Paul arrived at Art College at least forty years too late to be taken seriously. This lateness must surely be some sort of record, even for an art student, but it gained him no garlands.

On an average day, one of his lectures might begin: 'We will today look at the abstract relationship between casual patterns of objects, such as may be seen, randomly formed, all around us – arrangements of bins, piles of "rubbish" . . .' (A pause here, coloured by what may have been a smile, which seemed to ask: did you see those inverted commas?) '. . . in skips or at the edges of building sites, spills of oil or . . . you get the idea . . . and . . .'

But Paul was already sweating by now, fully aware that he had never understood the first thing about art before, and nor would he in the future. He could understand the secrets of mixing colours, developing a sense of form in line drawing, perspective; but this was kids' stuff. His tutor's video of a dead rabbit – all jumpy and cut on a loop – left him perplexed. He had been the only one to laugh, quickly realising his mistake and staring at his hands as the rest of the class turned their saddened eyes on him; but worse: his tutor had praised his laughter, describing it as valid, citing the near hysterics teenagers have after making an ill-judged dash across a busy road – 'The closer the juggernaut gets,' he said, 'the greater the laughter.'

Thus, month by month, Paul was slowly squashed beneath the stones of today's art, until he found himself at a point where just one more trapezoid installation would have flattened him. By the time of his final exam, crushed beyond caring, Paul had accepted his role as one of those at the bottom of the class. In life, a whole load of amateurs, awful at doing what they take pleasure in, is vital to the continued success of a sphere of learning. It is from this base that those with rare talent may emerge. Without thousands of housewives scrubbing away at the cello, for example, there would be even more empty seats at the great concert halls. Comforted by having found his true place in this part of his life, Paul hung on, scraped a pass in his final exam, then abandoned thoughts of any career in this direction. Meeting Eva proved to be a powerful anaesthetic and the rapture that this drug induced allowed him to fall with grace.

Eva's attitude to the decline of her boyfriend's ambitions remained unclear. She had come to London aged nineteen; he was now twenty-three and in the last year of his college course. The fact that Paul was already so far into his artistic demise confused her, but she supposed that many of his student colleagues were similarly insecure. It was probably a sign of the sensitive soul. That he met his obvious disappointments with what appeared to be gentle resignation was all that mattered. She admired his sensitivity. She also imagined that he was suffering some sort of hangover from his disturbed childhood.

Paul had spent his mid-teenage years repeatedly walking into trouble – and although he had been cut a lot of slack by his school (after all, his sister, one of the school's brightest hopes, had just killed herself), his attempted torching of the sixth-form block one night had led to his having to be, thereafter, educated at home (although he remained un-expelled: officially on post-traumatic leave). He told Eva about this in the manner of someone who has now come to terms with their life, but he gave her only the bones of the story, and nothing extra. If she hadn't quizzed him about his siblings – one, deceased – he might well have avoided telling her a thing; this, despite his almost schooled simplicity once she had asked.

He was, understandably, keener to talk to her about his post-school travels, which had been encouraged by his teacher parents, who thought that some time free in the world would help him grow up. Each day, Eva asked for the story of a different adventure. There was the ferry from Odessa, down the coast to Varna, or some other Bulgarian port – the smartly uniformed officials having been vague – which in fact docked, many weeks later, in Durban. A spell in La Paz (which had sounded more promising than it was), which Paul had reached after a seventeen-week bus ride from Caracas, which had seemed, before the event, to be a great way to meet people, but had become a descent into disorientation and confusion, leaving him almost married to a farmer's daughter somewhere in a 'hilly foresty bit' where he might still be living (like a soldier still wandering the jungles of Vietnam, lost to time and civilisation) had it not been for a hippie trekker, who turned up on the back of a truck of caged chickens one afternoon and, betraying her true roots as a history teacher from suburban Seattle, frogmarched Paul onto the next bus out of the place.

Paul had so many other curious tales, that during those weeks following her arrival in London – whilst she was still feeling like a refugee – Eva would spend all her time with Paul, revelling in his stories. He shared these with gusto, but she longed to ask not: How does a sheep's eye feel in the mouth? But: What happened to your sister, how will you ever get over that?

So, Paul had returned, aged twenty, from two years of random discovery with enough recent history to bury everything that flowed, poisoned, beneath – but in a position of such geological vulnerability that it was probably for the best that he looked only at the fresh surface, and prayed for the avoidance of earthquakes.

Eva's intention, once she realised that she did have the strength to leave Bjørn (and by extension, Norway), was to move into a room in a Victorian house in Hammersmith. This had been found for her by Paul, on the express command of her father, who, in his decorated English, had declared that 'If my daughter is following you to London' (his tone making clear who had caused this upheaval) 'then you are going to make sure she's fully safe and has a home to stay.' Paul imagined that his silence would be taken as humble compliance, but Eva's father went on angrily, firstly in Norwegian, then, upon remembering that Paul did not speak Norwegian, and becoming calmer, in English: 'Have you any idea how my wife is feeling?'

(More silence from Paul, this time correctly interpreted as 'No'.) 'She is a usually fully strong woman – she is now crying all days. All nights too.'

Paul made clear his wholehearted wish to help and was soon searching the London newspapers for suitable adverts.

Yet the Victorian flat that he found did not work out so very well.

The lady who owned the rambling Victorian terraced house in which Eva was to rent a room turned out to be a madam. That is to say, especially for the coy: her house was a brothel. Now, this seems a cut-and-dried failure of any landlady from whom one is to rent a room, especially if one is a girl who intends to earn a living in a more modern way, but the brothel that Mrs Lewis of Roseberry Gardens ran, although aspiring to provide a morally sound service for needy gentlemen, became known for its unusual extras, and as a result caused a scandal within the profession beyond that which might have been expected from any place offering a common-or-garden paid-for fuck.

Originally, in the days when the police officer walking his beat would come in during the quiet times of the afternoons for a tea in the kitchen, Mrs Lewis's establishment had been seen, by those who realised its true role in the neighbourhood, as a place of honest, adult relaxation. Almost all the customers arrived in well-fitted jackets, treated their hostess with the same respect as they would have afforded their own wives, and left quietly with not even a smug smirk on their gently shadowed lips. Later, some nasty incidents with foreign men were talked of, but nothing too unexpected, nothing perverse.

It was in the ten months before Eva was due to begin her tenancy at the house (at a time when the need to rent a flat in London was still too far in the distance for Eva to foresee) that the slide from respectability began. Mrs Lewis would remember it as beginning on a deliciously warm summer's evening.

A house on a Hammersmith side street, in leaf-lined respectability, but the ice has run out.

'Sorry, Mr Lafontaine, but you didn't come here for the gin, I presume?'

This question, offered to the room, was unexpectedly snatched at by the gentleman – as if he had been a previously contented lizard who had just seen an irresistible moth pass. Mr Lafontaine sat a while with the wings of the question twitching at the edges of his mouth. Then, having chomped and swallowed it, he paused in thought, before launching into a detailed appraisal of the brothel, and suggesting several areas for improvement. This was not what Mrs Lewis wished to hear, and it came as a great relief to her when a black-haired girl descended the stairs and, by way of a practised glance, bid the gentleman to follow her.

'. . . and the question of the kissing?' Mr Lafontaine asked, in all seriousness.

Mrs Lewis was not prepared to discuss the matter.

'I am not alone in my thoughts, madam, I am not alone,' and he allowed himself to be led away by the girl: away from an iceless gin, to a kissless screw.

Mr Lafontaine did not sleep at all that night; in the folds of his bedclothes grew rebellion.

It was four weeks later that Mr Lafontaine returned to Roseberry Gardens, and during this time he had abstained from all but the matrimonial bed. He had made sure that he was not the only one, and he felt the weight of his achievement in the dignified silence with which he was met at the door.

'You have made your point well this time, Mr Lafontaine,' said Mrs Lewis, once they were seated in the reception room. 'But how you came to know so many of my customers, is beyond me.'

She offered him a drink.

'Yes, a complete mystery,' he said, his eyebrow twitching with pride. 'Still, I think that this kissing might bring new glory to this old place. Quite a coup.'

Mrs Lewis imagined how this man's wife must have suffered. Her own gift to each house was twofold, she thought. First, she had a role in supplying an air of grace and calm to the bank managers and executive-class men who might otherwise be too jumpy for the good of others; second, she sincerely hoped, she lessened the demands made on such women as Mrs Lafontaine.

'It didn't go down at all well with the girls,' she offered as she turned and left.

No indeed, the staff at Roseberry Gardens were far from impressed, and an increase in charges had to be levied to offset the incentives that Mrs Lewis had to offer her workers for the provision of this extra service. 'Disgusting,' said one. 'If I had known this is what you were leading me into,' said another, 'I would never have started.'

But the clients were uproarious in their celebrations at this new service. Glorious, uplifting and enlightened, were just three happy comments.

'Sex as God intended,' was the consensus.

Yet it was from the clients that the trouble began. They started asking for extra kissing; kissing before the act; and, most upsetting-ly of all, kissing without the act.

'Lord help us!' demanded Mrs Lewis. 'Half an hour of kissing? What kind of perverts are these men?'

Although she stuck at her business for months more, three weeks before Eva was due to begin renting the side flat with its own entrance Mrs Lewis admitted defeat and gave all her girls notice that in six weeks they would have to find employment else-where. She put the house on the market, and within days disap-peared, disillusioned with her whole life, leaving only unpaid bills and one word, which she posted on watermarked white paper to all her client's wives: Treachery.

So it was that Eva arrived in London one Wednesday and made her way to Hammersmith: along the straight, left towards trees, a lit-tle wiggle – to be met by a closed-up house, for sale, gone from her path; leaving only one option in her mind: to move in with Paul (who saw this as a sign that they were, and always had been, meant to be together).

Eva arrived at Paul's flat (less than five months after meeting him) with the strange feeling that she had already lived out an entire

53

existence and that she was now in some sort of afterlife, a bonus, to be enjoyed or endured as she saw fit. Yet, though she had run according to a well-thought-out plan, spies from her remembered past reached out and found her still, although she had left a forwarding address only for her father, who would have passed it on to no one – except to her mother, who would never have asked. These agents of unhappiness would cajole, tease or threaten her, depending on when and where they found her: weaselling from the empty seat next to her on the flight to England; laughing with their scab-throated cackles when she sat in awkward silence next to Paul on the tube, her cases held around her like sandbags; whispering through taught lips in the hours of night when Eva could see her way neither back nor forward.

Days, though, were lived in more easily. And during that time, whilst a warm spring became a hot summer, Eva and Paul achieved a rare happiness.

§ 10

NOW ALONE, BJØRN WAS IRRETRIEVABLY LOST. HE STOPPED going to lectures and instead set himself the task of finding a job that required no teamwork, no qualifications, and as little thought as possible. He found this work at the fish-processing factory, where he was shown how to gut and fillet a fish in less than twenty seconds. The cold of the North Sea had not yet been allowed to leave the bodies of these fish, and Bjørn found this very therapeutic. The first ten minutes of each shift were uncomfortable, but after this came a wonderful numbness that left him able to use his fingers in only the most rudimentary way. He hoped that this feeling would spread up his arms and throughout his entire body.

Now that he had no intention of carrying on with real life, Bjørn found forgetful refuge in the beds of women. With their help he planned to make a lucky-charm necklace to counter the darkness of his dreams. Each girl would contribute a bright bead. He would collect these and add them onto his string one by one until he had been doing it long enough to forget why he had started in the first place. Bjørn liked his plan, and implemented it with such vigour that soon there were beads everywhere. Consequently, he made not only the necklace, but also a rosary, on which he could hail Mary, and amongst others: Ingrid, Hanne, Hilde, the Lundstrøm sisters, Ragnhild and Magnhild; and Marianne.

Bjørn passed Ingrid most mornings as he walked back from his work at the fish factory. He would usually see her somewhere between the vegetable market and the Hotel Norge. Sometimes they had smiled at each other. One day, instead of walking straight home, Bjørn stopped in Olav's square, sat at the base of the statue of the King, and waited for this pretty girl to walk straight towards him. By eight fifty-five he was already cross at her lax punctuality, but still he waited. He hoped that he did not smell strongly of fish. Cold, fresh fish smell of pebbles, but Bjørn knew that some girls could be funny about these sorts of things. He tried to detect an odour on his thawing hands.

Just after nine, she appeared. Bjørn got up and placed himself in her way, looking straight at her as she came nearer. He wondered if she would just walk around him, which would have been embarrassing, but, instead, she stopped without fuss.

'I've seen you so often, yet don't know your name,' he said, as if he needed to apologise for not being clever enough to guess it.

'Ingrid.'

'Well, Ingrid, I wonder if you would have dinner with me?'

She looked at him. He was not smartly dressed, but his eyes seemed very alive, and he smelled of the deep sea, as her father had done. She hesitated to say no straight away, so said, 'I don't think my boyfriend would like it.'

'He can come too!' exclaimed Bjørn, as if delighted by the idea. 'Is he interesting, like you? We will become great friends, I know it.'

The next week they had dinner, without her boyfriend. Bjørn remained well mannered and friendly throughout, as if he wanted nothing more than mealtime company. Then, outside the restaurant, he kissed her briefly on the lips, and said goodnight.

She phoned the next day and asked when they might next meet. 'How about lunch tomorrow?' Bjørn suggested.

During the following days, Ingrid revealed herself to be great fun. Bjørn got to know her, not through conversation, but by making love to her – mostly in the middle of the day, and always outside.

This lunchtime love suited Ingrid well, since she had an hour off work, and spent most evenings with her boyfriend. Bjørn, however, was soon finding the timing annoyingly predictable. He did not like being conveniently fitted into Ingrid's working days, and began imagining that she had pencilled him into her desk diary in between a meeting with the marketing department and a spell of audio-typing. Worse – during this time, Bjørn constantly feared that his insides were going to fall out from the gaping hole in his stomach that no one else seemed able to see. His experiments with tight-fitting vests and homemade corsets had helped not a jot – he was only ever free from the fear of a messy end when a girl had her arms tightly around his ribs.

'Squeeze harder!' he begged, as he felt his liver slip. 'Link your hands!'

Ingrid looked perturbed. 'Look, I don't do weird.'

One morning, against the run of the tide, Ingrid turned up at the fish factory and insisted that she wanted to have sex with Bjørn as soon as he was available. This should have been to Bjørn's liking, but, even though it was July, the wind in the car park was cold so early in the morning, and afterwards Bjørn felt pain in his kidneys that lasted for several days.

After only a few weeks, Bjørn found that the pleasure of screwing someone else's girlfriend in and around the parks of Birkesand had grown thin indeed. He phoned her at home one Sunday afternoon. She was obviously unable to speak freely.

'I think we should stop this,' he said. 'Your boyfriend wouldn't like it.'

After Yvette and Sonja came Ragnhild. Years after his affair with Ragnhild was over, Bjørn was unexpectedly reminded of the taste of her. Sitting alone in a Copenhagen restaurant watching the steam rise from his plate, he breathed in and was sad. He realised only then that the slightly bitter, yet inexplicably attractive taste of her kiss was garlic. Surprised by the force of this sudden memory, Bjørn had been unable to eat more than a few forkfuls. As he watched his dinner grow cold, he remembered that everything he had loved about Ragnhild had that same hint of bitterness.

Ragnhild was six feet tall, with black hair that seemed to eat the light in a room, and jade-like eyes that gave it all back out again. Even more compelling than her looks was her unpredictable and disturbing personality. Bjørn met her at evening photography classes, which although held at the school of art, were free to the students of the university. He had stopped attending his university lectures some months before but still had a student card and thought that there could be no finer place to meet interesting and sensitive lovers than here. He soon had cause to doubt his optimism, however, being very disappointed by the turnout at the first lesson. There were five of them in total, the two ladies of the group attending only because the cycling that both had been enjoying since their retirement ten years before had become too much of a strain on their arthritic knees. They were charming women, yet Bjørn saw in them the grim future that awaited any man who married a Norwegian girl who was fond of cake. Romantically frustrated, but always having enjoyed taking pictures, Bjørn decided to stay anyway. They talked about darkrooms that evening.

Bjørn's employment at the fish factory ceased the next day. He had displeased his boss over a period of many weeks by being repeatedly late, or absent altogether. This had not even been passed off as minor illness, and it was this lack of courtesy that annoyed his boss most. Taking time off sick to recover from drinking sprees or personal disappointments was the right of every worker, but such a brazen lack of any excuse gave his boss no way out. He had to act, which was very unfair. Bjørn was called in to be officially reprimanded. The next day he didn't bother to go back. He had, as usual, a filleting knife in his hand, but, instead of standing amongst dead fish, he sat on his own kitchen floor quietly cutting open his arm. Strangely, this seemed to help. Just the sight of the blood was very calming. He closed his eyes and let worms and beetles crawl out too. Centipedes writhed in amongst them as the whole offal-like mess slopped onto the floor.

At the next photography class Bjørn arrived early, ready to connect with the better side of himself. Also waiting was a newcomer. She was silent and Bjørn was unnerved.

'Are you, perhaps, tonight's model?' he asked, as if this might be a nice light little opening that would relax them both. Tonight's model looked somewhere between furious and amused. Bjørn had never seen such confused eyes. 'No,' she said. Then silence. During class, the new girl sat still as a pebble, but afterwards, Bjørn having managed a remarkable and disarming apology, she agreed to be taken out. That evening began the affair that Bjørn would always regard as a marker in time.

It seemed natural to Bjørn that, after he had begun seeing Ragnhild, he should photograph her. She was asleep one morning when he made his first effort. Having awoken early, Bjørn began to tidy Ragnhild's flat. He was sure this would be much appreciated. Within minutes, his efforts had uncovered many unusual objects. They perplexed him – yet he did his best to find drawers for nit combs and cupboards for garden trowels. He awaited Ragnhild's gratitude, but she slept on. Realising that this might be a good time to capture her image, Bjørn opened his camera and loaded a new film. He sat at the end of the bed and looked along her long legs, over her hips, a fall, a rise to her shoulder, then all that darkest hair falling about the pillow. He saw her nose, mouth, and knew then that he would never be able to record her beauty. It wasn't a well-cut magazine face. It was all that he knew of life in one place; he didn't even try to cage it. Instead, he worked to capture the atmosphere of that morning, as a girl he didn't know he loved lay sleeping, with him at her feet.

Ragnhild woke to the sound of the camera's shutter. She smiled when she saw what Bjørn was doing, as if pleased that he considered her worth the effort – but she didn't ask to look when the film had been developed. This remained their unspoken agreement.

Bjørn would be allowed to photograph Ragnhild in any situation, as long as he didn't expect her to pose, and she would not ask to see the resulting pictures, being content to watch the hungry admiration in her lover's eyes.

Over the next weeks, Bjørn developed dozens of films. He took Ragnhild as she chopped onions in the kitchen, as she bathed, as she slept in a chair. He became quietly addicted to seeing her through a lens. Her ankles, the curve of her back (her back!), her armpits, they were all he needed from life. Ragnhild had noticed this – and how he now seemed to enjoy following the line of her breast with a camera more than with his hands. Something had changed in him. More likely, she had failed to notice the obvious all along. He was a scientist, not a lover. A cheat too, because this had not been the deal. She was being viewed, rather than admired. Bjørn shot her not because he found her attractive, but because he was fascinated by her ugliness. The look on his lips as he starred at her thighs seemed suddenly offensive. He was looking at her with disgust. Her fat ankles and squat toes were worth putting on film, but not touching. How long was it since he had wanted to feel the shape of her ear in his mouth? Her too large serving-dish ears, which smelled of wax? He documented them as he might a spider or an oddly shaped fungus. One morning when Bjørn was out Ragnhild took his camera, spare films and the precious second-hand lens that he still hadn't paid off, and threw them in the bin. This did not seem to be enough, so she put the bin in a bigger bin and left it outside on the street.

Bjørn did not take the loss of his things well. He was not used to being more rational than his partner, and it disturbed him greatly. She would smash her favourite things if he didn't let her have her way. She became so cross when the gas lighter didn't work, that it took seventeen broken matches to start the strange-smelling heater that threatened nightly to kill them both. Life was lived on edge: but this was someone else's cliff-top. Within two months, he found that he could bear no more of this ruinously passionate woman, and began his retreat.

*

Meeting Birte was merely a catalyst to the inevitable. Bjørn had been introduced to her by his brother Karl, and, now that he planned to escape Ragnhild, he saw nothing wrong with beginning a relationship elsewhere. It was simply a matter of timing. Although he knew he would never feel as passionately for Birte as he did for Ragnhild, Bjørn thought that there would be compensations: like waking gently and lying in bed without worrying that Ragnhild was in the bathroom looking for pills. He also hoped that Birte, being ten years older than him, would surprise him in bed. It took several weeks for him to realise that she was not just waiting to get to know him better, before abandoning her reserve. She never would be up to much.

During this time, Bjørn was unthinking and careless; but letting a woman like Ragnhild discover this affair for herself was unwise. She called him one evening, just as he was about to leave his flat and have dinner with Birte. Standing next to his front door, dressed in a coat, and holding the phone receiver in a gloved hand, he wondered why he always picked up ringing phones. He should have learned by now to approach them more cautiously. Instead of skipping down steps on his way to a night with his new girl, he found himself connected with this old one. They had not spoken for two days, Bjørn having been busy helping his brother fit some new cupboards.

'Come round,' Ragnhild commanded. 'I want to make love.'

'Well, I'd like to, but I'm on my way over to Karl.' There was not much regret in his voice.

'Then come round afterwards, idiot.' She was doing well to control herself. 'I'm going to wait up as long as necessary. By the time you get here I'll be absolutely desperate.'

Unsurprisingly, the thought of a desperate Ragnhild was too much for Bjørn to resist. This would be his final time with her and he was looking forward to it. He left for dinner with renewed haste.

Birte had spent the afternoon cooking. She shared a house with friends and had taken care to consider this when planning the evening. She wanted to get everything right and knew from experience that an intimate dinner in this environment was possible only if the whole thing had been carefully thought through and all precautions taken. Her four housemates were either out or shut in their rooms. A scented candle masked the smell of damp, whilst the kitchen and bathroom had been re-cleaned at the last minute to guarantee piece of mind. No one's washing could be seen.

Birte had devoted hours to making a deliciously subtle fish curry. Where she had found lime leaves and fennel seeds, her friends did not know. It was clear that this youngster-brother of a friend had got to her.

Bjørn arrived with flowers, an excellent start; and he ate heartily. He could not have put more food away if he had been feasting before a prize-fight. But then, immediately after dinner, he got up to leave. Birte was very upset. For an awkward moment she seemed about to cry.

'But I thought you were staying?'

'No, my cousin phoned just as I was leaving, and she was in a terrible state. She'll be totally desperate now. I can't just leave her like that.'

When Bjørn arrived at Ragnhild's flat, still gently smelling of coconut, he was ready for a crazed encounter. He got one. Already having anticipated fury before passion, Bjørn concentrated on looking harassed, yet contrite. He waited outside Ragnhild's front door until he was sure that the look he had achieved was just right, then rang the bell.

Ragnhild opened the door dressed in black. All around were broken things. Plates, pictures, electrical equipment – all lay about the floor in pieces. Furniture had been shredded; a burnt curtain had sent soot across the ceiling.

'Jesus Christ, Ragnhild, have you had intruders?' Bjørn slowly entered the flat. He knew now that he was in serious trouble. As he looked around the scene, and thought how best to play the situation, Ragnhild hit him from behind with a fishing priest. Designed to kill a salmon, it only dazed Bjørn. A second blow brought him to his knees and a third knocked him out. She spared him a fourth, but when Bjørn awoke, he did so without his left little toe, which she had cut off with a pair of pruning shears.

*

Two weeks later, Bjørn made his first break with the past. Birte – who now that she was his only girlfriend seemed increasingly, indeed, alarmingly dull – had been talking about her childhood. Bjørn, who had not been paying complete attention, was suddenly ambushed by a question that usually he would have sidestepped. It was about his mother, a woman that he had not seen or heard of since she ran away across the sea, when he was eleven years old.

'Where's your mother now?' Birte asked. 'Your father, you say, lives alone.'

'My mother's dead,' said Bjørn, who was not thinking about anything other than Ragnhild. It was only after he heard himself say this, that he was shocked, and realised that, although it was most likely that she was not, to him his mother was indeed dead. And so, that day, whilst his mother did who knew what, over the ocean, in her new world, Bjørn buried her. He gave her no flowers or eulogy, but only the past, which now fell from him into the open grave.

The one mourner at this hasty funeral had begun to look terribly peaky, with a sweat rising from his cold forehead, and Birte, who was most particular about this sort of thing, insisted that he go to bed immediately. This could develop into a fever, which was always dangerous. He was probably still weak from his gardening accident. She went at once, leaving Bjørn alone with his vacant future and lost past. As he lay on his bed, he remembered a humid summer's afternoon, years before.

There is an empty garden, not well kept. Now a bird arrives to rustle about under the larger of two pine trees. A sound, and movement in the tree, sends the bird off elsewhere. There is someone here after all. It's a boy. He's in the tree. From his vantage point, he can see far further than anyone might have supposed. In fact, the heat of the afternoon is distorting the horizon, so it's difficult to tell if the view ends at all. Someone with his feet on the ground could never guess that, from up here, one can see eternity.

There's no one else about, and, in this silent picture, there does not seem to be much going on: but this moment is special. This is the place that the boy in the tree will spend years trying to find. It is here and it is now that his childhood ends.

Years later, as an adult fresh home from a funeral, lying on a bed, Bjørn has returned: and so begins his blind search for the future, from where he can start his life again, from where he will once more be able to look out from a height and see the whole world in one garden.

§ 11

FOLLOWING THE DEMISE OF HAMMERSMITH'S MOST ELEGANT knocking shop and the resultant accidental acceleration of their relationship, Paul and Eva each experienced the sort of romantic euphoria that life keeps in reserve for the young. Both of them had received a battering that year – Eva in a more literal sense – and the love they felt for each other had been heightened by this, leaving Eva often dizzy and Paul prone to feelings of enormous strength and invulnerability.

This rapture, unchecked by real life, led to a sudden marriage and a peak of happiness that, had it been mapped, would surely have shot skywards in imitation of the printout of a heartbeat. That they should marry so soon, in such haste, when surely they had many years in front of them, could be seen as the rash impetuous-ness of youth, or the acceptance of a romantic inevitability. Which was true is hard to say. Still, Eva had dreamed of marriage to a man who made her giddy and she had certainly been feeling disorientat-ed since the beginning of that year – and she had met Paul at the onset of this imbalance, though whether he had been the cause of her mood swings, her flushes and her irregular pulse was not cer-tain. And that Paul should wish to marry Eva should be no sur-prise: all other futures had withered in his mind within days of them meeting; Paul could contemplate none other. Their marriage ambushed them on a July afternoon.

One evening, Paul, who had been dreaming, opened his eyes to find Eva wrapped in shadow. She was possibly just tired, but Paul suddenly saw that Eva was quite out of place in his basement flat. Feeling that he must do something about this, but having no other living quarters to offer her, he stood up and exclaimed, 'Tomorrow we will go boating!', then sat down in surprise.

'Where?' asked Eva, excitedly.

'I don't know, I've never been,' admitted Paul. 'Still, it's a great idea isn't it?'

Eva nodded her agreement whilst Paul looked for a map. The map book, a recent present from his father, was of southern England and showed which activities were possible at different locations. Paul's father had hoped to encourage his son towards a more active lifestyle. There were horse symbols running at Epsom and Sandown; fish jumping in Hanningfield and Bewl; and rowing boats skittering over rivers and lakes on almost every page – so whilst Paul sat on their small sofa, Eva reclined, letting her legs dangle over his knees.

'Read me place names,' she said. 'Then I'll decide.'

Paul flicked through the book. His list was punctuated by page turns, which allowed Eva to weigh each place's name for beauty and promise.

'Marlow. Tamefield.' (Fiddle with pages.) 'Sketterbury. Walthamstow.'

Eva quickly sat up. 'Walthamstow!'

'Walthamstow? You're kidding me?'

'No. It is easily the best sounding so far.'

'It sounds terrible. Are you sure that you prefer it to, say, Marlow?' (Marlow, Paul let fall from his tongue in the way that he imagined a Shakespearean actor might.)

'Yes, Walthamstow. It sounds so romantic – let's go there.'

So it was that on a quiet weekday morning Eva and Paul hired a rowing boat on a pond in Walthamstow. They wobbled dangerously on entry, then splashed their way around an island to the far side. Paul was not a natural rower – a truth that had remained unconfirmed until that day – and he now spent some time trying to adjust his rowlocks, until it became apparent that they were functioning perfectly and the cause of the boat's slow progress must be hidden elsewhere. Then Paul lifted his eyes, and he saw that Eva was looking at him. She had been watching his faffing with a level of fascination that most would have reserved for a fine magician or concert pianist. Then Eva was unsteadily on her feet, so Paul moved across his seat to let her sit beside him.

'I'm a hopeless rower: totally uncoordinated. Still, can you imagine what fun I'll be on ice skates?'

Eva was smiling as she leant across and kissed him. This entailed her leaning uncomfortably on her right hand, so, as they were the only rowers on the pond that Tuesday morning, and they had drifted behind a small island, she moved to sit astride her lover and kiss from a better angle. This left Paul nastily pinched; he distracted himself by undoing the buttons of Eva's top and then the clasp of her bra. He stopped for a moment and found that the whiteness of her breasts had become one with the dazzle of the sun off the water.

A scene we all live for, yet Eva cannot have been lost in it, as she had the suspicion that she had heard someone laugh. She raised her head from where it had been resting on Paul's to see five boys on the nearest shore, watching. A larger boy hit a smaller one, possibly as punishment for laughing, then shouted, 'Come on, darling, show us all!'

Eva, fumbling with her blouse, shouted back at them in Norwegian. Paul, meanwhile, had disentangled his arms and begun to row in a circle – Eva still straddling him. Once this circle had straightened itself and veered to the left, the two lovers were once more out of sight.

Then there was time for Paul to stop beating the water and stare at Eva in wonder: 'Goodness. You talk like a fishwife.' He nodded approvingly. 'Yes. I quite like it.' Eva turned pink, then began to laugh. 'Your Norwegian is not so bad, after all.' Her laughter increased, Paul joined in, and soon they were hysterical, with only the weight of their attraction pinning them to the seat of the boat and preventing both falling overboard.

After a minute or two, with laughter contained, Eva began to wipe the droplets from Paul's forehead.

'God I love you,' said Paul.

Eva pushed her hand through his hair. 'Then marry me,' she said.

They did marry, within two weeks, without an audience and having informed no one. This greatly upset Paul's mother, who was unable to decide whether to be angry, sad or overjoyed. She had always feared what would happen to Paul if he ended up alone (knowing, as she did, that Paul had become incomplete and therefore needed someone to help balance those missing bits in order to prevent him falling over continually, like a sawn-in-half doll); yet she craved a chance to celebrate as a family (the last large gathering that had fallen to her to organise having been her daughter's funeral). The news that her son had married without her led to a fusion of happiness with bile that threatened to lead to the sort of breakdown that she had always feared for Paul.

Soon after her marriage, Eva was planning her future in a typically business-like manner; she was glad to be, once more, in charge of her destiny. Thus, her newly acquired blank future filled swiftly with structures that closely resembled those she had left behind, only without the violence and pain, in whose place came a husband who loved her.

So, given strength by her suddenly stable domestic arrangements, Eva was once more living her life as she had intended. In the early autumn, she enrolled at King's College. Here she was advised to begin her course from scratch, having missed a term of the first-year course in Norway, and seeing as she would now be studying in English. She agreed, restarting her studies in history without fuss, and was soon seen as a student of distinction.

§ 12

ONE MONTH MARRIED, PAUL WAS SURPRISED TO MEET A FRIEND in the supermarket. He had gone to the shop in order to buy some milk (the shop was close so he often bought only what he needed immediately) but found that they only had skimmed, which he didn't like. This frustrating lack of the basics might have driven customers towards other, further shops – but most felt a fondness for this local store which often mispriced things (one might pick up a perfectly good burgundy for the price of a child's toothbrush) and more than once had let customers decide the value of their goods when the tills had packed in and closing time was near at hand.

Paul stood, thinking, trying to decide if fresh skimmed was better than full-fat UHT, when he saw Margaret Atkinson stooped over the frozen pizzas. This may not have been the best angle from which to recognise anyone, but Margaret was wearing one of her trademark glamorous dresses, and she had an unforgettable profile in this bent position. Paul admired this, before going to her and saying, 'Have you lost your ring in there, or what?'

Margaret stood quickly, before recognising Paul and starting to laugh. 'Ha! It's you. Now for Christ's sake help me find a mushroom one. These all have pineapple.'

Margaret first met Paul when he had just arrived in London, from Sussex. He was new enough to his art classes to be only confused and not yet despondent; she was studying philosophy at Cambridge, but spent much of her time in the capital as her boyfriend worked there. This had not prevented her becoming romantically entangled with Paul, and the two now talked with the ease of those who have been to bed and still remained friends.

'So, do you live near here?' asked Paul.

'No, but I'm seeing someone who has a flat on the Isle of Dogs.'

'Mmm, shitty.'

'No! It's huge and rather wonderful, really.'

'OK . . .'

'Did you finish at the college?'

'Yes, about . . . eight weeks ago. I managed a pass, but who cares about that? I've just got married!'

'No! . . . Who to?'

'A girl I met in Norway. I've only known her since the new year.'

'Blimey. Fast work. Well done.'

The two left the shop without milk or pizza and soon sat drinking coffee in a shabby café. Here Margaret revealed herself to be an English teacher at a school in Wimbledon, and once she found out that Paul was at a dead end, she clasped her hands together, thrilled.

'You must come and teach art at my school – the art teacher has been sacked for stealing mugs . . .'

'Mugs?'

'Hundreds of them, over many years, apparently. Some sort of mania, I imagine. He sold them at car boot sales.' She paused to refind her thought. 'So you simply must come and help out.'

Paul was looking unconvinced.

'Wimbledon's only a tube ride away and it would only be part-time. If you're doing nothing else, why not?'

'But I have no idea how to teach. They'll want certificates or diplomas in teaching or something. And anyway, you're not in charge, are you?'

'No one's in charge. And at a private school as bad as this everything goes by the path of least resistance. You'll see – the head will be delighted. Give me your number.'

Only days later, Paul was interviewed by the headmaster.

'And Mrs Atkinson says that you are only twenty-eight. Still, you have done a lot of private coaching and seem to be much in demand.'

Paul, aged twenty-three, and never having taught anyone, just nodded.

The head went on. 'I've come in specially today and I must say I'm fantastically pleased to have this business wrapped up. I'm off to Devon tomorrow.' (He was already on his feet, ready to leave.) 'Mr Woodruff will show you round the school. Term begins on the 6th of September, you will teach on Tuesdays and Wednesdays, but Mr Woodruff will go through all that. And don't forget to look smart – wear a suit: gain respect.' (Almost a laugh.) 'One of my little mottos, that.'

During this time, as Eva restarted her studies and Paul began teaching, the couple lived in a two-room basement flat in Limehouse.

The entrance to this was down narrowing steps which seemed to suggest that, more than a century ago, the builder had run out of materials. It was to this dark hole that luxury gifts began to arrive. Often it was Paul who would take receipt, and the parcel would wait, smugly, on the side table until Eva arrived home. Then it would reveal itself, emerging as brazenly as a jeweled dancer might from an enormous cake: a crystal travel clock, a silver tray, a jade-handled letter knife.

These gifts came from Eva's father, who did not think of visiting in person, but would not forget a birthday, a saint's day or an anniversary. Eva's mother never signed the cards that accompanied these presents, and her father did not write her name next to his. It was always quite clear that, for this woman, a fissure had opened in the earth one day, and into it her daughter had fallen.

It was a great surprise, then, when a letter arrived one morning, fresh from Norway and addressed to Paul:

Dear Sir, how magnificent the hills looked this morning, with the sun shining on them, and they being still all wet from the rain. I ate break-fast in the anticipation of doing something special today, and look, I was right! This letter comes all the way from Bergen, Norway, and will bring with it all the joy of knowing that far away, others are thinking of you.

Paul read on in disbelief. The letter did not mention Eva, and did not explain itself, but simply arrived like the weather, and stopped when it had run its course.

Eva was shocked to learn of this development, but did not want to know the letter's contents, nor what Paul planned to do in response to them. Thus Eva corresponded with her father by means of extended thank-you cards, and Paul tried to develop a written relationship with his mother-in-law, who never gave a hint that she had received any message from him, instead sending random musings or factual reports from the town of Bergen, without reference to their connection, as if she was the sometime Scandinavian correspondent for the *Limehouse Gazette*.

DURING THE EVENINGS, PAUL AND EVA OFTEN WANDERED through parks or went to the cinema. The couple tended to spend this time alone, rather than with friends. Eva met up with her fellow students separately, with weekly nights out – girls only; Paul had left all his fellow artists behind him when he finished college, and functioned as an outsider at his Wimbledon school, being present for only two lesson-packed days per week. He rarely even saw Margaret.

Often, Eva and Paul would simply cook and then chat as they ate, perhaps with the television on. Paul would tell Eva what had been happening at school, or how his ideas for a novel were developing (thoughts of writing had landed upon him as soon as he stopped drawing). Eva would tell Paul about her friends, or how their oldest lecturer had been getting on since the worsening of his deafness.

One Wednesday evening, having prepared pasta again (cheapness was, for these two, a prerequisite), Paul told Eva about the business of the stuffed birds.

'Today something so odd happened, that it's worth waiting before I tell you about it.' He added a little more tomato concentrate to his sauce. 'Pour some wine, it's in the fridge. When we're sitting down I'll begin.'

In his art room, Paul had a variety of cupboards. Not all of these opened, and for those which were locked no key could be found. This did not matter to Paul, who had access to storage galore. One of the advantages of being an art teacher, he realised, was the size of the room he was likely to be allocated. Anyway, during morning break, Paul had gone to the staff room to get himself a cup of tea. He drank this at the edge of a gang of would-be militants, who were discussing the outrage of inadequate holiday pay. This was the sort of issue to involve the union in, apparently. Paul's position was sounded out, but when it became clear that he did not have one, the circle closed, leaving Paul as a dot on its edge. Not much bothered,

Paul returned to his room and got out enough paper for the next lesson.

Unknown to him, children had been present during his absence. He did not notice the broken lock on one of the unused cupboard doors. Inside this cupboard the children had found many stuffed birds, most in a rather moth-eaten state. They had taken them out of the room in their school bags, waiting until someone had a good idea how best to use them. By lunchtime, Godfrey Evans had hatched a plan. It met with instant approval. Each child would take a bird and place it in a classroom, on the teacher's desk – and together they would furnish as many rooms as was possible. The chemistry labs would be a problem, as these were always locked during lunch – so Godfrey would do these himself, using the back window to enter, which was often open to prevent the build-up of fumes. So it was that long-dead owls, starlings and sparrow hawks hopped their way into the light again, and, as a final touch, Master Evans suggested they each sellotape a speech bubble to their bird's beak. Then it could sing a tune appropriate to the teacher who would receive it. So far, this prank would have caused astonishment and laughter, but in giving free rein to each child as to the content of the speech bubbles, Godfrey had erred. The nightjar whistling 'Mrs Lemon: marry me' would have elicited a blush; the thrush singing 'Who's a pretty boy then?' would have failed to upset Mr Godstone, who, despite his sensitive soul, was a man who saw only the obvious, and would have assumed this to be a parrot-inspired call; but the tawny owl, daringly placed in the deputy head's office, should have known better than to hoot 'Mr Woodruff is a prize cock' – for although the wordplay was a move in the right direction, the deputy head was a man prone to sudden violence, and once he had exploded and thrown the large bird through the thin glass of his bookcase, sending razor-edged shards scattering onto the carpet, he needed someone to punish.

Paul was his first victim. The presence of the stuffed birds in the art room was well known to the longer-serving members of staff, and the deputy head considered Paul morally responsible for their actions. Paul was explaining the value of aerial perspective in painting when a sharp knock sounded on his door; through the window in this, Paul could see a furious face. He left the lesson and closed the door behind him. A patronising finger beckoned him to follow, and soon Paul was staring at the profaning owl. He looked to Mr Woodruff for a clue.

'Your owl?' spluttered Mr Woodruff.

A perplexed look from Paul.

'This bird has come from your room. How has this happened?'

Paul, still at a loss, began to assure Mr Woodruff that this was not part of some project involving him. The two began to argue, but before the situation could inflame, calls were heard from other parts of the school. The birds were causing a rumpus.

Eva listened to this, enraptured. 'Oh Paul,' she said, 'how fantastic. This is the sort of thing you should write about.'

Paul laughed. 'Yup – perhaps I should do so in the school magazine.'

Aged twenty-four, newly married, and with a hopeless beginning to his artist's life now firmly put behind him, Paul turned to writing with a new seriousness. His efforts thus far had been half-hearted, yet he had no excuse, having plenty of free time, which he might use wisely. He now saw literature as his true calling. This was a shame, as, unlike drawing, he had no ability at all in this direction. One might have thought that with such a rich past already behind him, Paul would only have needed to exercise a little editorial restraint in order to produce a book of thrilling intensity – but it was not to turn out this way. Still, he began writing with energy: his lack of any education in this direction did not deter him; neither had utter disillusionment at art college stilled his creative pulse. Really, as unlikely as it should have been, it was inevitable that the world of books would be his destination once he had run from the visual arts, the arena of dance and music being saved from his attentions by the luck that he had good ears and a sense of shame.

Writing, though, is something we can all try our hand at, regardless of ability, and Paul felt moved to write down those things he might once have drawn. Thus, during the winter following his just-scraped graduation from the East London College of Art, Paul began the search for his novel, which was to be a love story. This choice of genre was a natural one, as when he had previously been seated before a model or a tree, pencil poised, Paul had always drawn, not the thing before him, but a vision of his love. Now he felt sure that he could write this message clearly through a story not dissimilar to his own.

A circus ringmaster (not overly tall; dark, quietly dashing) meets a beautiful young schoolteacher from Leipzig. She is subdued and clearly has unhappiness in her heart: the ringmaster wants to help. Finding out her love for animals, he invites her to a guided tour of his menagerie, and introduces her to his favourite elephant, which, whilst performing tricks for her (and successfully drawing out her first smiles of the year), sits on her foot. The ringmaster carries the schoolteacher to hospital, where an emergency amputation is performed. But, during this operation on the schoolteacher, her surgeon falls in love with her, in theatre, and she wakes to his unwanted advances. Unused to rejection, the surgeon is driven insane and begins to stalk the girl and her ringmaster lover, who are forced to flee to Africa, where they start a charity – bringing animals into the homes of orphans.

Now, this plot was not without promise, but where before, in drawing what was before him, Paul had been able to indulge his heroic and romantic vision with impunity – here, for some reason, never lapsing into poor taste – his writing became obese and vulgar at the least provocation. He did not talk in this way, but perhaps felt the need to say more with a pen than his mouth. Possibly he imagined himself a prose-writing poet. This helped him not at all; he struggled. Simply: he had talent for something else. But a lack of ability did not stop him attempting a novel, and he began his new task with the vaguely directed vigour of a boy scout, who, finding himself lost in a forest, pluckily heads in random directions, refusing to notice his hopeless situation.

During that winter, above the hapless writer, the crows gathered.

§ 14

AFTER SPENDING A YEAR STUMBLING THROUGH THE LIVES OF local women, Bjørn was out of work, in debt, and seemingly beyond all help. He might have entirely disappeared from the world soon after, had it not been for a chance encounter with an angel. One Sunday afternoon, whilst walking through a park feeling the usual despair that a Sunday spent alone brought on, carelessly juggling ideas of suicide and emigration, he saw a friend stepping briskly across the grass towards him. From behind a flowerbed, Marianne shouted, 'I haven't seen you since last New Year!', and she was still waving her arms as she gave him a hug and asked, 'Are you married yet?' Looking more carefully, she saw the answer written in Bjørn's stubble, which clung patchily to his long cheeks. 'You look awful.'

The simple honesty of this cheered Bjørn up at once. 'Yes,' he said. 'Spring is upon us, and I feel like shit.'

'Well, let me buy you a coffee and tell you how wonderful life is.' And she was off ahead, holding onto his heavy hand, so that he was forced along too fast, as if he was walking a large puppy.

Marianne had been abroad studying history of art. She told Bjørn of the wonders of Italy, and, as she spoke, the dull spring around them began to recede. Watching her, Bjørn felt fascinated, but uneasy. She spoke with such alarming energy. He wondered if she had been drinking, yet surely her wildly dilated pupils suggested narcotics? Bjørn wondered if he should ask for some, but, so far, there had been no pause in her conversation for him to speak. Marianne spoke of food that tasted of something other than salt and water. She said, whilst smiling naughtily, that he couldn't be expected to fully appreciate what she was on about, since he had never been beyond Norway's barren shores, save for that time that he had spent in England, which if they were honest, wasn't up to much either. He was about to speak, when she went on. In Italy, mini newborn cheeses were the colour of porcelain. They could be eaten whole – not chewed, merely squashed with the tongue. Tomatoes were green, red, yellow – all at once, and wonderfully misshapen. They smelled of . . . She waved her hands in circles . . . For the first time, she was struggling.

'Squashed tongue?' suggested Bjørn.

'Summer!' she shouted, and everybody in the park-side coffee shop was surprised, except Bjørn, who was starting to think that he needed a holiday, preferably with this girl. He looked at his pastry and put down his fork. Here his life turned.

Bjørn had known Marianne for years. They had gone to the local school together, along with Eva, before Bjørn had been packed off to England. At school, Bjørn had thought that Eva and Marianne were friends, until the day when Marianne had come to tell him that Eva was, in fact, in love with Jacob, not him, and had instruct-ed her, Marianne, to tell him, Bjørn, to get lost. This, Marianne said, was a measure of just what a cow Eva was. Bjørn was con-fused (which is not surprising considering that he was only ten at the time). He had not thought it possible that Eva might be in love with him.

After their chance meeting in the park that afternoon, Bjørn had tried hard to further his relationship with Marianne. He was sure that she would bring some of her happy sunshine into his life, and into his bed, but knew that she was soon due to return to Italy for the summer term. The thought of this lovely woman bouncing off to Florence, leaving him to stew alone in his flat, made him desper-ate. He needed to make her his own, before she left, but it was tricky to get her where he wanted her. She was staying with her age-ing mother, and any visits to the house involved all three of them.

One morning, Bjørn took round some tulips that he had picked from the park, only to have them stolen from him by the old woman. She opened the door and stared with such dazed wonder at the flowers, still cold with dew, that he had no option but give them to her. This would have been fine if Marianne had been there to witness the gift, but she was in the bathroom, and by the time she appeared her mother had put them away somewhere, probably in a cupboard, and very possibly no one would see them again. Seeing

Marianne's patient devotion to her mother, and feeling the good-ness of her nature, Bjørn felt awkward. Every time he found him-self imagining how it would be to screw Marianne he felt a moment's guilt, before continuing.

Marianne wrote from Italy several times. Her letters were full of passion, but never specifically for Bjørn. They were filled with a love of all things and, most annoyingly, a love for other people. Young men and women from all over Europe seemed to have moved to Florence for the summer. Who could blame them, con-sidering the grace of the domes and the timeless balance of the bridges? Bjørn, writing not from some little café, nor from a bal-cony about to catch the morning sun, found that his feelings had more focus. He had but one source of light. Yet, still not knowing how Marianne felt for him, he thought he should stick to everyday subjects. He could not, however, bring himself to write about how he was looking for a job, nor about the condensation problem with his kitchen window. Having stopped seeking out interesting women to have sex with, he met hardly any fun young people. Food did indeed taste of salt or water, or both, as was certainly the case with his father's speciality, twice-boiled cod. (This double boiling had originally come about one dinnertime when his father had cooked the fish for its full allocation of twenty minutes, yet the vegetables were still not ready. Suddenly inspired, Bjørn's father had taken the fish out of its pan until the vegetables were nice and soft then re-boiled it very fast so that it too would be hot. He had found the result unusually tender and juicy, and had cooked fish this way ever since.)

The many letters that Bjørn sent Marianne were generally short, this being in Bjørn's view better than very boring. Thus, Marianne would receive twice-boiled letters that to her seemed neither juicy nor tender, but, rather, flaky and insipid. Fortunately for Bjørn, she was born wise, and knew instinctively that boring letters can come from exciting men. It was also Bjørn's good luck that, although writ-ten with monotonous regularity, the Italian postal system delivered the letters in sudden bursts after a decent pause, and lost most al-together.

Bjørn knew that, in order to interest Marianne for long, he would have to change. His first thought was to return to university, work hard, and impress Marianne with his intellect. He had loved his course, and the more he thought of it the more he wanted to begin again. He contacted his tutor, who remembered him, was glad to hear from him, and also hoped that Bjørn could return (most of his students being thick as turkeys), but could do nothing without the approval of the Rector. Bjørn should come to see him in a week, by which time things should hopefully have been sorted out.

Bjørn, who had not been to the university for a year, considered the timing excellent, as he could simply begin again where he had left off.

The next week, when he arrived, Bjørn was surprised by the shabbiness of his tutor. A year ago he had seemed like a man too caught up in intellectual thought to consider his dress. Today, he looked simply messy. Bjørn's dishevelled tutor sat him down and told him the way things were. Unfortunately, the Rector considered Bjørn, who had dropped out without warning or excuse, to be a morally redundant near-criminal. The university would not be reopening his place, and would be very careful to try to avoid accepting anyone quite as deranged in future. The tutor apologised. Bjørn wondered if he had known the Rector's daughter.

Having been academically thwarted, paying off debt and buying some new clothes were now Bjørn's priorities. In order to do so he took a job in the tourist office. This was numbingly dull, but Bjørn concentrated only on earning some money before Marianne returned. He dreaded her coming home to see him with fresh eyes. By now, she may have forgotten the details of his look. She was probably re-remembering him as he had been in the past. Upon her return she would be shocked. Had he really always been so grubby? Certainly, his letters were total crap, but she had forgotten this tramp-like appearance. She would run. So Bjørn turned up to his dead-end job on time, as if this might bring him redemption; and he was the only one in the office to take just one hour for lunch.

'Come on, new boy, give us a break,' his colleagues begged.

'How will there be any overtime to be paid for if you keep doing all the work?'

One morning in June, a letter arrived from Marianne. She had taken her final exams, and was coming back to Norway on the 8th of July. For Bjørn, instant happiness turned to worry. He was an idiot to have fallen in love with her whilst she had been gone. What kind of arse fails to fall in love with a girl whilst she is around? Then, given this failing, surely he could have waited for her to return before coming over all spoony? How can anyone cling to what's not there? He had found a way. As her homecoming approached, the pleasant summer weather changed. A cold front that had been marooned over Iceland pushed east, bringing skies the colour of rock and air that smelled of water.

On the morning of Marianne's arrival, Bjørn knew that the last thing she would want was to be met by him at the airport. It had been his idea to collect her – he had phoned. She had probably been making strained comedy-faces to her friends as he spoke. 'God, this guy's freakily keen,' she would have told them after hanging up. 'He seems to think he's my boyfriend.'

Bjørn waited in the arrivals hall of Birkesand's airport for more than two hours, during which time the few seedlings of optimism that he had managed to grow in the last days wilted, then collapsed. By the time Marianne strode through customs, Bjørn was able to smile only by grimacing then flaring his nostrils, which he knew had the effect of slightly raising the corners of his mouth.

'By God, Bjørn, you look as bleak as the weather,' Marianne said, as she put her arms around him and reached up to kiss him warmly on the mouth.

After Marianne had been home for a week Bjørn was fully captured. He awoke on Saturday full of energy and optimism, and knowing that the only reason for this was Marianne. He dressed smartly and walked to her mother's house.

Marianne was out trying to find paracetamol.

'I suffer, Bjørn,' her mother confided, as if this was something that she had, until now, been keeping secret. 'My head aches with each movement, yet if I sit still I can feel the blood pooling, ready to curdle, in my feet.'

Bjørn took her bony hand. 'You poor, sweet lady,' he said, leading her to the sofa. 'You must put your feet up on these pillows. I've seen verbena in your garden, I'll make us some tea.' And he walked off with such purpose that the old woman did just as she was told, staring for the next ten minutes at the extravagantly framed photos of her early life, which were nailed to a wall in a corner that no one ever looked at. Behind her, as she would have seen through the window had she been facing the other way, Bjørn keenly gathered leaves. Unfortunately he knew little of gardening, and whilst Marianne's mother recalled her past life and sank into a depressed nostalgia, he had been picking leaves from the wrong bush. He brought them to the kitchen and brewed up, but didn't like the result himself. Marianne's mother, on the other hand, drank several cups, growing fonder of the tea with each mouthful. The mania that this brought on surprised everyone.

When Marianne returned with the pills, she found her mother highly animated.

'Three and a half years!' the woman wailed. 'What malign blanket of sloth has come over me?'

Marianne had no answer.

'Anniversaries and birthdays have passed. My sister died – yet still your father lies unvisited and untended in his grave these last . . . Yes! Three and a half years!' She looked directly at Marianne. 'How has this been allowed to happen?'

A taxi was urgently called, and the three of them were taken to the cemetery. The old woman was now at the height of her rantings. She talked loudly about her husband's life as a pilot, and how he had loved the air above all things, even spending much of his free time in winter ski-jumping. Whilst it was true that he had died doing a job that he loved, how sad that his engines had cut out, sending him crashing into the foul North Sea. He had always hated the sea, with its rotting stink of ozone and ability to make him sick up his breakfast. He couldn't even swim. Far better if his aeroplane had leaked fuel, ignited, then vaporised in a massive fireball, sending billions of its pilot's particles into the stratosphere. How happy this would have made him! And what comfort it would have brought her during these last bitter and lonely years. Marianne, who was sitting with her mother in the back of the taxi, started to cry.

Having visited the grave, Marianne's mother became calm; the journey home passed in silence. Afterwards, Bjørn was invited to stay to dinner. He had known, even before today, that Marianne would soon find a way to escape her mother. She would find a job in another town (these specialised arty opportunities not existing just anywhere, you know), and this flight would leave him behind. He waited no longer to act, and whilst peeling swedes for Marianne's mother to chop, he asked her if she would mind being without her daughter for a few days. Only after taking an enormous sigh, and closing her eyes awhile, did she nod her consent – just the one nod, before resuming her chopping.

Bjørn rented a fisherman's cottage on an island less than two miles from the mainland.

'We are going to paradise,' he told Marianne. 'Pack only your flip-flops.' Although she begged to be told more, Bjørn didn't want to spoil the surprise, but did tell her that their island was somewhere between Cuba and Borneo. She thought, whilst pouting.

'Africa?' she asked, astonished.

'Well, it's more in a triangle between the three places,' said Bjørn – and she understood.

'Should I pack a raincoat with the flip-flops?'

'You think it's Norway,' he said accusingly. 'Just because I work at the tourist office, you think I must be poor. Well, let me tell you the truth at last. I am, in fact, the heir to the Reber fish soup business. I'm a millionaire!'

She reached up to hold his cheeks. 'I'm so happy that you're merely eccentric, you know I could never have become serious about a pauper. I shall give up my further studies and instead spend my afternoons learning to play the piano.'

'And the mornings?'

'Mornings will not exist for me.'

The island of Flekke is a large rock, upon which stand a few wooden cottages, sheltering from the North Sea in a dip. There is one shop, which is open on Tuesdays, and a small stone-walled harbour. The boats in this harbour are all of rowable size, and from them can be seen crabs, starfish and colourful wrasse, all swimming in the brazenly clear water. Bjørn and Marianne came to this harbour each day, after a late breakfast. Summer had returned, so after balancing along the narrow sea wall they would sit on the end, letting the reflected sunshine dance on their bare feet. Here they played games such as spot-the-anemone, and tried to catch fish on a bright orange hand-line. They soon gave this up and tried instead to slowly lower down the line and surprise any creatures that hadn't been paying attention. Being here, and listening to the sea, Bjørn, who had not been planning this, knew that he was going to marry Marianne, and having seen the certainty of it, he could not think of a reason to wait. He left Marianne with the hand-line, told her to catch dinner, and wandered back along the wall to the shore, where he looked over the tiny, pebbled beach. He was hoping to find a ring.

Returning to sit down next to Marianne a few minutes later, he began to work on a small piece of wood that he had found. Marianne watched, curious, as beneath his penknife the ring took shape.

'I always thought you utterly incapable,' she said happily, 'yet, look at that, you're making something . . . small.'

'Yes,' replied Bjørn, measuring it against her finger. 'It's a ring.'

Marianne wore it for the three months that it took Bjørn to afford a silver one. She loved the idea that he had made it for her, but although the sea had washed the outside smooth, the inside had been left rough by Bjørn's knife, and it scoured her skin, leaving a raw patch for its replacement to sit on.

§ 15

ONCE HE HAD BECOME ENGAGED TO MARIANNE, BJØRN FELT
that he should look for a better job than the one he held at the
tourist office. He needed to build some sort of career. Once, he
would have wished to astound the world of marine zoology with
radical theses born from his work at the University of Southern
California; he and Marianne would have lived partly on a yacht,
from which he would dive and she would write books about
artists. Now, though, his options were limited. He had no cash. His
father had no cash. Education would have to belong to Marianne;
he would provide for them. Viewed like this, in the abstract, it
didn't seem like a bad deal – so, evenings were spent with a copy
of *Bladet Birkesand* and a pen. He could quickly have found a job as
director of Esso, or as archivist to the Lapland Artistic Institute.
Those within his range were not so appealing. After two weeks, he
saw an advert for the position of shoe salesman. This did not, on
the surface, appear to be a job that would interest him, but it could
not possibly be worse than sitting in the tourist office, working
deliberately slowly. No salary was mentioned, but Bjørn imagined
that if he turned out to have a talent as a salesman, he might earn
enough to afford the rent on a flat that was less small and dark
than the one he had lived in since returning from the army.
Perhaps he would become a manager; then they could think about
buying.

The next morning, he called the number given in the advert.
After a brief chat, he was asked to come along straight away.

'But I'm due at the tourist office in fifteen minutes.'

'What, planning holidays already? Forget that. When can you
start here?'

Bjørn paused to think. His new boss spoke first.

'Meet me here in an hour. I'll be in the car park.'

So began Bjørn's life with shoes. He was soon travelling all over
Norway trying to encourage retailers to stock good, European-
made footwear. Importing from China? What do your customers

think of this? The quality. The detail. Look! And another sample pair would be produced.

Meanwhile Marianne studied for a doctorate at the University of Birkesand, and planned her small and inexpensive wedding. Thus passed a year, too much of it spent apart.

For Bjørn, time hardly existed. He was so regularly on the move that his watch often stopped altogether, as if in protest at all that constant fiddling – an hour lost here and two added there. Whichever timepiece controlled Bjørn was doing the same thing. When his father reminded him, one Sunday, that the wedding was only two weeks away, and that they had planned a family meal for the wedding eve, Bjørn checked the calendar immediately. This couldn't be so – two weeks until his marriage? He wanted to present the evidence to his father straight away, if only to reassure himself that there was at least a month.

Mr Olsen was right about the timing, though, and his plans for the night before borrowed something from the past.

When Bjørn and Karl had been children, the Olsen family spent summers in a rented house by Hardangerfjord. For the boys this was as good as going abroad, as it took many hours to drive their Opel estate car across the foot of Norway, on and off the ferry, then through the fruit-tree-mottled scenery of Hardanger. They always rented the same house. Before the car had stopped, the boys would jump from their already opened doors and run from place to place, checking if their den had survived the winter and that the karting hill was still as steep. The house had its own boat, which was tied to a wooden jetty in the sheltered cove below, and it was from this boat that Bjørn would fish. Aged ten, Bjørn caught his first cod.

All month, he had caught nothing but mackerel – endless rows of the things. Carrying them home sometimes proved difficult. Eventually, he worked out that the best way to carry them was to string them through the gills and onto a line. He bobbed into view looking like he was bringing home some huge decoration for the house.

'Are we to hang them from the rafters?' asked his mother, who had been forced to come up with ever more adventurous recipes for the cooking of these fish. Poached on nettles, with blueberry jam, was declared the best ever. But all his family begged Bjørn to stop bringing home the same fish for supper every day.

'It's worse than having a mouse-catching cat,' his father said. 'Let the seagulls have them. Take up kite-flying.'

On the last day of the holiday, Bjørn was once more aboard the little boat, rod bent far beyond what even four mackerel could have managed. He had been sternly ordered to throw back his catch, but when he held a bucket-mouthed cod in his trembling hands, he felt sure that they couldn't have meant it to apply to such a fish as this, so he took it home, proudly slung over his shoulder.

'Good God, Bjørn, don't you listen?' cried his desperate mother. She had been short-tempered ever since it had started raining, the week before. His father, though, recognising the magnificence of the animal, said that they would take it home salted and have it on Christmas Eve. The two of them went to the shop and bought six kilos of salt. They packed the salted fillets in between towels, which fitted neatly above the suitcases in the back of the car. When they arrived home, Mrs Olsen had thrown the towels away, but not before her husband had rescued the fish and taken it to the attic, where it was hung up to dry. The house had, apparently, not smelled right since.

Twelve years later, and a week before Bjørn was to marry Marianne, Mr Olsen sought a preserved cod, in honour of this memory. The pre-wedding meal was to be a nostalgic one and the salted fish had already been ordered from his friend Nils, who was also an architect, and was one of the only people that Bjørn's father had kept in touch with after leaving work. In his free time, Nils was a hunter and fisherman. He lived on a hill outside the town, in such simple isolation from all modern things that it seemed to anyone who visited that he lived in the time of King Magnus. He had a wooden outhouse in which hung deer, ribs or fish, according to the season. Each working morning, he would shave with an open blade, wash in cold water, then dress in an immaculate suit, before tiptoeing through his farm-like back garden, shutting the gate carefully behind him to ensure that no chickens escaped, then stepping into his executive car. When he descended the hill, it seemed to him that time changed too. As the stony track gave way to the road, he came through the centuries, arriving at the freeway at about the same time as he entered the real-time world. This double life pleased him greatly, and it was rare that he was caught in an agitated state, thinking of sea-trout, when it should have been sewage, or roofing materials, as an autumn stag stood, head wreathed in the mist of a final breath.

The bus stop where Bjørn's father alighted was at the bottom of the hill, leaving a mile's walk before he got to his friend's house. It had rained hard overnight, so he only got as far as the edge of the woodland before he had to stop. In front of him was the result of a small landslide. Rocks and mud lay across the road. A sapling ash tree reached out to him for help. He sidestepped it and approached the two workmen who were about to start clearing the way. One of them sat in a digger.

'I need to get past,' said Mr Olsen.

'Not for a couple of hours you won't. There's several tonnes here,' replied the one leaning on a shovel. He had the look of a man who measured time in half-day units.

Mr Olsen must have looked sincerely forlorn, as the workman in the digger beckoned him over, then gestured that he should get into the scoop of the machine.

'Hold on tightly!'

Bjørn's father did as he was told – was delighted, uplifted, and then was set down on the other side of the rubble.

'I'll bring you some blood-pudding!' he shouted back, as he walked on towards his friend's house.

Where the road became a small track, there was a clearing in the trees. Here sat a lady artist on a chair, with easel, lunch box and paints arranged about her. She had seen him, but Mr Olsen stood at a discreet distance to watch, as if by doing this he wouldn't disturb her. After some minutes, she turned around. Mr Olsen, who upon seeing the fragile curls of once brown or golden hair falling from beneath her hilarious pink hat had fallen in love immediately, stepped backwards and fell into the flooded roadside gutter. The lady stayed where she was and began laughing so loudly that Mr Olsen was sure that people would soon come from all directions to see what could possibly be that funny. Some would no doubt fall from the other side of the road and down the vertiginous slope, so disorientated would they be by this mad crowing; others, with their bellowing, might precipitate further rock falls and be swept, breathless with cackling, down into the swollen stream below, and thence out to sea. But once the lady artist had seen how terribly upset Mr Olsen was with the situation, she came across the road and said, 'Don't worry, you look like you needed a wash.' Thus, Mr Olsen was saved from further embarrassment by a growing anger. He got up as quickly as he could, staggering out of the muddy water and onto the stones of the path. The lady came near, and astounded him further by drying his forehead with her painting cloth, streaking him with rainbow colours and soft confusion.

'Come and see something beautiful,' she said, leading him over, beyond her easel. Raising her arms as if she herself was responsible for everything in view, she revealed the cliffs and rocks beneath them, aglow with damp; the white-frothed water of the fjord spitting at low-flying gulls; and everywhere islands, which seemed to move, as if floating on soup.

As a child, Bjørn's father had been a boy unable to keep still. This was not due to ill discipline, as his stick-tapping schoolmaster suspected, but was his natural, unalterable state. It was as if many animals had been forced inside a small bag. His arms waved from side to side at dinner; he had to get up from his chair (quickly) and shout during lessons – which was unfortunate, as his ruthless teacher knew about it even when his back was turned.

Now, in front of this heaven, this Norway, Mr Olsen once more felt the menagerie rumble and scrabble inside him. He started to vibrate – first his feet only, but then all parts joined in, until he felt nauseous and was sure he would be sick. Then squirrels, cats and crows would shoot forth towards the sea. The pressure inside Mr Olsen increased. Finally, to prevent bursting, he screamed: 'Marry me, you strange witch!'

Mr Olsen arrived at Nils's house seemingly drunk. He could only keep his balance by clinging to the doorframe with both hands. Nils, chastising him and ranting about how his drinking had almost killed him once, helped Mr Olsen towards a chair. He scowled at his scramble-eyed friend.

'We've talked about this endlessly, Harald. You promised me. Shame on you, shame – and with your boy about to be married. Get hold of yourself.'

Mr Olsen, finding a reply impossibly elusive, wet himself. Nils was struggling with his friend, trying to eject him from the house, when Harald spoke.

'A siren was waiting for me on the path.'

Nils stopped in alarm. Stories of these cliff-top women and their evil ways were well known. Flint faced, the two men sat on the floor. Nils was now looking dazed too.

'Harald, this is worse than I thought.'

Harald Olsen had indeed given up drinking. This had come about, not because he had been sure to die of it sometime soon – which, to him, seemed to have been part of the point of the thing – nor because he had, years since, run out of money and was now also running seriously short of things to sell; he stopped because he found that his son had fallen lower than himself. When he had seen that Bjørn was strong, he had no qualms about pulling himself up on his son's trousers. He had watched Bjørn do well at university, then drop out and become quite the most brilliant seducer that Birkesand had known – in this century, at least. But when, more than a year ago now, Bjørn had come round (probably just to check that his father was still alive), Mr Olsen had seen before him a wretch. No one, before that, had been able to rival Mr Olsen's depth of dilapidated squalor; yet here stood someone who had found an even lower level. Mr Olsen had not realised that there was one. Ashamed at himself for setting such an example for his son to follow, Mr Olsen had opened all the curtains immediately, and, later that afternoon, he went out, blinking, to buy a mirror.

§ 16

ON THE EVENING BEFORE HIS WEDDING, BJØRN SLEPT IN A chair. His work left him always tired, yet unable to sleep at night. Short rests taken whilst travelling had become routine, so that even when he came home he paced around at night and fell asleep in corners during the day.

Mr Olsen was in the kitchen, cooking. Having already soaked the cod for twenty-four hours, he now cut it into strips. Rehydrated beans sat in a white bowl. There were fresh things too: potatoes, carrots, onions and swede waited next to the chopping board. He worked happily alone, all the time thinking of the future and how lucky he was to be alive again. He felt as if he had been released unexpectedly from prison. His siren fiancée, his youngest son's marriage, Karl's imminent arrival – these were happy days. Why had he let himself sit alone in this house for so many years? (In the dark, drinking until he was ill and not fit even to see himself.) By chance, he had given up drinking on the same weekend that Bjørn had met Marianne, and although he wouldn't be introduced to her for a month or two after this, he had always felt a particular gratitude. Somehow, she was a rescuer. Had she not liberated his son from his wanton whoring? A veritable angel.

Mr Olsen began to sing, as he had often done two decades before, continuing to hum when he ran out of words, and only stopping altogether when he forgot the tune.

The house was already warm with the smell of salt-cod stew when Karl arrived. He rang the bell only once, which showed what a civilising influence his new love Kristi had been.

'Welcome.'

'And where's the groom?'

'Asleep in the living room – always tired.'

Kristi offered to help Mr Olsen, whilst Karl went to find Bjørn. Walking through the hallway, Karl could already hear his brother snoring, so, in keeping with the theme of the evening, and in homage to times past, he decided to recreate a scene from childhood.

Standing next to his brother, Karl first tested the depth of sleep by balancing a cushion on Bjørn's head. All was well, so he progressed to light but stable books, before aiming higher with a carefully placed lamp, which he then plugged in and switched on.

Bjørn hadn't moved, and Karl was concerned that he might be unwell. He went to get some ice to help him find out.

In the kitchen, Kristi was cooking with Mr Olsen. She had been warned by Karl about the quality of food she could expect from his father: but the aroma leaking from the oven was mesmerising. Mr Olsen confessed that he had bought his first cookbook only this month, having had the intention of making this evening's meal special, but just reading Hilstrand Knudlevik's *One Hundred Ways with Salted Fish* had inspired him to learn more. He vowed to Kristi that he would cook a new dish every week, possibly branching out into foreign cuisine. He had seen a particularly colourful Italian cookbook in the library, the cover of which showed a dish with pasta of three different colours – imagine! This was truly exotic stuff.

Just then, Karl came in looking for ice. 'Coloured pasta? Sounds disgusting,' he said distractedly as he headed for the freezer; but before he got to it there was a crash in the living room, followed by confused swearing.

'Ahh,' said Karl. 'Champagne instead of ice, don't you think?'

Then Harald Olsen's fiancée arrived, completing this new-born family; all of the younger generation were struck by how handsome she might once have been.

Dinner began with gravlax, which Bjørn had apparently loved as a three-year-old. 'Why do we always need an excuse to get together?' the diners asked each other. 'Let's do this often.'

Then came the salt-cod stew, and it was now that Bjørn started to become emotional. He was being dragged back across times that he had been hoping to leave behind. But the conversations about his future happiness with Marianne, and the many grandchildren that his father would soon be entertaining, held the past back – until pudding arrived. The dessert had been specially made, from a borrowed English recipe, by Kare Gilhus, the fiancée witch. During dinner, as this dessert heated in the oven, a strangely elusive memory fluttered around Bjørn. Briefly, he had seen it.

'What do you like about England, except sport?' the bag-eyed, sunken-mouthed Mr Olsen had asked the twelve-year-old Bjørn. Bjørn, who certainly didn't enjoy sport, added plum crumble to the list of things that he thought his father might like him to like.

'And what do they do to the plums to make them crumble?' asked Mr Olsen.

So it was that on the eve of his wedding Bjørn was brought a plum crumble by a witch. The dish sat on the table ready for Bjørn to serve, whilst all the other diners admired it.

'Oh, that's really special,' said Karl, as everyone smiled at Bjørn. Bjørn was unable to answer.

'It's right that you should be emotional tonight,' said his father. 'Nothing will be the same again.'

That night, Bjørn was drunk but unable to sleep: an odd situation; and it was as he muddled around in his old room in his father's house that he remembered his wedding trousers. He swore. They had been forgotten at his flat. The walk to collect them would normally have taken little more than ten minutes each way, so Bjørn, who was, after all, failing to sleep anyway, decided to fetch them now.

As he zigzagged towards his trousers, Bjørn was troubled by the plum crumble. The witch had picked the plums locally, which added a personal touch, but they were stone-hearted. When she tried one off the tree, her mouth collapsed. Spiteful things, unripe plums, so she had added half a bag of sugar and a pot of cinnamon to compensate. Had she been using English plums, she would have stuck to the recipe. The resultant mix, although strangely delicious, now seemed to be fermenting inside Bjørn. This was not helpful, as he was already much slowed by his drunkenness. He was hoping to collect his clothes without delay, yet when he eventually stumbled into the town's central square, now not more than a minute away from his trousers, he saw two men wrestling.

Bjørn sat on a step to watch. Fights between drunken young men were not uncommon, but here was something a little different. Both men were huge, and wore only their underpants; and they were fighting in the classical style, trying to unbalance and throw one another, rather than merely brawling. A clear opportunity for a punch to the chin was refused. Then the man in purple pants got the better of the one in black and held him on the ground under his considerable weight. Bjørn got to his feet and warmly applauded. The two men now got up and, comparing bruises, came over to Bjørn.

'Do you like wrestling?' the one in black asked. His Norwegian had a strong accent.

Bjørn, feeling cautious, said that he did, but only ever as a spectator. The large men looked disappointed.

'We are here in Birkesand for a strongman contest,' said the one in purple pants. 'We are from Latvia.'

'Ah,' said Bjørn, feeling less steady as the night deepened. Then there was silence, which Bjørn, being the local, felt responsible for. So he asked vaguely, 'How strong are you, then?' The men looked at each other. Bjørn went on. 'Could you pull up that lamp post, for example?'

There was a sad shaking of heads.

From now on the men spoke only in Latvian, which had the effect of disorientating Bjørn even further.

'Ignatius, I bet I could lift this man over my head twenty times without stopping.'

'Dropping him to the ground each time, or down to your knees?'

'Knees, you twat.'

Ignatius shook his head. 'Too easy. Instead, lets see who can do it fastest.' Ignatius looked at his watch and raised his arm. The second hand approached a new minute.

Bjørn was thinking of his marriage and, reminded of the late hour by the large man's watch, he began to excuse himself.

'So, good luck then,' he began, as Ignatius's huge arm fell . . .

Grabbed by his belt and jacket, Bjørn was held horizontally, then thrust up and down.

'Stop wriggling!' commanded Ignatius. 'You're slowing him dreadfully.'

The strongman pumped. Despite the cool night, he was already sweating.

'He's surprisingly heavy, Ignatius, surprisingly heavy.'

At sixteen lifts Bjørn was thrown to the ground. There was much cursing. Ignatius was now not so confident of making it to twenty either, so he suggested that his challenge should be to run back to their hostel with Bjørn held above his head. It was agreed. Bjørn had by now passed out, so he was left on the ground as the two men returned to their clothes, which lay in piles by the side of the square.

The next morning, the police received reports of a body dumped in an outlying suburb. They were relieved to find just another drunken groom, whom they woke, then took home. Resuscitated by a Turkish-style coffee, Bjørn told his family of his ordeal. No one believed him. Keep drinking water, they said – and hurry up, we'll need to fetch your trousers on the way.

Not long after, a small group of people watched Bjørn marry Marianne at the Birkesand registry office.

The just-wed couple honeymooned in Scotland, and these two weeks made obvious how much time had been spent apart. Bjørn vowed to speak to his boss as soon as he returned: 'I need more time at home,' he would say. 'No, damn it, that isn't good enough.' For the moment, though, such things could wait.

Argyll reminded Marianne of Norway, but with more purple and green. In fact, it was like home with colour. This prompted fantasies about living abroad that she dared not share with Bjørn. She had other hopes too, but these she did not keep to herself.

One evening, after dinner, Marianne and Bjørn played cards in the hotel bar. They were alone, even the bartender having left them to each other. A bottle of the cheapest wine stood on the table next to some upturned cards. Both had seen the other's hand, and were proud of their sneakiness, but had decided to let the other win. The game was going in circles.

'I want a family,' said Marianne, casually picking up the Jack of spades.

'You don't need that Jack!' exclaimed Bjørn, exasperated.

Marianne looked at him sideways. 'Are you cheating?' Her voice reminded Bjørn of his favourite schoolteacher.

'That you haven't noticed until now is baffling.'

She put down her cards. 'Did you hear what I said?'

Bjørn's eyes remained fixed on his cards long enough for her to wonder if she had misjudged things. 'Tell me that you want a family, too.'

'Yes,' confirmed Bjørn. 'But I must make it clear that I want no more than eleven. Mostly girls.'

That night, they made love in the way of their grandparents, with no barriers. But as Marianne (who liked to be in control of most situations) knelt over Bjørn, then sunk him deep inside her, she felt a chill on her back. This was likely have come from the window, which also lay ajar, but Marianne stopped, aware that she would never again be here, at the beginning of her life. So she waited, stilled, determined to slow down time.

The next morning, Marianne was awake before Bjørn. From their window, she could see the shore of the loch. Beyond, a small boat headed towards the open sea. Upset that someone should be enjoying this morning before she was even dressed, she pulled on clothes, put her hair up with a clip and padded excitedly out of their sleep-filled room.

Haar still clung to the far side of the loch, but the air was not cold. She walked down to the water and over wet seaweed, taking each new piece of land as soon as the receding tide allowed. Emerging rocks became mini-islands, became part of her new world. It was all hers. Taking oyster shells from around her feet, she threw one at a time into the water, counting. Eleven, she said. Eleven.

In the bedroom the air was damp and heavy . Bjørn rolled over, with a smile, only to find that his wife was gone. Light was falling through the partially undrawn curtains. He walked towards them. Still smiling, and now pushing his hair back with his hands, he looked out and saw Marianne. At this distance, back turned, monochrome, bobble-headed, she still could not have been anyone else. She stood alone on the shore.

§ 17

speaking to his boss.

'I simply want to spend more time with my wife,' he said. 'Isn't there a role for me here, in town?'

'You've only been with us a year, Bjørn.' (His boss was thinking. It was clear that he wanted to be helpful.)

Bjørn pushed. 'I know that I haven't been here long, but things are different for me now.' He watched his boss, who was uncomfortable. A car started behind them.

'I can give you a better job in sales, in the meantime. More money. Then, in another year maybe, it should be possible to bring you here as a manager.'

'Not now?'

'Not a chance. This is more than I should be offering.'

Bjørn thought for no more than a minute before accepting. At least he had secured the future. But his new job required him to spend even more time away. He explained to Marianne that this was just for the short term. It was his only way in to a better position. Really, his boss was doing him a big favour.

As Bjørn was now often away, and her wedding was past, Marianne was able to concentrate on her thesis – but she didn't feel much like a student any more. Most of her time was spent at home. She went out with friends only occasionally. Italy was a long-distant memory, and more than this: those memories increasingly seemed to belong to someone else. What had happened to the carefree girl that she had been only one year ago? And what of her dreams? She would soon become a fatter version of her mother, no doubt, and Bjørn would return home one day to realise that the young woman he loved had been lost. These were Marianne's thoughts as she visited the library one Wednesday to consult a book on the Renaissance. She was distracted from this book, and her unhappy thoughts, by Ulrikke – a girl she didn't know.

Ulrikke, having recognised Marianne, came over to say hello, although the two had never been introduced. This stranger was in her first year, studying philosophy, and carried with her a thick volume on Kant.

'That looks like tough going,' ventured Marianne, after the two had exchanged names.

'Yes, it's a bugger really. Still, one advantage of being single is that I might get bored enough to actually read it.'

'A bit of peace is wonderful at times,' said Marianne. 'I think I'm going to do a good job on this.'

'Who needs men?' They laughed – Marianne a little less.

Bjørn had not been mentioned, and Ulrikke took from their conversation that Marianne was single. With no further thought she shared her relief.

'Thank God you got rid of that arse Bjørn!' She seemed genuinely delighted. 'Hetty, my sister – you remember her? – had a terrible time with him. But then, who hasn't?'

Marianne remained silent, and Ulrikke said she looked quite ill. Ulrikke was now thinking that she might have gone too far. Perhaps Bjørn was not long gone? Or maybe Marianne had, like Hetty, discovered him in bed with a friend? Or two friends? This would not be something you'd want to be reminded of. Ulrikke, chastened, departed.

Marianne was dizzy. No one likes hearing from their husband's past lovers – or their sisters – yet Marianne would usually have forgotten it quickly. Everyone has a past, and she knew a little of Bjørn's. Before, though, it had not seemed so important – and this had not been the only time that she had heard bad things about Bjørn. There were some very upset people out there. About a month before her marriage, she had been sitting at the back of this same library, with an impressively large book on Poussin open in front of her, lost in thoughts of an allegorical nature, when she had heard the rustle of gossip. Some girls, just out of view, were mentioning her future husband's name in none-too-successful whispers.

'He did what?'

'Turned up at the hen night.'

'And this was in front of you all?'

'Yes. He told her: "Seeing as you're to be married, I think we should stop all this secretive sex, don't you?"'

There was half-muffled giggling.

'But then he went on about how a vicar's daughter shouldn't be doing it in a church anyway! Poor Hildebrand. She just ran out crying.'

Another witness spoke. 'And then he said – with all of us staring at him and cursing: "Just thought we should get that straightened out this side of the big day."'

The conversation moved on at this point, and Marianne was not ever sure that she had heard all of it correctly, but she was haunted by doubts. Later, when she had convinced herself that Bjørn's past was not her business anyway, and that she should concentrate on the future, she asked him about it. She was a little vague, and as a result Bjørn wasn't sure who this girl might have been; but Marianne wanted to know, specifically, how many girls Bjørn had slept with. Had there been many? Bjørn looked as if he was really trying to count them, but he became confused and gave up, saying: 'Good God, about half the town I should think – which is how I know for certain that you're the best girl in this place.'

Marianne had assumed he had been joking, but knew that there must have been more than she would like. She hoped to get used to the idea. Now though, thinking about it again, she flushed.

§ 18

PAUL SPENT MONTH AFTER MONTH WRITING ON HIS FREE days, and sometimes at weekends too, or during evenings, especially when not much of use had been accomplished during normal hours – and those months passed quickly, being full of weeks that resembled previous weeks. Time was measured in term-sized blocks for both Paul and Eva. Schoolchildren grew somewhat older and university courses rolled onwards across the capital.

Then, during spring, after two years of his staccato efforts, Paul's novel was ready. That is to say, it had been completed in a rough way, which was cause enough to celebrate. He took Eva out to dine at a vegetarian Chinese restaurant in Bethnal Green, which someone had recommended in a newspaper.

Paul's next move, in the search for publication, was to send his efforts to an assessment firm that advertised itself as: 'Total Writing Solutions – a professional and thorough editing and assessment service with contacts in the trade'. Paul thought that this might be just what he needed and sent off some two hundred pages, along with a cheque to cover the charges, which were broken down into: editing (per page), critical feedback (per page), and administration (one charge fits all). Then he waited, at first impatiently, then forgetfully, for a response.

When after eight weeks a reply came, its enthusiastic tone and upbeat prognosis surprised Paul as much as Eva. In truth, Eva had not read much of what Paul had written. The reason for this was twofold: at first she did not read it because Paul had been shy and reluctant to give her any of his work to read (perhaps sensing a lack of quality?); then, secondly, once Paul had become used to the idea that Eva might read his writings and had given her a hundred pages to tackle, she had found them full of words that she did not understand, and felt that the plot had become too rambling to follow. She did not tell Paul of her doubts – for a start, English was not her first language – but Paul had misgivings of his own. So, when his assessor described the plot as 'full of richness' and 'surprising the reader with sudden twists that, nonetheless, seem remarkably true to life', Paul laughed with delight. His assessor went on: 'The work is full of promise, but needs some further thought before it is ready to show an agent.' Then came a list of ideas relating to structure, pacing and characterisation. Paul read these comments keenly and began to make notes with a new energy. 'Yes,' he told Eva (who was now becoming more enthusiastic about Paul's writing, having been, at best, sceptical before), 'this chap is full of bright ideas.'

And indeed he was. The assessor, Dean Spencer, a sometime journalist, was also the owner of Total Writing Solutions – and the brightest of his ideas had been to start a sham company in order to extract money from the countless sad loners who thought that they had it within themselves to write a book. His partner took phone calls and replied to letters, also arranged publicity and cashed the cheques. She had been working at a call centre in Gwent when Dean Spencer met her in a pub and took her to bed. Finding her to have been the most talented of all the lovers he had bedded that year, and having only recently stumbled upon the idea of his writing consultancy, Dean persuaded her to follow him to London, where, once her flawed character had been revealed, he introduced her to his plan for making money. 'I've always admired writers, Dean,' she told him, before negotiating a slightly larger cut of the takings than he might have been anticipating.

Total Writing Solutions operated from a flat above a newsagent's in Whitechapel, and they had a standardised format for their critiques. Dean would briefly skip-read selected pages of the book in question, in order that he might at least enter the character's correct names in his assessment template. Then things were quickly dealt with. Firstly, the reply would state, as a fact, that nothing could be guaranteed in the world of books. Then it would say, '. . . but in the work you have sent me I note such promise that I see every reason to be hugely optimistic as to your future as a writer' of poetry/ literary fiction/ romance/ or whatever.

Next, the reply would list achievable changes that had to be made in order to present the writing in its best light; these were always the same. Once these improvements had been put in place (the reply went on), attracting the attention of an agent was, whilst not quite guaranteed, then highly likely. A reduced fee was offered for a resubmission, at which time, assuming that the advised work had been done, the assessor would be in a position to pass the work on to the owner of the company, who would in turn pass it to his contacts in the trade.

Resubmitted work followed a similarly standardised formula to that employed for the first reply: Dean Spencer would pass the writing to his lover, who would take a look and say (without fail), 'This work, Mr Spencer, is total shit.' Then she would throw it in the bin and the two would retire to the White Hart pub for a drink.

Later, a letter would be sent emphasising that the hopeful author had been warned that nothing in the writing world could be guaranteed, and that, furthermore, the assessor was disappointed with the quality of the resubmitted work (which lacked development), so that it was felt at this time that there was nothing further that the company could do to help. The letter always ended: Good luck.

Still, Paul's work was of such low quality – using words such as 'peregrinate' and 'bounteous', where 'walk' and 'full' would have done – that Total Writing Solutions thought that they smelled a rat. They carefully toned down their response, but still made sure that there was enough honey to make their victim, should he be real, feel sweet.

Hopelessly excited, yet still trying to be realistic, Paul began work on the changes that he felt sure would bring his novel to the highest level. 'You know, just because someone says it's good, doesn't necessarily mean much,' he told Eva. 'There's still plenty to improve.' But he felt his enthusiasm bubble, and found himself thinking (in moments when he should have been writing) about his soon-to-be-glorious future. And during this time, whilst Paul was motoring towards what he thought would be literary stardom, Eva decided to buy a bicycle.

The impulse for this change of transport (she had been taking buses and tubes thus far) came from the combination of an imminent tube drivers' strike and a chance encounter with a free newspaper. Eva sat down next to this paper, on her way to lectures, at the same moment as the driver of the underground train that she was on began a propaganda announcement over the train's tannoy system: '. . . and we ask passengers to be patient, because the walk-out on Thursday is in response to . . .' Eva switched off – but to fully ignore the driver she needed something else to focus on, so took up the newspaper next to her. This contained nothing but adverts, almost exclusively for second-hand cars, but as she flicked through them she saw a column of bicycles resting against a row of washing machines and she was struck by the memory of freewheeling down the hills of Birkesand. 'Sod this tube,' she thought (she had always suspected them of being unhealthy anyway), 'I'm going to cycle from now on.' And, as usual, she stuck to her word. She bought the bike from a woman in Bow, and that Thursday, as the tube stations closed, she breezed past legions of unwilling summer-time walkers – although, in truth, the joy of this was tempered by car fumes and her constant fear of being run over. Arriving at university felt like an achievement in itself, strengthening Eva's bond to her bike – so, when on her way home again she saw a felt-tipped sign offering 'Free security coding for your bicycle – protect those wheels', she decided to take up this opportunity. The sign read: 'Tonight, June 24, Stepney Green, 8 p.m.' So Eva set off after a light supper, declining Paul's offer to take the bike himself.

Unfortunately for Eva, this bike-coding event was not all it seemed. She too was about to become a victim. (This constant exposure to the threat of crime was, she soon realised, one of the problems of living in a great city.) Two Turkish brothers, who had a clothing manufacturing business off Commercial Road, had become addicted to card playing and had run up debts beyond an amount they could hope to repay. The other members of their card-playing circle were violent, ignoble types, as indeed were the broth-ers, but all were united in an unusually generous view of debts run up at the table, putting them, if only for a short interlude, in the same category as sportsmen of the previous century, who loved the act of participation over the thrust of winning. When the brothers had been found short in the middle of a hand (one having lent all he had to the other early on in the game), the oldest gentleman at the table shook his head with such sadness that the brothers expect-ed to be ending their days that night – and to be spending the next years feeding Epping Forest seedlings. But to their delight, the old man began to talk to the others at the table about a suitable forfeit, leading one of the brothers to begin crying in a way that threatened to jeopardise his health. Once the youngster had been silenced, the card table patriarch announced the agreed penalty: the brothers were to travel from London's East End to Beirut wearing divers' wetsuits and using no money to help them. (A hollow laugh and shrugs from around the table.) They would leave the following night and make a camcorder documentary of this odyssey that they would present to the old man's son in Beirut, who would post it back to London, leading, in the event of satisfactory compliance, to a cancellation of the debt, and in the event of failure or attempted deception, to a back-street bullet. The brothers kissed everyone at the table, surrendered their wallets, and quickly left.

So when Eva turned up in Stepney Green with her bicycle, dismounting next to the park gates, she unwittingly pushed her bike onto the stage of a comedy film. 'Ah, I see we have our second cyclist,' said the larger brother as Eva approached. 'It's still not eight, but shall we begin?' The smaller brother sighed, then produced a home-movie camera from his bag. As his sibling ripped off his trousers (revealing his wetsuit underneath), Eva and the other young woman (who had also arrived early for this show) abandoned their bikes and backed away fast. After a hasty disrobing, the rubber-suited boys clambered on the bicycles, waved and set off south, the smaller one looking all the time through the eye of his camera.

This event could not be fully appreciated by Paul and Eva, who had no idea what to make of it. Having wasted four hours at the police station, waiting to give their evidence, the couple realised that, often, the police don't know what to make of things either. So Eva returned to the tubes and Paul patched up his novel, and soon it was time for a holiday – which they took in Wales. 'Damn – that was too boring,' Eva said later. 'Let's do something better next time, eh?'

At this point Paul was ready to unleash his improved writing on the world. He sent the masterpiece to Total Writing Solutions; he needed a larger envelope this time – and more postage. This he took to be a sign of progress.

Four weeks passed, then came his reply. The feeling of let-down that hit Paul when he read this kiss-off was magnified by the fact that the first reply had been solely responsible for dispelling his doubts about his own writing. Furthermore, the ideas for bettering his work had given him a sense of purpose and energy that he had never previously known. He thought that he was getting somewhere. Now, to read ' . . . and so it is with regret that we must conclude that there is nothing more that we can offer you at this time. We wish you good luck' made him feel like a bride jilted at the altar. All his self-doubt returned at once, and he was left with the impression that he was lost in a darkening forest.

§ 19

AFTER A YEAR OF MARRIAGE, AND HELPED BY HIS PROMOTION, Bjørn became able to afford the deposit on a small house in the suburbs. The house was really only a cabin, being arranged on a single floor and having been built entirely of wood; unfortunately, it was often in shadow, sitting beneath a steep hill and many pine trees; but Bjørn was joyous. He imagined filling it with children.

They brought their few belongings from the rented flat in Bjørn's embarrassingly old car, then spent the evening drinking wine and making wild and uncosted plans for their new home. The next day, though, Bjørn set off to sell shoes with renewed vigour, leaving Marianne to consider her unfinished thesis, and the responsibility of providing a new Olsen to live in the second bedroom. What had happened to Bjørn's job as a manager? It was somewhere in a pipeline, no doubt.

The thought of her future, with a family, had always helped Marianne feel positive, and yet, after a year of trying, she had failed to become pregnant. At first, she had been relaxed about conception, thinking that it would be the natural result of their married union. In fact, part of her had been glad that she had not become pregnant straight away: there was no rush. Now things were different. Alone in her dark house, Marianne became obsessed. Instead of studying the history of art, she was learning how to conceive. *The Nutrition of Fertility*, by Dr Jens Stockhausen, was sensible but dull; *The Cosmos of Conception*, bizarre and difficult to believe; Dr Zak Bluhm's *Pregnancy Food Bible*, simply annoying. Yet Marianne read them all with great zeal, underlining salient points and making notes in the margins.

She bought a calendar and marked with red circles those days on which she was most likely to become pregnant. Blue circles highlighted days on which the biology was wrong, but the planetary alignments were at their most advantageous. Black squares denoted dates of no worth at all, when the best policy would be to rest and save energy.

Following the advice of her food bible, Marianne altered her diet. She forced down many steamed tripe-and-vegetable lunches that were quite disgusting to her – but, she thought, perhaps all the more potent as a result.

Bjørn, who was unaware that there was a grand plan under way, was perplexed by the strange foods that had started to appear at the table. He thought that it might be that Marianne was over-keen to show what an imaginative cook she was going to be over the next decades: never a dull meal. Yet if devilled oysters on kelp was to appear just once more he knew that there would be an argument.

After these culinary assaults, Bjørn was in no mood for sex. Perpetually worn down by the weight of his shoes, he would have been lethargic anyway – but having been violated by his dinner, he was fit only for a troubled sleep. Some nights Marianne, it seemed, agreed. At other times Bjørn was savagely used, whenever he happened to be home and regardless of what else he was doing at the time. Books were left on the ground, part-read; teeth were half brushed; telephone conversations were urgently truncated. Bjørn was beginning to wonder what sort of woman he had married.

A year and a half into their marriage, and still not pregnant, Marianne saw that she must up her efforts. She visited a Chinese woman who gave her a herbal pessary, which failed in its intended effect, instead causing Marianne to have blurred vision for more than a week, during which time she risked death every time she left her house, either at the foot of a ravine, if she tuned left, or under the wheels of a car, had she walked towards the centre of town. Frustrated, she sought help elsewhere. A man in a kaftan sold her a crystal that he told her to swing in clockwise circles over her womb, which she did until her arms ached. She slept with it and woke with an indentation on her belly that she considered a propitious omen, until nature proved her wrong. Patience, she told herself.

On the 25th of February – a day when the stars were singing – she set Bjørn to work after a particularly invigorating meal of beetroot dumplings. Afterwards, while Bjørn lay defeated on the sofa, Marianne quickly went to the bathroom and spent a full ten minutes standing on her head. It was not as easy as she had remembered from childhood. Blood filled her ears and her eyes bulged, but only when she was sure that, in continuing, she risked permanent damage, did she fall over, exhausted, onto the tiled floor. She lay there for some time, looking nothing like a beautiful young woman with something of a glow about her, but every bit the victim at a crime scene.

§ 20

AFTER HIS DECISION TO ABANDON THE STRUGGLE FOR A career in visual art, Paul had not felt lost. Perhaps he should have done, but the way his relationship with Eva had rushed onwards, followed by the accident of his falling into a teaching job, had given his life the illusion of momentum. Time, of course, moves on without giving a hoot who feels ready to come with it – but whilst a man is able to deceive himself that he is at the helm, steering his life's course, he may enjoy the feeling that all is well and that he will always turn only where he wishes to go (the impossibility of being able to reverse can be ignored in this happily blind state). Now, cruelly early, Paul saw the true nature of things, and being aware that he was absolutely not in control of his future gave him an edginess that had previously been missing.

Eva saw the situation too. Being in the position of watcher, however, she felt strangely in charge – an illusion akin to that enjoyed by a swimming teacher who cheers as her little charge thrashes unaided from one end of the pool to the other, whilst she mentally works to keep them afloat. This new situation, where Eva felt for the first time able to give Paul career advice, came as a relief because, where before (when her idea of an artist's work was an abstract one) she had rather liked that Paul was a bit different, now she had begun to feel rising frustration.

When the first, positive, reply arrived from Paul's assessor at Total Writing Solutions there had been hope for a career in writing – Eva, naturally, did not then share her views on the subject of work with Paul. (She had also been very busy ensuring that her degree would be a first-class one, and maybe she wanted to give Paul a sporting chance to make something of himself.) Now that it was clear that any writing success would be a long way off, if it was to happen at all, Eva felt not only able to steer Paul on a straighter path, but duty-bound to do so. Even given this steely business-like approach, Eva, who loved Paul, wanted to find a way of cushioning the impact of her husband's fall, and this led her to gently float the idea of a full-time position at the school. 'You do seem to have an unusual flair for the work,' she said. 'Why don't you try it for a year or two?'

Thus Paul found himself talking to the headmaster, who referred him to his deputy, who, to Paul's relief, showed the sort of total forgiveness in the matter of the stuffed birds that would have been becoming even for a man of the cloth.

It seemed that Paul's talent for teaching had been noticed, and the school was glad to offer him four almost full days a week, starting from the beginning of the autumn term. This he accepted, but without the gladness that might have been expected of him. Paul, in being highly gifted in something he did not value, suffered the fate of a man, long married to an admired lady, who has, nevertheless, spent years being hopelessly in love with someone else. In such ungratefulness is tragedy born.

Eva finished her undergraduate course in the summer, three years and three months after arriving in England, and once she had graduated she sought a well-paid job. This disappointed Paul, who had imagined her continuing her studies. She had always had an interest in early Nordic history, and Paul thought she should pursue this. Eva felt otherwise. To her, a directionless quest for knowledge (which is how she saw such esoteric study) was no more than self-indulgence. Watching Paul whilst he tried to write only stiffened her resolve to start work on something solid: something that would pay monthly, releasing her and Paul from being obliged to live in a flat paid for by Paul's parents. She had been increasingly unhappy with this dependency, but her pride was hobbled by her need for a degree (the passport to her well-paid job) and the fact that she was studying in English, which slowed her down and precluded the taking of part-time work.

In any event, after obtaining her first-class degree, Eva spent some months establishing contacts in the business world, during which time she helped out the uncle of a university friend with lots of dull filing at his thriving City law firm. Then, on a sparkling autumn morning, she made her thrust into the world of six-day weeks and addictive salaries.

That morning, Eva was up early: Paul could feel her energy from beneath his sleep.

Got to get up, he thought. Got to show some willing to be part of this event. Having risen, he began to make coffee. The flat was cold, but from outside, and above, it seemed that the sun, like Paul, felt it necessary that it be seen to make an effort. Setting two cups on their mini-table fulfilled Paul's breakfast ambitions, and he began to flick-read a free local paper. An article on a lady who thought that the exhaust from the Limehouse Link tunnel was responsible for turning her window box strawberries into marrows was absorbing Paul, when Eva came in. She wore the second of the two suits she had bought with her summer's earnings (combined with her savings, which for the daughter of such wealthy parents amounted to very little – plus any other bits of cash she had lurking around: some of it Norwegian), and looked young.

The young don't often notice how fresh their lovers appear; they have to wait until they are older, and this accounts for much melancholy; but Paul saw with timeless eyes that morning, and the picture of Eva that he framed – on the morning of her first interview, in her second suit – hung heavy in his mind.

Life was moving on, and it was leaving him behind.

SOON AFTER STARTING HER SHINY NEW JOB, EVA TOOK OUT A mortgage, without help from Paul, and bought a house in Wapping. 'You've been paying for me for too long,' she said. 'Now it's my turn.'

In moving from a rented basement to their own three-bedroomed house there was, of course, reason for celebration – but Paul could not help seeing this as a statement of superiority from Eva. The day of their move brought what he had achieved next to what she had, and separated them by only a ten-minute drive. So, whilst the recently built terrace they arrived at was hardly glamorous, it benefited from the comparison with their just-left flat, which had desperately tried to prevent their leaving by the trick of a loose-hinged door. Watching Paul try to lift the door back into place, Eva was reminded of a nurse supporting a weighty geriatric, whilst a young relative looked on in discomfort.

In this new house Paul kept up a more constant rhythm of work than he had been used to and dreamed of a second novel, whilst Eva left before breakfast and arrived back at any time between seven and midnight. This move to Wapping was accompanied by a change of mood in the lives of both Paul and Eva. Paul felt this key change immediately – and his perception of it was given shape by the move itself, the discomfort of which seemed to signpost a darker future.

One Friday evening, as Eva and Paul made plans to leave their rented flat, a split in their outlook had become apparent. Eva, who was intending to throw out most of what she owned anyway, said, 'I've called some removal companies – one's able to come tomorrow to give us a quote.' Paul, who had anticipated hiring a van (there was one often parked nearby that advertised a great daily price, painted on its side), said, 'Fine.' (He told himself: You do not need to feel in charge of this move.)

The next afternoon, a large middle-aged man called round. It did not take him long to see that this was a small job, so, having done some measuring and made a few notes, he promised to send an estimate. 'Can't you tell us now?' asked Paul. 'A rough figure?' This amateurish guessing was not to the removal man's taste, but he had a son of a similar age to Paul, and wanted to help. 'Well, I can't be exact, but it's not a lot, so, perhaps . . .' An ambulance screamed past above them at this point, so the sentence was increasingly drowned out. Still, Paul could see the price in the movement of the man's lips. He gasped. 'How much? For the few things we have here? Just down the road? Bloody hell!'

Eva apologised, following the man into the street to say how sorry she was about her husband's rudeness, and how the price seemed very reasonable to her. These conciliatory words had little calming effect. Eva returned to the flat in a fury.

Still, Paul got his way, and on the morning of the move he and his friend Ronnie carried furniture and bedding, a fridge (which was astonishingly heavy) and cookware, along with all the oddments that a couple might collect in their first few years together, up those irregular steps and into a van that looked as if travelling to Wapping was about as far as the most optimistic mover might risk.

The fridge had been one of the first items to be loaded into the van and Paul felt increasingly unwell with each heavy upward step. He desperately wanted to stop and put the thing down, but Eva was watching from below, and he feared her ridicule, given that he had shooed away paid-for help.

In fact, Eva watched with nervousness, not spite. She had noticed Paul's decreasing vigour over the last months – even as they walked to the shops she had to slow right down to keep next to him. She had assumed this to be linked to Paul's sedentary and strange way of working (compared to those she knew who rose by five and spent their mornings bouncing around the bank achieving things), but watching him struggle with their little fridge (three narrow shelves and an icebox), she feared that a hernia might be one step away. Still, she did not mention her concerns, as Paul was extremely sensitive to criticism, especially that concerning his physical ability. Once they were settled in Wapping, things were sure to improve. Paul was now teaching four days a week, which would liven him up; also, such a lack of light cannot ever have done good to anyone – and for the last two years Paul had been spending three days a week underground, digging a tunnel towards his novel's end. Now things would be different. Yes, light was what they needed, then all might be well again.

Ronnie too noticed Paul's difficulties and he tried to take as much weight as possible himself, in order that his friend might be able to continue. As the two hobbled upwards, he was put in mind of a job he had undertaken six months previously.

Ronnie was a cellist. But, as a freelancer and sometime member of several mediocre London orchestras, he was unable to meet all his bills. He was, therefore, forced to search for other, additional, employment. He found this as a part-time deliveryman for a local furniture company. A violist friend of his drove a minicab and was sure that Ronnie would find this work more gentle on his hands – but Ronnie hated driving in London, preferring his role as passenger, so stuck to his heavy lifting. One day he turned up at work to find that his partner (and driver) was ill. There was, however, a table that needed delivering, as it was overdue, and the lady who had ordered it had telephoned to make clear that if it did not turn up in time for her wedding anniversary dinner, she did not want it at all. This would have been a problem, as the table was a bespoke item that would be impossible to sell to another client (having 'Alfred and Hilda, forty years together' etched into its slate top). Thus, Ronnie was told to deliver it on his own and unload it with the help of the lady's son, who had said on the telephone that morning: 'Yeah, sure, no problem. There are a few steps though.' The furniture company's manager wanted to make certain: 'It's got a slate top – it's really unusually heavy.' This was, apparently, not a worry.

So Ronnie arrived, winced when he saw that his client lived on the seventh floor of a Victorian block, jogged up 140 steps and rang on the bell. Already breathing hard, he walked back down with his would-be helper.

'OK, mate, you take the front – the back's harder off the lorry,' said Ronnie. 'Take care, it's pretty heavy.' Out they went, not a word of complaint from the helper – slowly up six steps, then a sudden stop.

'No, no, dear God no.' The helper appears to be near tears.

'Do you need a rest?'

'Not a chance.' He ignores the question. 'Oh Jesus.'

(A pause.) 'Shall we go on?'

(A look of anger crossed with despair.) 'Are you crazy? I can't do one more step.'

And with that, he limped off up to his parents' flat. Ronnie took four hours to get the table to the flat, and was unable to do anything but lie down for two weeks. Once he could stand again, he decided to ignore his hatred of traffic, and took a job as a sandwich courier.

Now, on the day of Paul and Eva's move, Ronnie remembered why he had given up his job. He was surprised by Paul's tenacity. Still, his concern for his friend's health prompted him to ask if all was well – but only once they were out of Eva's view, alone in the van.

'Indigestion or something, I suppose,' replied Paul.

He did not even convince himself.

§ 22

DAMASK ROSE, SPIRITUALLY ACTIVATED QUARTZ, SEA URCHIN.
Nothing had succeeded in bringing about that which Marianne had imagined endlessly. It was time, she decided, to go to the doctor, and she dreaded hearing what was truly wrong.

'My dear girl, we will of course run the usual checks,' her physician said, 'but the solution may be more simple than you imagine. You say that your husband is often away. Well this cannot help.' He laughed, before going on. And as he spoke, Marianne felt relief flood her limbs. Stress, anxiety: these were bad. Tests would be taken at the hospital, but whilst they waited for the results she should be calm. Throw away the charts. Eat cake. Go for a long walk. Marianne left, smiling.

It was May and the blossom was out, carrying the scent of spring. It was enough to make her want to bounce. Little skips found their way into her walk until she could contain them no longer and was compelled to break into a child-like run. She ran past the cinema and along the streets of the old quarter, her little handbag flying around her, so that shoppers outside Hansen's department store asked each other whether she was all there in the head, and an elderly man on his way home from the fish market remembered the day the Germans had invaded.

By now, Marianne was feeling wobbly, so she slowed, eventually stopping by the statue of King Olav, gasping through her refound smile, feeling as if a little more joy was all that was needed to send her rocketing skyward, ready to explode. Bjørn was home from his trip to Århus that evening, and, as luck would have it, this was not a time that she was at all likely to get pregnant. Thus, they could have a relaxed dinner then perhaps watch a film on television. How simple.

That afternoon Bjørn arrived at Århus airport carrying a present for his boss, Odd Rådal. It was a life-sized mannequin, and had been given by the director of a Danish distributor. The dummy was most unwieldy, and had slapped and kicked a number of people already. Bjørn carried it under his right arm, it being light despite its size. In his left arm, Bjørn had his usual case.

'She reminds me so much of Odd's first wife,' the Danish director said. But Bjørn was not keen. The dummy did not look in good condition anyway – it was fit for a skip.

'Couldn't she go by courier?'

This unwillingness seemed to agitate the Dane. 'No, no. That won't do at all. Today would have been their anniversary. I only found her this morning and thought, given what Odd's said about you, that you wouldn't let me down.' These last words held something of a threat.

'But will he be happy to be reminded of an ex-wife?'

'Yes, of course. He hated her, true, but how many laughs that lady provided us with over the years.'

So Bjørn lumbered towards the check-in with Odd Rådal's first wife tucked under his arm and sweat running down his neck. He dropped his case as he presented his passport and ticket. 'Just the two items to check in today, sir?' asked the attendant.

'No, these will come as hand luggage.' Bjørn was already looking around for the stall selling drinks that used to be here.

'Not the lady, obviously,' laughed the attendant. Bjørn nodded; the attendant looked askance, so Bjørn explained things slowly, as if to a dull-brained child.

'You've got loads of space on board, this flight's always almost empty.'

'Sorry,' shrugged the man. 'I'll mark it fragile.'

He now took hold of the dummy's head and began pulling her towards him. Vexed, Bjørn jerked her back, by the feet, causing both her legs to pop off and clatter to the ground. The two men stared at the lost limbs.

'Just send her as three bits,' Bjørn said, with strained quietness. He picked up the legs, passed them across the counter, then took his case, ready to go.

The attendant waived a hand. 'I'll have to weigh the case, sir.'

Bjørn tightened his teeth.

'Just put it up here, sir.'

Sure that he could find it within himself to be calm and mature, Bjørn complied, and smiled. The attendant nodded as if he had known all along.

'It will have to go as cargo.' And he pressed a button that started a belt that took Bjørn's case off towards the hold.

'Give me my case back, you little shit!'

People stopped where they were to watch, as Bjørn screamed.

'You pulled the legs off that girl!' He gestured violently in all directions so that everyone looked in different places to see. 'You've got the case, now do you want my shirt too?' The attendant was clear that he didn't, but Bjørn was already undressing.

'Here, have this!' His belt flew off. 'Trousers?' The attendant looked away. Everyone else, however, was enjoying this. Bjørn was down to his underpants when two much larger men in uniform approached. They took hold of him. The crowd was to be disappointed.

'Calm down,' they said. 'And whatever you do, don't show us your dick.'

All the fury dropped from Bjørn when he looked down at his bare legs.

'Come on, don't stop there,' someone said – but everyone looked away as Bjørn came past, on his way to a spartan room, where he would sit on a plastic chair, looking like he had just been the victim of a humiliating interrogation.

Possibly because he had kept his pants on, Bjørn was not charged by the airport police – but Scanlink Air banned him from their flights. So, the next morning, he returned home to Marianne with a different airline, relieved to be free, but furious at the pettiness of airport officials. Mr Rådal, not for the first time, received his anniversary gift late.

Bjørn spent his extra night in Århus at an airport hotel. By the time he arrived the kitchen had closed and the only thing he could find to eat were biscuits. The night porter, being unusually helpful, and having seen that Bjørn was in some distress, provided him with a half bottle of whisky. He would take no payment for it, nor would he share a drink, so Bjørn thanked him and went up to his room. Here he sat on a round-backed chair, which seemed to have been carpeted rather than upholstered, opened the bottle and poured into a glass that he had found in the bathroom, which may, to start with, have smelled of toothpaste. Each mouthful steadied him. His fingers stopped twitching, his feet shuffled more slowly. Soon his eyes were coming to rest, like a child's just-left spinning top. By his third glass, Bjørn was approaching clarity. Crumbling a shortbread biscuit, he began to think . . .

How had he got here? A not unclean room, decorated in the style of a modern train, stuffed with plastic. Was this home now? He thought about Marianne. He had phoned her from the airport. 'I'm afraid I'm delayed,' he said, eventually conceding that this was partly his own fault – yes, he had over-reacted – yes, they had talked about this before – yes, he was now regretting it. Yet Marianne had not been cross. She had come across as . . . (he was almost there – just one moment) . . . motherly.

'There are so many more important things for us to be thinking about,' she had said. 'Deeply important things.'

Bjørn had agreed, without knowing what on earth his highly distractable wife was talking about – but now he heard these words slow down, and hold still in the amber of his glass. Seeing them captured there, he understood at once.

Suddenly standing up, he slapped his face then danced on the bed.

Was Marianne pregnant? Had he even been awake these last months? No – he had spent a year asleep: more! No, no . . . He thought about it further. She had certainly not been pregnant when he left. He calmed himself. Not pregnant – yet. Bjørn finished the bottle of whisky in the spirit of celebration, after which he was fit for nothing but falling asleep in a bed-top sprawl.

He was woken early by a whirring sound. It was impossible to see in the darkness, but it seemed to be coming from the wall lamp beside him. Perplexed, Bjørn turned on the light. As he did so, the whirring became high pitched and frantic. Something in that glass-bowled lamp was accelerating. A mouse, aware that it was about to catch fire, was trying to escape – moving ever faster, until it became a smoking blur, shot upwards out of the lamp (soot falling from it), bounced off the ceiling and fell behind the curtains, from where it ran off towards the bathroom without a pause. Bjørn saw beside him the remains of his biscuits and smelled faint notes of burned fur. His eyes hurt, so he turned out the light and fell back into sleep.

That morning, Bjørn laughed at the airport, on the plane and in the customs hall – so that by the time he was hugging Marianne, he was vibrantly awake and feeling extremely husbandly. Marianne had been deprived of her planned evening with Bjørn. Still, she was in a light mood following the previous day's happenings, and looked forward to a meal without unwelcome but nutritious additions. For once they could relax.

Bjørn, however, raced through his fishcakes as if he was keen to be done with inconvenience of lunch. When she had also finished, Marianne went to fetch dessert. Before she was half way to the kitchen, Bjørn had pinioned her against the wall.

'Come on then, sweetheart,' he said with alarming energy. 'Let's screw.'

Marianne threw him off. 'Stop it Bjørn, what on earth are you thinking of?' She unruffled her top. 'If I had been detained overnight in Denmark, I would be feeling a little more humble today.'

With that, she went into the kitchen, leaving Bjørn to wonder at the fickleness of women. Dessert was eaten in silence.

§ 23

ONE DAY IN JULY, MARIANNE WOKE LATE WITH THE SUDDEN feeling that the world had been enjoying the morning in her absence. She had been lying in contented stillness, lazy as a summer trout. Soft air moved over her, bringing with it the sounds of birdsong through her open window. A lawnmower hummed in the distance.

Her eyes sprung open: a lawnmower? What time was it? Sticking out a hand, she found her clock. Eleven-thirty. Early risers would have been up for six hours by now! Her cousin, Ludwig, would have been out at four, rowing the fjord as he trolled for sea trout. He would already be sleepy: eleven-thirty? Time for a lunchtime nap.

Quickly, Marianne went to the bathroom, splashed all over with cold water and pulled a dress over her head. Outside, the sun dazzled. In its full beam, Marianne ate breakfast, coffee adding to the ripening heat. Come on, girl, she said to herself. Is summer not short enough? Get to it.

Ever since her doctor had given her leave to continue living, Marianne had been planning her garden. Days without obsession were so much more beautiful: there was time to notice things. Her garden was, strictly speaking, oblong; but it was really no more than a slightly squashed square, a large part of which was taken up by ill-fitted concrete slabs. Some years before, no doubt (probably on a day similar to this), others had woken up bursting with gardening energy. Marianne hoped that she would manage a better job than they had. Those slabs would come out first. She could store them on the other side of the fence, there being nothing but forest below them on the hill.

Next, she would tackle the roses that rambled, out of control, in the far corner. They had grown into woody monsters, and looked not unlike the teenage boys who gathered at the bus stop on summer evenings, with gangly limbs and unkempt heads. What she was meant to do with these, she did not know, but it would be a shame to dig them out. Pruning might be needed. Patchy grass completed the look of the unloved garden, but Marianne was not perturbed. The challenge energised her. She took her breakfast cup and plate inside, washed up, and returned to the garden wearing a pair of old skiing gloves. They might not have been made for the job, but they would do nicely for now.

First, she attacked the paving. The slabs were already wobbly, which helped her get hold of the edges – but they were heavier than she had imagined. Each square had to be unevenly rolled across the middle of the garden and helped through the fence, onto the hillside. Several of them slipped a few metres down it. It was satisfying to remove that paving, but by the time that she was watching the last of these blocks slide to its precarious resting place, the lawn appeared to have been ploughed. Never mind, thought Marianne, it was a hopeless case anyway. All I need is seed. I'm pretty sure that grass grows from seed.

She planned buy some that afternoon – there was a DIY and garden centre on the main road back into town. Now, though, she eyed her roses, before going inside for the scissors. These proved to be almost useless at cutting back plants, and, by the time that she had finished, the bushes were torn and broken more than pruned.

I'll get some secateurs as well as the seed, thought Marianne; and some ready-grown plants in pots; and a book, too – there's obviously more to gardening than I had imagined.

It was then that she saw the first of the snails. Squatting down, she could see more of them sheltering on the shaded base of the wall. Snails, she knew, were bad. She was going to bring fragile young plants into her garden, and these things were lurking in corners. She went back inside, then came back out carrying an empty glass jar, went to the (now subdued) roses, and plucked every snail from its sanctuary. Her mother would have stamped on them, whilst shouting: It's no good throwing them down the hill – they'll be back! But Marianne wanted a garden free from violence. She secured the lid on the jar of snails, then popped them into the car, planning to throw them into a bit of woodland far from here, from where they could crawl into someone else's garden.

After a snacky lunch, Marianne set off to the garden centre. She drove an indirect route, thus ensuring that she would pass a suitable spot for her snails. At a particularly leafy part of the forest, she wound down the car window and slowed to a crawl. There was no one about, so, as the music from her car radio frightened the birds, Marianne flung snails into the wild from her still-moving car. She steered with her knees, laughing, as she imagined what Bjørn would make of this.

Six weeks later, Marianne was told that she would never have children. 'It's a one in ten thousand chance,' said her consultant. 'Which basically means never.'

The full impact of this on her was not instant. Only over the next days did the news settle within her bones and sink into her belly. From there it entered her blood, which took the feeling to all parts, leaving her nails brittle, her eyes opaque and her breasts wrinkled. Within a week her teeth yellowed.

Bjørn was away for this first week of Marianne's decay. It was a very trying time for Norwegian retailers. A strong dollar and rising interest rates left many people fearing for their jobs. Households across Norway worried. Bjørn, who, at work, was trying to make himself appear indispensable, was due back for only three days before an important trip to Bonn. He had, naturally, been stressed recently. He and Marianne had argued about trivial things. She wondered what would happen now that she had this to tell him. He might leave her. His whores around Europe might start to seem more important than his dried-up wife. Maybe one of them was already special to him. Not merely a fuck, but a mistress. How much warmer would her round thighs feel under him, now that he knew that he had a desiccating lizard-wife back at home? He would pray that she did the decent thing and hung herself from a tree – a fertility offering so that this new Mrs Olsen would start birthing babies now, and for the next decade. Kids would turn up as regularly as Christmas presents. Dozens of them eventually, falling about this house sicking and saying Mummy.

It was Friday afternoon and Bjørn would be home shortly. Marianne went to a corner and tried to disappear. When Bjørn let himself in, he found her tight as a ball, lying on the floor, reciting a prayer made up entirely of names, as if she was an old woman before a war memorial and was reading from a list of the dead.

That night, Bjørn sat on the end of the bed for more than two hours, listening to Marianne sleep. Finally he took some of her sleeping pills himself and lay down, heavy fog arriving like a longed-for killer. But he could not stop himself dreaming.

He was in India, having been promoted to shoe-seller to the world, and a large family stood before him. They were surrounded by lots of homes, making him feel quite claustrophobic. Although he could make out none of his surroundings clearly, he was increasingly convinced that these homes were little more than plastic sheeting and boxes. An intense smell, disturbing yet vaguely attractive, strengthened as the breeze stilled.

A small, elderly man stood nearest. He seemed to be the head of this family. Bjørn looked down. 'Goodness, sir,' he said, seeing the unshod gentleman's broken feet. 'You certainly need my help.' Bjørn opened his case. It contained myriad footwear.

'It is very important,' the old man said, 'that our shoes reflect our personalities.'

Bjørn seemed moved. This man saw the world as he did. After

some thought, Bjørn reached for a pair of London-made chestnut brogues.

'Very classic. Old-fashioned, some might say. Still more would call them timeless.' Bjørn passed them to the patriarch, pointing out the detail in the stitching as he did so. The old man looked delighted.

The man's wife came forward. Having taken her character in with a glance, Bjørn presented her with his choice of shoes: high-heeled slingbacks in faux leopard. She took them with a sneer. Some of the family laughed as they all shuffled excitedly forward. Next came the son and his wife, then aunts and children, some of whom may not even have been relations. All were shod, and, with a couple of obvious exceptions, everyone was happy.

Bjørn smiled, his lips now papery, his teeth crumbling. He began to add up the bill on his calculator. 'US dollars?' The older man looked surprised and shook his head. Bjørn fiddled with the numbers once more, then showed the amount to his customer.

'But we cannot afford this!' exclaimed the man, who then began shrugging his shoulders to his family and pulling faces, as if Bjørn was some charlatan thief. But he did not move, or appear ready to give the shoes back.

'Perhaps you have something to exchange?' asked Bjørn, who was always ready to help out a client. His eyes moved between the ladies of the crowd, but settled on a small boy. There was a gasp from a very dark woman, who then began crying – but the patriarch nodded.

Bjørn took the boy's hand and dragged him away.

The next morning, Bjørn woke with dust in his eyes. So, whilst Marianne slept on, he went to wash himself clean as best he could, only waking her up when he became concerned about how many tablets she might have taken. After a silent breakfast, he told her that he was canceling his trip to Bonn. They needed time together – they could go somewhere for a few days. He was surprised by her answer.

'Go to Bonn,' she said. 'A holiday won't do anything for us.' And having made this statement, she left the room.

Bjørn did not know what to do next. People sometimes needed to be alone. They had to grieve. Lamenting the death of the unborn would be a superhuman task. It was like having someone just disappear. Were they gone? Perhaps they would return. The fact that he had lost the most important thing that he had never had, made Bjørn sick. Yesterday morning, all the unborn children of the world were wobbling about in God's vast nursery; by the time Bjørn returned home, his kids had been found, taken aside and shot: one bullet each. What pit they were then thrown into, he would never know. There were not even bodies to bury.

And what of Marianne? He tried further conversations throughout the morning, and over the course of the next day, but was always told to go; nothing further, just go. So he did. Two days later his bag was packed. He carried it into a taxi and thence to Bonn, leaving Marianne to imagine whatever she chose.

She had been waiting with increasing alarm for Bjørn to declare (loudly, over her go-awaying), 'No! I'm going to make the decisions today. Work can go to hell.' Yet what had he done? Paced around the house as if he couldn't wait to escape, packed his bag in good time and stared at her with an aggressive silence. He had left at a trot. What did that suggest?

§ 24

BJØRN, PACKED OFF AS IF HE WAS IN THE WAY, OF NO USE TO his wife in this crisis, was enjoying his own lonely breakdown. He knew that Marianne blamed him for their childlessness. It was not she who had brought this upon them: he had done so, and had needed no help. A year's whoring might not have condemned him to hell, but he would never atone for Eva. He had smashed her to pieces. He had done all but kill Eva's child himself; she had only spoken the lines that he had written for her. One New Year's Eve, not so long ago, he had sliced his own child in two: but it was only now that the blood was really running.

*

It is the recent past. He can still touch it. 'Hello?'

'Bjørn. Do not call me again.'

'How can I not call you again? We've got to meet. I love you.'

'Bit late for all that.'

'I'm going to come round anyway.'

'No! I said it's too late.' There is a pause from both of them.

Then, Eva speaks. 'Look, perhaps I'll call next week.'

Next week she has gone. She is still close enough to touch, though.

Bjørn is in the Thorsens' garden.

'She wants to talk, I know she does.'

Mr Thorsen is digging.

'She wants never to see you again.' He seems serious.

Bjørn won't leave. 'I know Eva. We're engaged, I have a right.'

'You have rights, do you? What about my rights?' He's about to get worked up. The digging has stopped. 'You're in my garden, for example. Piss off.'

'I won't move. She wants to speak to me, I know her.'

'So you know her, eh? Then I suppose that you know she was pregnant?'

This is said in the manner of a statement. It has the intended effect of silencing Bjørn. Mr Thorsen approaches. It takes him a lifetime to walk those few steps.

'She had an abortion because of you, you little shit!' But words are never enough, and it's his shovel that starts to sing.

Within weeks of being branded as barren, Marianne became a recycling addict. As a girl, she had never even considered the possibility of recycling things, knowing that only smelly old women did things like bring egg boxes back to the shop to have them refilled. Sensible people threw empty things away. Really fun young people often threw almost full things away, just because they could. This innocent view of waste was crushed beyond recognition one afternoon whilst she was drinking coffee with Bjørn. The long summer sun filled his side of the room, so that he was made to blink more often than was natural.

'Do you want some milk in that?' he had asked, never having been able to read her whims on such things – whims which should, quite frankly, have been obvious to a husband.

'No, but you have some,' she had said, passing over the just-opened carton. Bjørn felt its weight.

'Where's the half-full one gone?'

Marianne replied that the half-empty milk, having sat out for most of the day where Bjørn had left it, was where it now belonged – closer to God, in the bin.

Bjørn – who had been fretting silently for months about his job, and how he would ever earn enough money to escape it – looked at Marianne with a desperation that could have easily been mistaken for contempt. After a pause, during which he suppressed a wail, he simply said: 'You wasteful woman.' He had not said such a thing before and nor did he mention it again, but Marianne felt those words fall on her like thieves. Ever since, she had thrown away almost nothing, hoarding old wire coat-hangers in cupboards and keeping dry scabs of soap that were always left over, no matter how long she used them, in a plastic bag under the sink. She also began recycling – starting modestly, but, by August, she did not stop at putting out some bottles each week; letters had their stamps removed; carrier bags began fighting their way out of already full drawers. Clothes that needed washing were put on once more.

That morning, as Bjørn scattered shoes around Europe, Marianne combed her neighbour's bins. She lived surrounded by wastrels. In five minute's scavenging, she had rescued a sock, seven glass bottles, eleven carrier bags and a totally unopened jar of pasta sauce. Marianne sat in the kitchen and stared at her haul.

§ 25

DURING THE TIME AFTER EVA BEGAN HER JOB AS A CITY banker, Paul lost an important memory. In fact, he may never have had this memory to begin with, but his unease at discovering an empty space, where there should have been the map of where he had stored his soul, safely waiting untarnished until the day that it might be needed again, strongly suggested to him that he had one to start with, but had recently misplaced it. It was at this point, upon discovering that he had left his identity somewhere else, that Paul began to become seriously unstuck, although many might have argued that he had been entirely lost for the last dozen years and simply, through the grace of God, had not had the vision to realise it. Into this gap within Paul slid the first tendrils of death, and they came disguised as trouble.

Now, several troubles had colluded, in order that they might bring about Paul's demise more effectively than each would have managed alone. The first of Paul's unhappinesses was an obvious one: hardly any young men can bear with grace that time, a few years after their education has concluded, when everyone else begins to realise that they will never be a staggering success. Paul had worked on his novel for two and a half years, and although there was a full stop at the end of the final page, the thing was a reject and remained as unfinished as ever. Moreover, all could see that he was not the highflying sort, and that it was Eva who would bring this couple all their glory. This bothered Paul, despite the fact that he was not at all ambitious. At twenty-seven, he saw himself at the end of the world's longest cul-de-sac.

The second unhappiness to come upon Paul related to the first; indeed, they were brothers. It began to occur to Paul that Eva, now that she was set up in her second life, as a banker with great prospects, had begun to see him as a facilitator. He had admirably performed his role in her life – being a human bridge – but was now outstaying his welcome. He was not sexy. Nor was he rich. He had no use, now that it was clear that he was neither artist nor writer. It was time he exited the stage. That the two were bound by marriage was a regrettable inconvenience, but the bonds were not insoluble.

At least this is how Paul thought that Eva might see it. Quite how Eva viewed the situation would never be established, because Paul now doubted himself, so did not ask her, being wary of exposing his flanks to further fire.

The third member of this loose coalition of like-minded ills was real. Strangely, at first, this had the effect of making it almost invisible. But sneakily posting itself in a position of importance was an illness that Paul had only recently begun to fully acknowledge.

This magnificent triumvirate now started to work strategically, leaving Paul hopelessly outmaneuvered. Still, he played on, as innocent of his doomed situation as a chess amateur.

A summer's Sunday morning with the heat already building. Eva and Paul are at home, in Wapping.

'Paul! Come down.'

He does.

'All this sitting around in your room isn't doing you any good. And we have to leave.'

Baffled silence.

'The beach, remember? Philip and Louise, lunch at the beach?'

You've never mentioned this – and hang on just a minute, I haven't said anything yet. But she doesn't: 'Quickly. We're late already.'

So the couple hurried into Paul's old car, and off they set for the Sussex coast.

'I have no idea where I'm going.'

She produced a map, but began directions before opening it.

The time this journey gave Paul, he used for stewing. And his opening thoughts were about Eva's new friends. Philip was for now only a name to Paul, but what a git he was sure to be. Philip was a success, of the young and boastful sort. Philip's name began too many of Eva's sentences these days. He was, no doubt, not just good at selling bonds. Philip would be good at everything.

The heat was still rising when they arrived at the beachside restaurant. The other couple was already at the table, drinking chilled wine.

'Hi, Philip. Hi, Louise. Isn't it a fabulous day?'

Philip and Louise agreed.

'This is Paul.'

Philip and Louise were very handsome, and they offered Paul gender-defining handshakes. Then, once Eva and Paul had taken their seats, Philip began to recommend what they should order.

'Lobster's the only thing to eat here,' Philip said. 'Anything else just won't do.'

And Eva nodded keenly.

'Four lobster and chips, plenty of mayonnaise,' confirmed Philip, as the waiter came.

'Philip and Louise have a house here,' said Eva to Paul, who was the only one who seemed not to be listening.

Instead of answering, Paul conversed with himself: A second house? This man is in his twenties. But I won't ask, in case he turns out to be younger than me. And mayonnaise? I don't want mayonnaise, I'm too hot. This is an awful day. The next thing Eva'll do, just to really bugger me, will be to suggest some beach volleyball. That would really finish me off! There, I still retain a sense of humour. No dignity, but at least humour. Well, perhaps the one is hiding behind the other.

When lunch had petered into a mess of shell and the feeling that there was time to kill, Louise suggested that they should walk along the beach.

'It's just so beautiful at this time of day. The sand will be too hot to stand on and we'll have to hop and dance.'

Eva loved the idea of it, and Philip added, 'And we must swim.'

The briefest shared glance confirmed the worst to Paul. In Eva's extraordinary handbag, which held anything anyone might ever need, she had packed his swimming trunks. Horror.

'I'll pop home for towels,' shouted Louise, who was already jogging off.

'Come on, then, let's go,' said Philip, smiling. 'And Paul, you must tell me all about your teaching.'

The tide is pulling from the left and they are swimming towards a red buoy. Paul is well behind. He's not giving up yet, although his sense of humour is lost. The others are far ahead and the shore is long gone. The buoy remains a sometimes-seen possibility. From what can be gauged, between the sharply moving waves, Philip has already swum round the buoy. Now he is heading back. But an audience is not what Paul needs. The thought of it tightens him, so that he can no longer work in the rhythm of the water. Splashing and coughing, he is barely afloat. Panic arrives, smelling an opportunity more ably than any shark; now he'll find out what it's like to drown. The waves are ready to receive him. The unexpected suddenness of death comes as a surprise.

But panic was soon to be beaten from Paul – and in its place came limitless shame.

'You all right?' Philip is alongside.

You think I can answer?

'Lie on your back. I've got you. We'll go in together.'

§ 26

EVA WAS NOT A WOMAN PRONE TO EMOTIONAL OUTBURSTS, and this did not bring her closer to happiness. For, in being an island, she unwittingly fell victim, repeatedly, to the principle of the first glance, which can hold sway in a relationship for a surprisingly long time. In fact, the principle of the first glance is less often a problem for such people whilst they are in the first stages of a relationship, where intelligent sorts assume that there must be more to their new friend than meets the eye; the real dangers come later, when intimacy has been achieved, and still there remains a coolness in the air. And this is the point that Eva and Paul had reached.

Paul had been happy until recently. Thus, previously, he had no reason to look for faults in his wife. Now that he had noticed a certain unravelling, however, he pulled at any loose strings that he came across, and of course this only made things worse. It was now that he felt the need for someone to blame, and his eyes fell on the person nearest at hand.

Paul thought: Here I am, teaching instead of writing. This is

Eva's fault. She decided on me teaching four days a week. And the reason she did this is clear – she likes to spend all her time at work and, like a modern mother, feels the need to ship me off somewhere whilst she does as she pleases.

He continued: And I am ill. This is obvious. And she does nothing. Never mentions it. This is because she sees it as a weakness. Either she hopes that, by ignoring it, this problem will go away, like an occasional wart. Or she sees our marriage as an irritation to be risen above, until such time as it becomes necessary to take firm action. She sees me as a temporary setback.

He summed up: I knew she was like this. I saw it immediately. She was always trying to mould me.

So Paul assumed that he had seen Eva's coldness early on; had been a hopeless and misguided optimist in imagining that this ice was only on the surface; and was only now confronting the uncomfortable truth: that his wife loved only herself.

But this list of faults was false: Paul had concocted it solely because Eva had not been a strong crutch for him, now that he found himself in need of one. She may have caused men to bleed tears in the past (although probably she would have denied it), but this was hardly Paul's business. With him, she had never wanted to cut. That her inability to open up to him was her only fault, and that it might be as much of a pain to her as to him, did not cross his mind, for he was now becoming lost in his own world.

Eva's life was also developing in a way that she did not want. Certainly, she had a job that she had chosen, and a husband too. The pillars to support a happy life, one might have assumed. But happiness eluded her.

For a start, the husband she had chosen was no longer pinging about the place in a mesmerisingly random manner. He was, instead, turning in on himself. Eva had tried to help, but in doing so had failed to apply her intelligence, instead guiding Paul to do what she would have done herself, which had the effect of making the situation worse.

Furthermore, Paul was becoming sulky and aggressive. He did

not seem to know how to act, these days. It was as if he had gone back to being a confused child. Did he not realise that she depended on him for survival? He was her warmth and air – her atmosphere. Now that Paul wobbled, she was as helpless as an astronaut cut adrift in space.

Paul was imploding. Eva was being sucked towards a cosmic void. Neither knew what to do about it. Paul had no idea that his wife dealt with crises in silence. He only saw her strength. If she had just said, 'We have a crisis,' he would have felt better. But she did not, having spent all her life hiding things inside herself, where others couldn't see. In this, she was like a Russian doll who, ashamed of her own face, adds shell on top of shell in the hope that she might eventually cover herself. Such impossible tasks always last a lifetime.

The afternoon of Paul's rescue from drowning, Eva was reminded of a feeling. This began as no more than a sense that she had missed something, but as she remembered the last months, fishing for the elusive missed thing, this feeling became more real, until it deposited itself in the form of two overpowering headaches, one behind each eye. That she had been working too hard, and that this had led to a gap opening between her and Paul, was now clearer to her than before. But it was not the memory of her unnecessarily long working days that gave Eva her twin headache, it was the remembrance of Paul, and a night spent at Mr Butter Chicken's.

The back streets to the north of Wapping and the west of Shadwell smell. This is not to say that the odour is universally bad, or that it is the same from one end of an alley to the other: simply that, in a place of such hotchpotch muddle, there is never an absence of perfume, because even on the day after the bins have been collected, at six in the morning, when the restaurants are not cooking, or on Sundays, when the pubs are not taking deliveries, there is, in the absence of anything else, always the scent of confusion.

On any evening in that final part of the twentieth century, had you walked along those streets, as Eva and Paul were doing, you may have pulled several faces: but you would have smiled at the aromatic generosity of the little café serving Indian food that Eva called Mr Butter Chicken's. The couple had come upon it by chance whilst walking around the streets near their new home, and it had been a favourite ever since.

Eva and Paul arrived at the restaurant. There were few tables, but as ever the place was not full. As they sat down, the waiter brought the menu. Now, despite his calm manner, Paul felt uneasy. Going out to eat had been Eva's choice. 'Come on,' she had said. 'It's a Sunday. Why not?'

This was a question that expected no reply, but Paul wrestled with it anyway. Perhaps he was just looking for a fight, but when Eva asked 'Why not?' Paul had an answer behind which hid every one of his life's worries, in single file. He kept his answer back.

Eva put aside the menu. 'Butter chicken,' she told Paul, who was not looking at the menu either. The waiter approached.

'Ah, yes,' began Paul, in the manner of someone who was not about to order two butter chickens. 'Can I ask you about . . .' He opened a menu, then took a diversion. 'Can your chef do me a healthy option?'

The waiter looked surprised but helpful. 'What is it you would like?'

'Um, well, a chicken breast just done in the oven.'

The waiter was sure that the restaurant could do better than that.

Hereafter followed a nasty few minutes, with the waiter extolling the health benefits of many of the restaurant's dishes, trying to accommodate Paul, but failing despite his efforts. When the waiter, having exhausted all the other menu options, suggested chips with curry sauce, Paul became red-faced, got up and left. Eva apologised and ran out after him.

'Paul, what's wrong with you? What are you doing?'

He approached her slowly, ending up very close, so that she began to feel a discomfort that she thought she had left behind in Norway. A pair of cold eyes watched her without moving.

'Wrong? Every. Single. Thing.'

And this is when Eva realised that she had the rare ability to cry inwards. Nothing came down from her eyes, and her face remained impassive, but instead of sadness falling out from her, to its true home at large in the world, she knew that, somewhere else, a vat was filling with tears. It would do so now and, without her having realised it before, it had been doing so for years, so that it was already topping up nicely. In just a few months, quickening little bits of time, her tank would be full.

Coming home late on a night before Christmas, during that dying end of a century, she fell right in that tank and drowned. And although for decades afterwards a woman going by the name of Eva Thorsen was seen and noted in the richer circles of the money-making zoo that is the City of London, she was but a fake. Everything that was Eva had gone for ever.

§ 27

AUTUMN TURNED SUMMER INTO WINTER FAST THAT YEAR, SO that it seemed not to be a season in itself, but merely an agent of decay. It was the first week in October, and the morning light had already lost its colour. Even the plastic-framed windows appeared to be closing in, tightening their guard in advance of the first snow. Another day alone began for Marianne. She did not change from her dressing gown before she started to work, instead just pushing the remains of breakfast to the side of the table then opening her books. The portraits of Ingres needed further analysis; his debts to past painters needed to be taken into account and influence on future generations discussed. One painting in particular needed to be interpreted in detail. Marianne leafed through the pages of her vast borrowed book. She stopped when she came eye to eye with the lady she had been looking for.

Ingres' portrait of Madame de Senonnes was, in Marianne's eyes, a masterpiece, not because of the virtuosity of the technique, but because of its subtle darkness. It held mystery. Marianne loved the woman's expression. Was it amused or flirtatious? Superior? Yet there was something sluttish in that look too. Fleshy hands were home to precious rings. Over this lady's fattened curves fell velvet, in rich burgundy. Above this, luminous skin burst through sheer silk. Her eyes talked through time. She was alive even now: a ruby earring wavered.

Marianne looked again. Behind was a mirror reflecting darkness. Someone was concealed in that gloom. A lover? No wonder this woman smirked. Gentlemen's calling cards had been hastily tucked into the mirror frame; some had fallen down behind her embarrassingly plump cushions. What a whore! Bjørn had rushed from his home to exactly this sort of woman. No doubt he would find swift pleasure on a bed such as this.

Marianne shut her book, hearing the heavy cover fall with the weight of a tombstone.

So this is it. The future.

Marianne stood, today, in the garden. It was unspeakably cold. She didn't put a coat on when she went out, and had only her pockets to keep her hands warm, whilst her breath formed clouds which were gone before they had a chance to drift.

She looked over the empty garden.

'Time to come in,' she said.

'Not a chance,' sang the reply.

'There's not going to be any soup left when you do. I'm going to eat it all up, right now.'

'I'm a bird, so I can't understand you.'

She put her hands on her hips and simply said, 'Soup.'

'Birds don't eat soup. And from here I can see across to Hernes.'

'And some sort of hat wouldn't go amiss.'

'You can't see me anyway, I'm invisible.'

He's up in the tree. She can see him there from inside, when she is at study, although she finds it hard to stay in on her own and watch. But it's true: now that she's outside, he is well hidden. He really might not be there at all; everywhere there is silence. She'll go in again soon, she always does, but not yet. Not with him out here in the tree. Not with it being so cold.

*

Some days presented themselves as little more than spaces within which to contemplate loneliness: white rooms. The walls of these spaces were undecorated, so Marianne found pictures from her memory to put up. She would spend hours sorting these images. At the end of such a session, she would look up to find that, invariably, the pictures had become blank paper within a frame. It was as if she had done nothing during all this time.

Still, she was a determined woman, and promised herself that she would avoid the endless repetition of this hell if she could, so, one Tuesday, when she came out of her bedroom to find blank white walls, she made herself a coffee and looked out her lifetime's photographs. They were stored in envelopes in a large cardboard box (which she had kept for the purpose after the move). Firstly, she took each envelope and lined up the pictures from it on the floor, trying to refind some order to them. Then she arranged all the envelopes by time. Some of them were, no doubt, wrongly sequenced, but, after an hour and a half of sorting, her life lay before her, as chronologically accurate as she could manage.

She looked at family snaps, first boyfriends (who didn't look too good in the increasingly harsh white light), Italy. Then there was her wedding. Then came nothing. Since her marriage, there was no record that she had lived at all. The pictures of her past were disappearing now, too. Soon all that remained was the white room.

All that white was oppressive, so Marianne looked at her feet. She wore red knitted socks. Then she saw that there was something in the room, after all. A large area of floor had been divided into segments. Each box contained a name. The only ones clear enough to read were: Trudy and Olf. She didn't even like these names; they were awful. But the made-up names were going now – due somewhere else perhaps – and in place of everything, came nothing. It was hard just to tell where wall became floor, making space seem unending: an eternity of nothing.

On another day, convinced that her philandering husband was planning his escape, Marianne disembowelled the house. She was entirely thorough, gutting one room at a time – not moving on to the living room until their bedroom had been destroyed. All those places that an ingenious villain might imagine safe were torn open. She unpicked the curtains; checked the edges of the mattress with careful fingers, before taking a bread knife and slicing it apart. She rolled back the carpet. The result was such profound chaos that after an hour Marianne was able only to stumble about helplessly, vaguely flapping at furnishings and eventually just sitting amidst the wreckage.

Then, after calming down, and whilst clearing up after the cataclysmic damage that she had brought on her house, Marianne found a photograph. It was unhidden, which was probably why she had missed it to start with. In it was someone that she had known well – Eva.

She looked closely. Bjørn had his arm around Eva; next to them stood Mr Olsen. Bjørn was smiling strangely; it was a bright day. Perhaps the sun was in his eyes. His father wore a jacket, which he seemed to have borrowed from a larger man. Only Eva stood proud. What a strange picture. Why had Bjørn kept it? Marianne wished that he had not.

There was nothing as annoying as hearing Bjørn speaking fondly of Eva. He was vague about all other women, leaving Marianne to imagine how he felt for them, yet with Eva he said openly how he should have behaved better. He never said a word against her. Yet Marianne knew for herself that Eva was a nasty, self-obsessed sort. Bjørn had loved her – she who didn't deserve him. Marianne knew that Bjørn wouldn't stay around long if *she* treated him so badly. He had loved Eva more.

Maybe he still did.

Marianne thought: What had become of Eva? Bjørn did not talk about her, unless prompted, and then he came out with terrible rubbish about how it was he who had been an awful fiancé. Marianne, sick at the idea of him with her, never pressed for more. She still, periodically, gave Bjørn the chance to call Eva a slut or even just callous, but he always came out with the same old tat.

Where was Eva now? Marianne had heard that she was abroad and married. She could not be far enough away. After an afternoon obsessing, followed by a night spoiled by ever more elaborate ideas of how Bjørn might still be meeting with Eva in secret, Marianne knew that she must find out some truths for herself. She had only one place to start, so wrapped a scarf around her neck, and set off for the house that Eva had grown up in.

Marianne remembered Eva's house well. She thought about it as she walked there. Years ago, there had been many afternoons spent dressing up; later, gossipy hours with music on loud enough to make it hard for them to hear each other, let alone for Eva's mum to eavesdrop. After almost half an hour, and having skirted the edges of Birkesand's north-west suburbs, Marianne walked, once more, up the road that she had visited so often as she was growing up. The houses looked much the same as before. Most would have the same owners, but not Eva's house. It had a different front door, and a more open garden than before. Marianne walked up to it and rang the bell with confidence. She had a plan, and she almost believed her story herself.

'Hello?' Here stood a middle-aged woman.

'Oh, good morning. I'm sorry to trouble you.' Marianne began her tale. 'I have just returned to Birkesand – I've been in Italy – and I used to be great friends with the Thorsens, who lived here back then. Well, I was friends with their daughter, especially. But, having been away – for several years, actually – I've lost contact with them, and her, and wondered if you knew their address . . . or hers.'

Marianne, smiling at her muddled introduction, was not surprised to be encouraged inside.

'Yes, please do come in. No, you can leave your shoes on.'

The two women sat in the living room, where Marianne had spent rainy days, years before. The elder lady was apologising. 'They moved to another part of Norway. If I remember rightly, it was Stavanger. Or, no, that may have been the Helbecks. But I'm sure it wasn't abroad. Lovely couple.'

'Lovely.'

'But it is their daughter you really wanted, wasn't it?'

Marianne looked attentively at the older lady.

'Yes, their daughter had already moved by the time we bought this place. I remember them talking about her, though. Well, Mrs Thorsen talked, at any rate. We struck up a bit of a bond.'

Marianne nodded, encouraging her helper to continue.

'If they hadn't been moving in order to leave this place behind – and some bad things that had happened – I'm sure we would have kept in touch. But my husband said: No. Leave them in peace, they want to forget this place.' The older woman shook her head. 'You know how men can be.'

Marianne confirmed that she did. She wanted to know more. 'I heard there'd been some trouble, but I only came home recently, and as I said . . .'

'Oh, yes. It was with your friend, the trouble, that is, I'm afraid to say. A man.'

'Ahh. There was someone around at about that time.'

The older lady looked towards the window. 'She told me his name. Now, what was it?'

Marianne looked vague. 'Eva had been with someone called Bjørn, before I left.'

'Yes, that was it. Bjørn. A bad sort, by the sounds of it.'

'I never liked him myself, but what happened?'

'Hit her, apparently. So much so that she ran off to another country, I think. Or at least, up north.'

Marianne felt as if she had been hit herself. Her face reddened. 'Hit her? No.'

The older woman looked at Marianne questioningly. Marianne felt defensive. ' I mean, I didn't think them suited, but he's not violent.'

'Do you know him?'

'Knew,' said Marianne. She had lost all appetite for this game. 'Knew him, and he didn't seem that sort at all. I just find it hard to believe.' Marianne swallowed. 'Poor Eva.'

Reassured, the lady continued. 'Well, people don't leave town that quickly unless there's something really wrong. Bashed her to bits, apparently.'

Marianne looked beyond to where a bird sat, near the window. It opened its beak, but through the double-glazing she couldn't hear it sing.

§ 28

WHEN BJØRN RETURNED FROM A WEEK-LONG TOUR OF THE Netherlands, he did so to a house that reminded him of how his father used to live. In the kitchen, books and papers had collapsed across the table. Unwashed dishes littered the surfaces. In contrast stood neat rows of empty cans, bottles and jars. Marianne had also, for some reason, filled an old margarine tub with used coffee grounds, which had now overflowed and begun to smell of smoke.

'Marianne?' Bjørn called as he walked through the house.

She was in the living room, watching television.

'Hello,' he said, concerned that she hadn't even looked up.

The television laughed.

'How was Holland?' she said, her voice hinting that she already knew.

Very nice. Really, really good. Cosy and warm. So full of possibilities for the future?

'Just fine,' he said. 'Get dressed and I'll make us lunch.'

The next day, Bjørn met his boss in the car park – on exactly the same spot that they had met for the first time, more than two years earlier. These outdoor meetings were much preferred by Mr Rådal, as his office was windowless and home to a large grey box of electronics, which breathed out a continuous exhaust of strange-smelling fumes that he assumed to be toxic. The mystery box could be switched off by removing a fuse, but this, as Mr Rådal had discovered, resulted in every appliance in the in the building shutting down. Having lived all his life in fear of computers, all things electrical, and, indeed, electricians, he now left the box untampered with and dealt with the situation by escaping at every opportunity.

'Hello, Bjørn. Thanks for coming along. We need to talk about the New Year, don't we?'

'I'm sorry,' Bjørn said, 'but I must give up the job.'

He spoke with such finality and resolution that Mr Rådal was temporarily frozen. Seeing not even a blink of understanding in his boss's expression, Bjørn went on.

'It's my marriage.'

Not even a twitch.

'I'll do everything until Christmas – including London and Vilnius, but that's it. London's where it ends.'

After some silence, and having recovered limited movement, Mr Rådal, who knew first-hand how debilitating marriages could be, asked simply, 'Can I persuade you to stay?' His weak question told them both that he already knew the answer.

After Bjørn left, his boss took out an enamelled pillbox and swallowed the contents.

At the house, Marianne is motionless, waiting for something. When she hears the sound of keys in the door, she hurries into the hall.

'It's done,' he says.

Bjørn comes in from the snow, and as he takes off his coat the last of the daylight falls from him.

Marianne had been so shocked that morning, when Bjørn had told her he was giving up his job – today, no room for doubt – that lengths of her thorn-dry hair had begun to fall out. Horrified that her husband was about to witness her total collapse, she took refuge in the bathroom, where she expected her nails to rot black and her teeth to clatter into the sink as her body raced to disintegrate. But not one eyelash drooped further. As her husband tried to explain through the locked door that he had seen the future and it did not involve shoes she found that, slowly, her blood began to flow more freely, reaching places where recently it had not been.

We want a family, said Bjørn, so lets start by making sure the two of us are never going to fall out of love: and her toes turned pink.

We've hardly looked for answers and Birkesand's not famous for its doctors, you know, he said: and her nipples tightened.

And, if we can't have children, then that's as we were meant to be, and we can adopt – how awful for any child to miss out on having you for a mum; we will probably end up with twenty: her ears warmed.

By the morning, life had returned to Marianne, as promising as a crocus through snow, and as fragile. In celebration of this, she discarded all memory of Bjørn's past and fell only towards the future. During that night, hope grew back deep inside her, seeding itself silently, dividing away unseen.

It was agreed that further decisions could wait until after Christmas. For now, they were simply relieved to abandon reality.

Marianne spoke first. 'Let's just tread water for a while. I'm too tired to do anything else.'

Bjørn smiled, unconvincingly. 'All right. Get back your strength, though, because it's going to be hard having me here all the time, leaving socks and teabags around the house.'

'We could make this place as lovely as your old flat.'

'Now there's a challenge.'

They were both wearing strained smiles now, Marianne for Bjørn, Bjørn for Marianne. Dual complicity.

So Bjørn slipped back into his travelling routine, gutted of hope, but unable to think what else to do. He convinced himself that his job now had a point, and the point was that soon it would all be over. Viewed from this angle, the great pile of shoes that had been blocking his path seemed climbable.

He took trains and ferries to places that he had been to so many times before. None of them had changed. He drove his tired car onwards across the foot of Norway. The pace of these travels heated up as winter deepened, but Bjørn didn't mind. The faster he moved, the quicker time passed and the less he was able to think of anything – which only made him melancholy.

Christmas approached, and with it an unguessed-at future.

Although physically undaunted by his frenetic travelling, Bjørn was having trouble keeping his mind in the right place. Once, he woke up in Hamburg, delighted that he would have a chance to look round Harrods and buy some expensive shortbread for Marianne.

His thoughts now on food, he dressed to go down to breakfast, wanting nothing more than strong tea and marmalade toast. The cold sausage and cheese that greeted him did not go down well.

'Your food is awful,' he told the distressed waiter. 'I didn't come to England to eat cheese for breakfast, you know.'

He was presumed to be American.

Another time, whilst in Stavanger, he met a man looking for directions. When this man approached him, map in hand, wearing an 'I'm looking for directions' face, Bjørn stopped him before he had said a word.

'I am from Norway.'

The man retreated, in case Bjørn proved to be unstable.

Bjørn also started to leave his clothes all over Europe. A jumper stayed in Lithuania, whilst Bjørn continued to Estonia. His spare trousers found a new home in Newcastle, whilst he returned home to Birkesand. These garments were never returned, and Bjørn had no idea where they might have gone.

'Come on, Bjørn,' insisted Marianne. 'Where were you last? Phone the place up, tell them to send your things back.'

Bjørn stuck his finger between his closed eyes (I'm really thinking hard here) but he knew that his mind had leapt into the future, where it was now waiting for him.

Thus Bjørn's clothes found new lives, mostly with happy new owners – although one student from Lübeck, who bought a tight but very well-priced jacket from a second-hand shop, was most unfortunate to lose his girlfriend, after she found a heart-shaped chocolate in the pocket, which had been put there by Marianne.

Increasingly, Bjørn was caught without the necessary attire. On these occasions, he did his best to buy something suitable. This was not always easy. More than once he could have been found banging on a closed shop door at five to nine, making pleading faces at the staff through the glass. That year, during the two months before Christmas, Bjørn became known as a man who would probably turn up in fancy dress, and as likely as not, would try speaking Danish at you. In the end everybody was glad to see him go.

Marianne was also wondering what Bjørn was up to. She was

sure, however, that he was not hoarding his clothes in a wardrobe in Krakow. Nor would he be thanking some well-shaped girl for having laundered them since last time. She had no need to worry when he went away.

Kiss kiss.

§ 29

ONE SUNDAY, TEN DAYS BEFORE CHRISTMAS, MARIANNE VISITED her mother. Every such visit brought with it the fear that sanity would have faded further. Her mother was quite deliberately letting her mind slip, hoping that she might, as a result, be able to manufacture some sort of reunion with her long-dead husband. Marianne arrived on a sharply cold morning to find that, the night before, her mother had taken another happy leap towards oblivion.

At first, nothing seemed wrong. Coffee and cake went well, with effortless Christmas conversation. The cake had, according to Marianne's mother, been brought round by her neighbours in order that she could celebrate St Maagrid's day in style. Marianne looked doubtful. Her mother beamed.

'How lucky I am to live next to such kind people.'

The cake did, indeed, look good. The old lady took up a knife. It was blunt enough to cause the cream filling to spill out from the middle. She let the fat slice that she had cut Marianne fall on its side. Meanwhile, Marianne poured the coffee. They were using the little cups that her parents had been given on their wedding day. Apart from the bit about St Maagrid, the conversation was as lucid as any Marianne had remembered in the last few years. She was much relieved.

Though doubtful about the obscure St Maagrid, Marianne wanted to thank her mother's neighbour for such a generous seasonal gift. She had spoken to this neighbour before, and up until this afternoon had never liked him. Their conversations had always centred on whether Marianne's mother should be in a home – and they had argued on their last meeting. Now Marianne saw her chance to make peace. She kissed her mother goodbye and went next door. 'Thanks so much for bringing that cake round for my mother,' she said. 'It was really delicious.' She was met with silence, so continued. 'I didn't realise it was St Maagrid's day.' Still nothing. Then, as if he had only now decided to move at all, the neighbour invited her in, but he did not offer her a seat. As they stood on the inside of the door, he talked.

The night before, the sky had been absolutely clear. When Marianne's mother had gone to the window, just before retiring to bed, she had seen the heavens close. She pulled the time-stained nets to one side. There, in her dressing gown, she communed with eternity. The stars though, were not so tranquil. As she looked on they awoke, unfroze themselves from the sky and started moving around. Marianne's mother stood up and pressed her face to the window. The cold glass drew her nearer, but at the last held her back. Beyond, one star stood still.

'Gunthe?' She had not said her husband's name aloud in ten years. Now she said it over and over, in a great chord of remembrance. The star acknowledged her by winking, but she couldn't see clearly through the dirty glass. Her husband was winking at her and she was trapped behind this fucking screen. It was like watching a child drown under ice.

'Gunthe!' she screamed. Her spit stuck to the glass.

Running out of her kitchen now, and in her slippers, she fell out of her house and into the road. 'Gunthe, I see you!' She threw herself upwards towards her dead husband. 'I'm coming!' But she was not coming, being unable to soar towards the stars because her slippers had frozen fast to the ice-covered pavement. Holding her arms up as far as she could, she wailed into the night.

Her neighbours, alerted by all the noise, had put on boots and coats and come running to her aid. But she did not want help – she wanted a cosmic end. So she was forcibly bundled, writhing and cursing and biting, into Mr Neaveson's home, where

Marianne now stood listening in horror to his report, which spared no detail.

'Having calmed her down – and I take no pleasure in telling you that her eyes were quite insane, bulging indeed – we decided that my wife would take her home.' Mr Neaveson stepped forward for emphasis. 'It's my wife's birthday today.'

'Happy birthday,' managed Marianne.

Mr Neaveson carried straight on. 'Then your mother took hold of my wife's boxed cake and refused to leave without it.'

Marianne got out her wallet. It would have been cheaper to have gone for tea at the Hotel Norge.

Despite this crisis, the season brought a child-like excitement to Marianne. Others might have found her enthusiasm manic, even unbalanced, but Marianne had no other way of living now. She allowed herself to be carried onwards by a torrent of unreality.

By the beginning of December she had already ordered holly from the island of Stord and a tree from a near neighbour who had a friend with a plantation. Marianne described the tree she wanted – with even, lively-looking branches, no thin patches, and a not-too-long tip, which had to end with a bushy bit. She was very particular about Christmas trees and wanted to go to the plantation herself to make sure of the choice, but this was, apparently, not possible.

Humming with festive anticipation, Marianne even went to the trouble of collecting her own birch twigs to steam the Christmas ribs on. When she woke up on the Monday of this last week before Christmas to find a clear sky and every chance of sunshine later, she cooked herself a proper breakfast of fried egg on toast, in order to fortify herself for a morning's tramping through the forest. Bjørn had introduced her to the concept of fried things for breakfast. 'It doesn't sound like a good idea,' he had agreed, 'but it is.' And, as if sunshine at the start of the week before Christmas was not enough, when she cracked open her fridge-cold egg on the side of the pan, there before her, twitching in the hot oil, was a double-yolked egg. Marianne began to sing.

*

Outside, snow broke underfoot. Above, between the path-side tree-tops, the sky gleamed. Within the forest it was darker. Marianne walked on until the spruce made some room for birch too. Here, birdsong fell through the branches. Everything else was still. The snow lay like dustsheets in a forgotten house.

Marianne took Bjørn's penknife from her pocket and with newly ungloved hands cut small sticks of silver, which she put in a bag. Then she wrapped her soft pink hand around a frosted branch and felt winter melt. She mouthed her thoughts to the trees – I shall make spring come early this year – and the words floated unsaid into the crisscrossed canopy.

She looked around to make sure no one had witnessed her boast and saw that there was only emptiness, and that the birds had stopped singing. The silence made her embarrassed. She had surprised herself, and, blushing, she re-gloved to hurry home.

Then, on Tuesday, with all of life's excitements rushing within her, so that her skin had been declared mysteriously radiant by all who saw her during those days before Christmas – during those happy times of insanity and promise – Marianne's world broke into ugly, splintered pieces. Bjørn had phoned five nights before, to say that doing business in Vilnius was incredibly slow and best left to the Mafia, and that, consequently, he was well behind and would have to fly directly to – where was it now? – and then . . . some place or other, before going straight on to London. In London he would stay three nights and that would be it. The end.

He had sounded cross and clearly did not want to talk much. Marianne was glad that this way of life would soon be over. So, anticipating the new beginning that was coming her way, Marianne put on her duffel coat and set off to the shops to buy some cheap meals for the next few days. No point spending money now. She was saving for the New Year.

An hour later, when she returned home, she saw from the door-way, before she had even taken her boots off, that a fax had arrived. Her breath formed clouds in the cold air, which refused to disperse, so that, even when she had closed the door, it seemed about to rain. She had a look at the fax before putting on the lights.

It was probably from Bjørn. She saw immediately, even in the half-light, that there were two faxes. One was indeed from her husband, who was currently staying in the Premier Guest House near Piccadilly, and sent his best wishes. He hoped that Marianne was eating proper meals and not just endless packet soups. The other fax was in English and was mostly written in obscure technical language, making it difficult for Marianne to fully translate – but she did know who Eva Thorsen was, and now also knew that Eva was staying at the Premier Guest house too. In fact (why deny the obvious?), staying with Bjørn. Three days of fucking and laughing without a pause.

Marianne stood holding the two faxes in the dull light for several minutes. Her heart beat in her ears liked muffled drums.

It was only later – when her clubbed-dead future had not even had time to discolour, but there had been a pause to think things through – that Marianne knew what she would do. Eyeing the number printed at the top of Eva's fax, she imagined calling it, and began to talk. She spoke directly to the page.

What if I'd just found out that my old friend Eva was pregnant? Yes, we were at school together, it seems a long time ago now, but I've lost her address. So I phone you. And I really want to send her and her husband a gift – something really . . . special. Yes, there is nothing as important as a new baby. We agree. Well, would you be careless enough to tell me where she lives? I'm very plausible, aren't I? But the pregnancy thing is meant to be secret. And now I realise that I've said too much! Clearly you didn't know and now I'm all embarrassed and giggly. Certainly you're as thrilled as I am. We're both so very, very happy.

That afternoon, Marianne hurried to the post office to be in time for an overnight delivery. Eva's bank had eager-to-help secretaries, just as she had expected: getting the address had been no problem. Marianne briefly thought about going to London herself – but she decided instead to send an emissary. Her agent was death.

§ 30

IN THE MIDDLE OF THAT SAME DECEMBER, AFTER A YEAR OF living in Wapping, and having been forced, by the daily task of walking up a hill, to confront his failing health, Paul arrived at the hospital. Now that he worked four days a week, he found himself unable to ignore the obvious. This displeased him, but the incline of the road leading to his school was becoming unmanageable – and when a pupil or a colleague caught him, then decided to walk with him, he was unable to explain away his need to stop. In October he had finally visited his GP and been ordered to undergo *tests*! Tests! Tests! Today, on the second day of his Christmas holiday, Paul was here, in hospital, for the results. X-ray and echo; ECG and MRI; walking, blowing, pushing and panting. The invalid Olympics were over; today the prizes would be awarded.

Paul entered the outpatients' waiting room and looked around for the reception. The place reminded him of an airport lounge that he had once been forced to sleep in on a trip to Russia; except that here people went outside to smoke; and instead of a bar, there was a faded children's play area that, for no reason that he could pin down, Paul wished wasn't there. Having been told to take a seat by the lady at desk A Paul picked up a discarded newspaper and found a free metal chair. He flicked through the paper, but the headlines were unusually dull, leaving him unable to concentrate. Getting up, he went to browse through a row of leaflets on an opposite wall. He picked out, at random, cards on HIV, ectopic pregnancy, plague, and a rouge recipe card that had probably been left by the last person to visit this wall, who, upon discovering that they had the symptoms of bilharzia, cancer and piles, thought that they would not, after all, have much appetite that evening. Walking back to his

145

seat, Paul rubbed the assorted cards slowly together. His thoughts drifted beyond this place . . .

A young man called out Paul's name from a doorway that had, until now, been closed. This doctor could not have been much older than Paul. 'Mr Askew is on holiday,' he said, shaking Paul's hand, 'so I'll be seeing you today.' Paul sat down and adjusted his position. Then he uncrossed his legs. Yet now that he thought about it, there was unlikely to be much wrong with him at all. Senior consultants see very ill people, whilst their just-qualified juniors deal with cases where the imagined tumour turns out to have been wind.

Paul eyed the doctor, who looked a little upset. Instead of speaking, he began to draw on a blank piece of paper that he had taken some time to find amongst the many sheets on his desk. Paul could not work out his sketch at all. It might have been a map of the Nile. No, the doctor kept drawing and it was looking more like an elephant. By now, the doctor was talking, explaining things, so Paul, having missed the first part, started to listen.

'. . . and then there was no separation at all. None!'

The doctor stopped, sure that he had made his point. 'Do you see?' Paul did not. His doctor nodded quickly several times: Yes, I see that you don't see. And had someone walked into the room, they might well have mistaken who was the patient. The doctor got up, excused himself and left.

'Extraordinary,' thought Paul. He looked around the room, which had very small windows and no personality. An orange cardboard folder lay on the desk. It was the brightest thing there, and it had Paul's name on it. Not knowing how long he might be alone, Paul thought he would flick through it. Inside he spied letters and X-rays; interpretations of test results (that were annoyingly obtuse); and at the base of a mass of results, he saw a conclusion from the consultant who was enjoying two weeks in Austria with his family. It ended spectacularly. Paul read the type: 'Inexorable progress towards death.' A pencil note added, 'A year, tops.'

'Damn, it's Thursday and I didn't put out the bins,' thought Paul, with the bit of his brain that still worked. Footsteps sounded

146

in the corridor. There was little time. Notes fell to the floor as Paul rushed for the window.

Paul spent the next days not telling people that he was ill. He did not tell his mother when she phoned for twenty minutes of chat about the state of her kitchen: Did I tell you that they cut the wrong size hole for the sink? I said: Take it back and start again!

Nor did he tell Richard, the friend who dropped round one evening to suggest a game of chess: Not in the mood? Shame. How was the second book coming along? Oh dear. These things can't be rushed.

And he did not tell Eva. In fact, Eva was pushing to clear a backlog of work before Christmas. She was a thing glimpsed in the dark; even Saturdays were not sacred.

He might well have told a neighbour when he chatted to her in the street, but his neighbour didn't ask how he was – Sorry to hear that. Do go on. No, really, I have all the time in the world.

So, instead of talking, he stirred his thoughts around in his head until they became a porridge of confusion; and he wrote to his sister.

Unable to be calm, Paul decided to take some exercise – he would go for a walk. This was bound to be good for him, but by the time he had mulled over his decision and mixed it up with all the indigestible fear that had fallen upon him in the last days, it was already late. He opened his front door to a foul, dark evening. Even the houses hung back in the shadows as if to shelter from the rain. Still, Paul set off manfully, opening a big black umbrella, turning up his dry, warm collar, and telling himself that this passing shower was clearing the London air. He would walk to Limehouse, and then, if he felt really good, continue as far as Canary Wharf or north to Stepney Green. He pulled his front door shut and struck out into the gloom.

Whilst he walked, he thought about his initial visit to the GP. He had been dissatisfied, as, although he had explained clearly and in detail how he felt, and, more importantly, what he thought his GP should do about it, the doctor showed little interest. Instead of addressing Paul's problems, he had set off in his own direction, and had begun to ask questions in the manner of a pollster. Do you exercise? – A bit. Do you smoke? – Hardly at all. Do you drink? – Yes, wine and water, I'm quite religious about it.

Paul went on: 'Shall I tell you about my grandmother?' The doctor scratched an ear.

Paul's grandmother had always enjoyed a drink. She had a thin, strict face, to which age had added an extra veneer of grimness. These harrowed lines were not, as many imagined, the result of a hard life that had slowly made haggard her once pretty face. They were the product of an absolute addiction, from her teenage years, to Persian cigarettes and absinthe, which she continued to drink until she was ninety-two. She had married an Algerian, who wooed her whilst she was still a student at the Sorbonne, and introduced her to more than drink and tobacco.

After following her to London, the Algerian had set up an amorphous import-export business, which for forty years funded an existence of joyful overindulgence. It was this couple who had introduced deep-fried foie gras to Bermondsey, and when Paul's mother had been christened fifteen pounds of caviar had been imported, shielded from customs within a large diplomatic bag, thus cancelling a debt owed by the Lithuanian ambassador's secretary.

Regularly there had been run-ins with the criminal group who controlled the safety of the businesses of Southwark. As a result, cases of cognac and sauternes had to be gifted to the appropriate families. These gifts never amounted to more than the sum that Paul's grandfather charged a rival group of criminals for information that he came upon in the course of his dealings, relating to the first group's activities. In fact, he made money from the deals, which invariably came (albeit through convoluted channels) from the families that received the cognac and sauternes in the first place. If they had just bought the drink, instead of extorting it, it would have ended up costing them far less.

Yet, whilst Paul's grandfather thrived on such intrigue, his grandmother wilted. These sorts of business adventures are not calming to women, so, after four whirlwind decades, and having recently survived an audit by the Inland Revenue due to the good luck of a warehouse fire, Paul's grandmother insisted that her husband retire. His friends had agreed, speculating that very soon the stress of his work would topple him prematurely into his velvet-lined coffin. So he moved to Devon.

Within two years this formally vibrant man had gained three stones and sunk into a depression so great that only lethargy prevented him buying a rope and taking a walk into the forest. He died of a torpor-induced seizure in his study one Sunday, but it was not until Tuesday that his wife realised that that he was not merely indulging his love of Turkish poetry whilst consuming rows of chocolate-covered figs that he kept in boxes under his day bed. The men who arrived in a private ambulance shortly afterwards found it very difficult to carry him down the stairs.

Paul's grandfather was buried in a coffin so costly, due to its size and extravagant fittings, that at the cremation service even the undertaker had cried.

After her husband's death Paul's grandmother had eaten only cheese biscuits and had given up smoking entirely; but her passion for absinthe had been thwarted only when she became too deaf to order it over the phone, and too frail to struggle beyond the local shop, which sold nothing stronger than gin. Driven by an unrefusable need, she began to experiment with cleaning products, yet she had lived until ninety-seven – the last five years being enjoyed in a state of total stupefaction which had, in more lucid moments, reminded her of first love.

Paul did no more than begin on this story, before his doctor raised a finger and said, 'I'm going to send you up the road for tests.' He indicated that Paul should leave, and gently smiled, but with the look of a much older man, as if Paul had said, 'God, isn't life hard?' and he had agreed.

Walking alone through the rainy evening, along the sometimes ill-lit passageways of Wapping, Paul was pleased to imagine that he had his GP with him. These family doctors knew a thing or two and Paul saw a chance for some free advice. He got straight to the point.

'So, how do I tell my wife that I'm going to die?'

The doctor did not answer.

'No, really. I'd be glad of your ideas on this one, because I've been thinking about it, and have come to the conclusion that there is absolutely no way I can tell her.' Paul checked quickly over his shoulder, to make sure that his doctor was paying attention. 'You probably get asked questions the whole time, by patients you bump into in the shops, or friends calling you up about their kids' rashes, I know, sorry, but I'm guessing that you have a better grip on these things than me.' Still silence.

'Also, assuming we've still got that patient confidentiality thing going, I'll admit that I'm in no state to decide on what to have for breakfast these days, let alone something as big as this.' Paul checked the two of them were alone in the street, before continuing. 'Quite frankly, I think I might be going a little crazy. Not fully-deranged-lala-psychotic, you understand, just a bit wobbly on day-to-day living.'

Paul nodded. 'Your silence tells me that you've sensed as much – and as for telling Eva? I can't bring myself to do it. Maybe I need more time? A few more days, yes, to get my own head round it. Yes, good advice, a few more days, many thanks.'

The doctor was no doubt glad this interview was over, as the weather was, if anything, worse. The continuing rain had, by this point on Paul's walk, made so many puddles that it was impossible to avoid them. He did not even get as far as Salmon Lane before turning for home.

Then came a cat. Paul had never liked cats much, and, on another day, would have been content to walk by this darkly furred thing, wearing the smallest of scowls. If he had been cycling on a night such as this he might have tried to splash the cat – but on this Thursday night the cat was about to cross his path, so Paul stopped to let him do so.

Then, with his luck fully recharged, Paul could go home and put on the radio. After opening a bottle of wine, he would call Eva at work and ask, 'When you say late, how late?' He would pause to listen. He would smile. 'Then I'll stay up and cook us something nice.'

The cat, however, had not obliged. Instead it had stopped, and now it sat down. It was still raining. Cats aren't meant to like water, thought Paul. Looking more closely he saw that the cat was far from a true black, it was simply mottled and a bit dirty. Move on, Paul told himself; but desperate for any luck going, he thought that he should give the cat every chance. He took down his umbrella, which may have been scaring it. The cat licked itself, whilst a man on his way home passed by. As the rain rolled down his neck Paul felt suddenly inspired. He reached for his keys and jangled them enticingly. His aunt's cat, years before, had enjoyed this game.

The cat got up – promising. Seizing the moment, Paul threw his keys across the path. They landed in a puddle, and a woman, who must have seen all of this, hurried past. The cat looked at the keys, then at Paul, then at the woman disappearing into the dark. Realising that he shouldn't have thrown the keys into a puddle, but at the cat, Paul felt for a coin. He found only pounds, but the cat was worth it. He threw two. Both missed and went into a bush.

Had Paul been able to leave it there, he might have gone home laughing. He might have fallen asleep in front of the telly, getting up only when Eva came home. 'I threw a pound at a cat today,' he would confess, as she put the kettle on.

But Paul was not able to leave. The cat had not finished with him yet. It got up slowly and walked off, but not across Paul's path. Instead it moved backwards, as if it had been trained in dressage. Then, just before reaching a bush, the cat disappeared.

Paul wanted to cry, but couldn't. He had to make do with the rain, which smacked his cheeks, then dribbled down his chin. Getting onto his knees, Paul looked into the nearest bush.

'You'll never find them now, love,' crowed a woman from a window above. 'You shouldn't be throwing things at cats anyway.'

Looking up, but unable to see much, Paul told this mystery woman, 'I'm looking for the cat, not the coins.'

'Coins, eh? No wonder you're on your knees!'

Getting up quickly, Paul shouted into the night, 'I know where you live, bitch!', and she hurriedly closed not only the window but the curtains too.

Things were now unreal. Nothing was able to be as before. But accepting this is hard. The day that brought an end to his life was itself dreamlike. It may not have happened at all – and if it did, then it might have been one huge mistake. I mean, how can a pleasant, well-educated man in his twenties kill you with a few words? (He was surely no more than early thirties.) Paul was certain that he had badly misjudged the situation. He should have been severe. 'Look, I don't want to become too personal, or be the cause of any long-term self-doubts, but you really are a terrible doctor – no, no, that won't do, I cannot hide the truth from you forever – you are an assassin.' Then Paul could have risen to his feet with dignified contempt, adding only, 'Goodbye, I trust you will never subject someone else to such an obscene assault', before leaving without hurry or flap. He most assuredly should have avoided trying to leave via a window.

What's more, he was assuming that the prognosis had some basis in fact, yet the National Health System is notoriously careless – something to do with having a million employees, probably; or so many ill people. The wrong organs were often removed; sawn left limbs fell to the floor whilst cancerous right ones remained; babies went to the wrong homes routinely. Five years later, fathers were looking at their families and thinking, 'This kid looks nothing like me. There's not even a vague similarity. For Christ's sake – he more closely resembles my best friend.' Yes, the NHS was screwing people all the time. Somewhere else, in a house or flat a bit like this, a man was, no doubt, sitting calmly. 'Thank God this wheezing and coughing's nothing to worry about,' he was thinking, as his arteries constricted and stiffened within. He would stagger around a bit, probably, happy that there was nothing seriously wrong, before dropping dead in the butcher's one day: just another cooling corpse. This could be so.

And what if Paul had not even turned up? He might have missed the bus, been mugged, been sent last-minute tickets to a matinee performance of *Der Rosenkavalier* at Covent Garden – and who would turn them down? If this had happened he would still be alive and the glory of uncertainty would have filled his future.

And Eva didn't know. This was a good thing. He hadn't even told her that he needed hospital tests, hoping to simply share the news that he was fine after the event. That hadn't quite worked out, but in her world he was still healthy – somewhere out there he lived again! He would have to tell her soon, though. Soon. Then he would start to die in her mind too.

After his rain-soaked walk Paul went to bed alone, reasoning that even the doomed can escape to their dreams.

It was morning, and Paul was uneasy. He paced the living room, walking evenly, then stopping suddenly to sit down, then get up – breathing more heavily now and more calmly then – before repeating the sequence, twice.

Then, at last, he went to his desk. From this, he took out a pad of white paper, and, after foraging awhile, a chewed ink pen that may very well have survived from his schooldays.

The letter that he wrote came in short bursts and was punctuated by long silences of inactivity. Then he seemed totally lost. One time he stopped on the word 'and', and went to the bathroom. There he made a small boat out of loo paper and set it afloat, before sinking it in a torrent of piss.

Dear Clara,

I thought about you the other day, and was shocked to realise, after a bit of counting, that we haven't spoken for more than ten years. Worse than this, after the first years, I began to think of you less and less and am now sometimes totally unable to recall your face.

Before now it hasn't even occurred to me to write. Thank God you never were a girl to hold grudges! If you had been, you might have spent a lot of our childhood pretty pissed off.

I have spent some time thinking about it, and realise that I can't remember you cross. This is making me smile. I knew it was a good idea to write! That I have not done so before baffles me.

It was a short letter, considering how long it took to write, and it was not signed. Paul put it in an envelope addressed with only a name, and took it to the bedroom. Here he put it in the pocket of a seldom-used jacket and left it, as if it was a letter for Santa and had no need of posting by conventional means.

§ 31

ALWAYS HAVING HAD PERIODS OF INTENSE DREAMING, IT WAS not surprising that Paul should, in his lonely vortex, spin round and round to the rhythm of his dreams; and not all these were filled with horror. On the third day, he remembered returning to a flat in Birkesand, early one January. How things came back to him he wished he knew: then he could have lived through the highlights each night. He never could work it out, though – but perhaps it was only that he had a slight cough then too, and a cold nose that had begun to drip.

In his dream, Paul returned to Norway, and to his first meetings with Eva. He remembered things exactly as they had been. First, he walked over barren streets, then across a courtyard, as he had done when he followed the flower-carrying waitress, but this time he was not there by subterfuge – he had been invited to visit, by Eva. He blew his nose, which he could no longer feel, and wished there was a mirror. A deep breath, and he rang the bell marked 4A. Nothing happened. He re-rang Eva's bell, but only after a pause long enough for her to exit the bathroom, without haste, had she been in it. Nothing: he might be the only person here. There were no signs of life. Then, having closed his eyes (as if concentrating on a magic trick), he decided to give her one more go. Only after this third ring did he see that the piece of paper, stuck into the plastic holder by the button that he had been pressing, might have belonged to its neighbour. If this was the case, the button he had been pressing was probably defunct, as all the other flats had neatly typed labels by their bells. Only Eva's was confused. This adjacent button, he thought, must be the one he needed, but it was entirely unclear. Paul pressed it a few times, hoping it was the right one – he had no wish to display his awful Norwegian if he was wrong.

Eva's voice answered. 'You sound keen! Is it very cold?'

She had answered quickly, as if she had been standing by the door, ready. Perhaps she had seen him crossing the street. If so, she would be wondering what he had been up to for the last minutes. Buzzed in, Paul thought no more of it as he made his way upstairs towards his destiny.

The lady in the flat on the ground floor, to the right of the entrance, dined out on the story of those minutes for years. On that evening, she was in her kitchen, which faced the back of the block, getting ready to prepare lobster mayonnaise for a late supper with her sister, who was travelling from Tromsø to be with her. She had bought the lobster at the fish market that morning, her favourite stallholder having set aside his freshest animal.

'This,' he assured her, holding the beast up, 'was landed this very morning. The finest, freshest, most vigorous lobster anywhere.'

Indeed, he did look large and lively. The fishmonger even put an extra band on each claw to ensure his customer's safety. Eva's lady neighbour thanked her market-man and headed home.

Now that she stood in her kitchen with the lobster, her mouth watered. But though the animal had been docile whilst wrapped up in the fridge, he was looking rather frisky out on the counter.

The water was up to a full boil. It was now that Paul, having blown his nose, rang for the first time. The lights in the ground floor kitchen went out.

'Stuff me!' exclaimed the lady, fearing another power cut. Periodically, parts of her apartment were cut off like this. A new fuse box had not cured the problem. In the continued darkness the sound of claws scraping along worktop could be heard. 'Stuff me!' the lady screamed, turning, and running into the table. She fell over, whilst the lobster dropped heavily onto the floor. There was mad screaming from the back of the apartment block as Paul, unable to hear anything at the front door, considered whether to ring once more.

When the lights returned, Paul having rung again, the lobster was somewhere else. The lady, bruised on the thigh and already shaken, looked around her feet, hopping and jumping until she was sure that the clawed marauder was not near. She reached for her rolling pin. She had an especially brutal one, in marble, that she kept for patisserie. She walked slowly towards the fridge and got down onto her knees to look under it. She was raising her club when Paul tried for a third time.

Sudden darkness, and the lobster was on the move. As Paul climbed the stairs, the lobster scratched across the floor towards the lady, who was now in tears – then, contact, and . . . Smack! Smack! Smack! A delicious dinner lay, dead, on a freshly dented wooden floor. After negotiating the table and switching on the light from the main switch, the lady surveyed her smashed-up crustacean. It was now only good for soup, which was made, and eaten, in the security of candlelight.

Whilst the soup simmered, upstairs Eva was kissing Paul for the first time. He had a cold nose, but a warm mouth, and a gentleness that made Eva want to cry. After kissing, Paul wondered what to say. He immediately regretted coming up with the dull 'Do you have two bells?'

Eva had obviously been asked this before. 'No, but I know what you mean. The one next to mine doesn't do anything. I have no idea why it's there.'

Back in the present, and four days after his visit to hospital, Paul almost kept a lunch appointment with a friend. Maurice had lived in Mexico for the last two years – his wife having been appointed to some excellent job or other that Paul, as yet, did not understand. He appreciated that this job was, however, good enough to move across the sea for.

Paul's friend spent the first months abroad trying to find a new role for himself, before discovering a passion for sculpture that surprised everyone who knew him. He worked almost exclusively on models of local women, and his art would have been shockingly explicit had it been anywhere near life-like. As it was, he made his untitled sculptures from rubbish that he found in the streets (of the red-light district, as it happens), and no one could make much of the mess that resulted. This suited him well, as he could show his work to anyone who voiced an interest, without any risk of upsetting them. Back for a family wedding, Maurice had called Paul to arrange lunch. They agreed to meet on Long Acre, Covent Garden, at one.

Paul was sitting on the tube, wondering how best to get to Covent Garden. In the past, he would have walked from Embankment. Today, though, he did not feel up to doing this. There is a hill that rises northwards from the Thames that Paul planned to avoid. Leicester Square was the obvious choice, but this route would involve changing once, then walking up quite a few steps. Bugger: steps. Could get a cab – that would be another fiver.

Meanwhile, the tube train's doors closed on Embankment station. When Paul finally looked up, having decided to spend the fiver, the train was pulling into Victoria. Oh shit, Victoria. (Steps: one billion; cab to Covent Garden: a tenner.) But wait – not so bad, not so bad – he could change at South Kensington. From there the Piccadilly line was direct. He probably wouldn't even be late. The thought of the natural light of South Kensington cheered Paul further. Not only could one see the sky: buddleia and ferns grew out of the walls and up towards the sun. He knew this area well, a childhood girlfriend having lived nearby. Yes, Veronica . . . terrible name, but lovely girl. The two of them had spent happy hours in an awful fast-food place on Thurloe Street. Paul wondered if this restaurant was still there. Those days were not that far gone, after all. And what had happened to Veronica? Paul tried to remember the last time they had met. It might have been the time they went to a Prom concert: quite Veronica's type of thing, that. They had gone with her mother. Afterwards the three of them had eaten Chinese. Was this the last time that he had seen her? They had drifted from each other in a friendly way, so that no one episode stood out clearly.

On the tube, Paul was becoming alarmed that such an important part of his life had already begun to recede into that part of the past that is so blurred, that it might not actually have happened. He tried hard not to panic.

'The High Street, Church Street,' he said aloud. No one else in the carriage paid much attention. 'Or was it Earl's Court?' They had taken a cab. He held Veronica's hand under her coat. It had been too hot for coats, but she had a nice one that she found hard to leave at home. It had become an essential part of Veronica, in Paul's mind.

'Hi Fat. Wonton.' It was woeful. The name of the restaurant eluded him too. He had recommended it to someone not so long ago. It was his lungs that were supposed to be buggered, not his brain. This was all too much.

Paul got off the tube at High Street Kensington. There, having forgotten his lunch appointment, he hoped to follow a path through his memory and come out in front of that unusually posh Chinese restaurant. It seemed not unreasonable to imagine that, if he found this restaurant, Veronica, still sixteen years old, might appear too.

In the shopping centre above the station Paul stood still, pulling breaths in as if they weighed more than usual. He hoped that he looked like someone who was waiting for his date to arrive. Normal people waited too. After a decent rest, and a bit of self-encouragement, he would walk out onto the High Street and cross it via a traffic island, waiting half way for the next green light.

Whilst Paul walked northwards from High Street Kensington, then stopped, then walked some more, he drifted again. In his mind, he was back in the year of his just-discovered love for Eva.

It was a Thursday in late January, during an unusually mild British winter. Paul was walking down towards the river, thinking away to himself, in a mood more suited to autumn. He passed Limehouse Basin, stumbled on a cobble, then pulled open the door of a pub. He was early, so ordered a pint before sitting down in a corner with a view of the door, and waiting for his friend, Ronnie, to arrive. Ronnie was a dawdler, leaving Paul with at least twenty minutes to himself. He spent this time looking vacantly towards the window at the far end, under which flowed the Thames, although Paul could not see it from this angle.

Norway had been a shock to Paul, with its barbarous chill hiding behind soft whiteness. The lasting impressions had been of his throbbing toes, and Eva, a girl worth dying for. He remembered her black eye and squashed foot as if they had been freshly made, even though both must have become fully healed. At least he had been only responsible for one of those assaults.

The pub was almost empty, and the barman hurried around, doing things that he should have finished earlier.

After Paul had passed some time sipping and daydreaming, Ronnie arrived.

'Sorry. A bit late.'

'I know, I know. I usually factor it in.'

Another pint was bought. Lunch was discussed and ordered. They stood at the bar whilst they waited for the food.

'How are you then? Still love-struck?'

'Taunt all you like, I'll not deny it.'

'Got a photo?'

'No, but you'll be one jealous loner when you see one.'

Some girls came in and sat at a table nearby. One lit a cigarette.

'Sure she's real? You can tell me, I'm your friend.'

Paul considered this part of the conversation over. A horn sounded somewhere out on the river. 'Are you going to be a twat all through lunch, or can we talk like big boys?'

'And if I pretend that we can, then you'll tell me lots more about this imaginary friend, right?'

'Listen, she's just great. If she's in my imagination then long live insanity. I've already bought a ticket to go back.'

'And she's similarly loopy?'

'Who knows?'

'You, I would have hoped.'

'It's not quite so simple. She's going through a nasty time at the moment. She doesn't say much about it, but there's an ex hanging around.'

'Never ideal. Sure this isn't going to turn into a full-scale car crash?'

No response. Someone else ordered food. The barman went to

the kitchen with the order, and returned with the smell of sausages.

Ronnie went on. 'But she has said this other bloke's out and you're in?'

A cursory nod.

'And what, she calls?'

'Well, I've been writing her letters.'

'Letters, plural? I though you'd only just got back.'

'Almost four weeks, Ronnie. Almost four weeks.'

Ronnie had nothing to add, here.

'Tell me, she keeps on saying that my letters should be shorter but that I must send her more drawings. Perhaps the writing is not romantic enough?'

'But at least she likes your drawing. You're an artist, so that's good, yes?'

'I'm not saying it's not good, just that I'm worried about the words. I'm not much practised at that sort of thing.'

'She's foreign, she probably can't read them easily. Don't be so touchy.'

'Even so. I don't think that's it.'

'Well, you want my advice? Make them gush.'

'I do. To go any further wouldn't feel sincere.'

'Look, here's a general rule, passed on to me by my dad – if you get to the end of such a letter, then read through it and think: This is a bit dicey, I'm not sure if I haven't gone too far this time – then you haven't gone nearly far enough.'

'And you speak, here, from experience?'

Ronnie half-raised a hand, put his head briefly to the side, and had a drink.

Soon after this Paul is in Norway once more. It's the middle of February, and Birkesand feels harsher than before. There is more ice than Paul remembered. He is inside, though, and Eva is making him tea, having bought some specially. He enjoys watching her move freely – her foot is almost completely better.

Outside, on the frozen pavement stands a man that Paul knows is Bjørn. Darkness is already falling, but according to Eva he'll not move for a while yet. Paul is watching him from the very edge of the window.

'And this is why I must use the fire escape at the back?'

'Yes, and get away from that window.'

She comes over to draw the curtains, making rather a show of it.

'So he's a complete fruitcake then?'

Eva is confused.

Paul sits down. 'Why can't I go and biff him on the nose?'

Eva looks softly at him. 'Because he'd kill you horribly.' She thinks a little more. 'If you met him on a staircase, of course, he wouldn't stand a chance.'

He shakes his head. Having put the lamps on, she gives Paul his tea, and now sits down too. In the lamplight he can see how sad she is, though she thinks she hides it.

§ 32

BACK AGAIN IN THE PRESENT (ALTHOUGH HE STRUGGLED against it), Paul was downstairs in the house in Wapping. It was the fifth day of his new life as a victim and now he received a special surprise. The morning post had brought a bill and a circular. Also, by special delivery, had come a handwritten letter. This last envelope bore a Norwegian stamp and was addressed by a feminine hand. Paul knew that this would be from his mother-in-law, Birte. She would write unexpectedly, with no pattern to her correspondence, having been, for example, inspired by a recipe that she wished to share.

> *The ladies from church not only quietly prayed before lunch, but riotously afterwards – joyously thanking God for this revelation of brawn and nutmeg – yes, nutmeg! Truly a blessing to rejuvenate even the most jaded of Christian palates.*

Sometimes the ladies from church would drink.

Paul's lucky-dip letter seemed to carry a postmark from somewhere other than Bergen, but the stamp was indistinct and it could have said anything. Why it was worthy of overnight delivery, Paul did not know, but he did not open it straight away, as the feeling of looking forward to anything at all was beautiful, and to be savoured. Indeed, Paul would have been well advised to wait considerably longer than he did, as his letter came not from his mother in law, but from Bjørn's wife, Marianne, and it had been born, not from the afterglow of a church luncheon, but from the depths of hate and loss.

In innocence, Paul spent ten minutes acting out normality. Only after dressing and making himself a pot of tea did he sit down in the kitchen, ready to open this poisoned letter from Norway. For a moment he remembered the feeling of nothing much, which is what it had felt like to be alive. Then he filled his cup and opened the letter.

The first thing that Paul noticed was that the letter was really more of a picture. The picture had been made up on a computer, and had the look of a child's photomontage. It really was a most unusual mind that had thought of putting an old and poorly-cut-out photo of Eva's head onto the body of a goat. Drawing close was Bjørn's smiling face, twinned with the body of a large and very masculine pig. This image would revisit Paul often in the next days. There was writing below.

Your wife has been having sex with my husband, Bjørn Olsen, many times recently at the Premier Guest House in Piccadilly. As you are living closer than me, will you go round there and tell them to stop? I have enclosed a photo. Perhaps you could pass it on?

Paul read it twice, then fainted.

There was a room, mainly white. Plastic and metal were everywhere that they should not have been: twin tormentors. It was difficult to move, here. A starched sheet lay, uncomfortably unruffled, stretched out before him. His world.

Despair ate into his arm. Clear tubing led to a clear bag. Something living came near briefly, then turned to leave. Gentle scent fell like iced water.

'Please turn the machine off.' But he had imagined the words. 'Please.'

Somewhere nearby, a woman left.

Staggering to his feet, who knows how long afterwards, and seemingly having thought things over as he lay unconscious, Paul put on a coat, took his car keys, and went to the garage. The door was wonky and the light didn't work, just as usual, but Paul found a hose, cloth and tape with enough swiftness to suggest that he had thought about this sort of thing before. He put his bits in a bag and added, as an afterthought, a box of matches that were to hand. He left in a hurry.

Paul drove as if he was a passenger. Looking out of the window, he saw things pass: warehouses, a traffic light on red, a tunnel that might never have ended. Not that these registered – his thoughts sat quietly on the back seat, later lying down, eyes wide open.

It was only once he had driven outside the M25 that Paul began to feel more alert; and, as he woke up, he became vexed that he didn't know where he was heading. He really ought to have worked out a route, not to mention a destination, so he pulled off the main road and soon after drove into a pub car park.

Paul had a map. This he found neither in the glove box, the back seat, nor the boot. It must have been back at the house, probably in the spare room. He began to cry, which is surprising, as one might have thought that forgetting the map was the least of his problems.

All suicides were, by their nature, experimental, Paul thought. Still, his own final day was a shambles. His whole life had been, now that he thought of it. OK, he could be more specific – why not admit the truth now that he would have to live with it for so short a time? Life had gone straight down the shit-hole when his sister had died. And she had managed things better than this, had she not? Yet she had been only seventeen.

Paul beat his head against the steering wheel whilst he pondered the toxicity of exhaust. Unsure of the time it might take to kill him, and not a great fan of pain, he decided to forsake gassing and opt instead for poisoning. A quick trip to Asda and the necessaries would be in a bag, in the car, then in his bloodstream. He would be in a drugged and drunken stupor before he could feel a thing. This was a much better idea – were paracetamol not painkillers?

'Forward planning, I see,' the kid at the checkout would say as he scanned the pills after the gin.

So Paul put his keys back in the ignition, ready to search Kent for a superstore. But, suddenly thinking better of it, he took them out and went into the pub. Swing doors swung, and the hugely comforting smell of beer and old smoke held his cheeks. Two women sat having lunch whilst at the bar stood several men. As the thought that he shouldn't kill himself passed behind him unnoticed, Paul approached the bar lady.

'Is there a supermarket or off-license near here?' he asked her.

'Our drink not good enough for you?' She didn't seem to be joking.

Paul was quite apologetic. 'No, it's not that. I don't just want a drink, you see?'

'We do crisps.'

Paul smiled sarcastically, and in a tired voice said, 'I just wondered if there was a shop nearby. That's all.'

The bar lady stared at the developing bruise on his forehead.

'Is this idiot pestering you?' asked a man in overalls.

'Yes.'

Paul was disbelieving. 'Fuck off, I just asked for directions.'

'Don't dare speak to Lilleth like that!'

Everyone in the bar looked on expectantly as the man stood up, then came close to Paul. 'You cunts come here from London with your posh voices and filthy language. Well, you can take this back with you!' And he stamped on Paul's foot, before head-butting him on the nose.

As Paul bled, Eva was calling home. It had been an unusual morning at the City bank. The receptionist, whom she hardly knew, had begun the day by calling Eva over, from where she had been waiting for the lift, and trying to start a conversation about her recently pregnant sister. Over-wide smiles had filled any gaps.

Then, when Eva had escaped to the twelfth floor, and settled her-self behind her desk, she had seen next to her, outside on the window ledge, a falcon. She looked at it sideways for a moment, exactly as it was looking at her, but when she turned full round to stare, it leapt from the ledge and flapped from view. Amazed, and wanting to tell someone about it, Eva looked about the room, but saw only people who would suggest it had been a pigeon, and others who, accepting the truth of it, would have waited for her to get to the point. She had been defensive around her colleagues ever since her appraisal, three weeks before. There, she had been told that she was perceived as pushy, and ought to work on her team skills. Eva spent her time on the tube going home each night wondering what team skills were, and how she was ever going to know if hers had been getting any better.

Next, whilst she had been thinking whether to call Paul, who might be doing some work, or might not, she felt an unexplained anxiety at the thought of having spoken to Bjørn the day before. The feeling passed as soon as she recognised it, but would return malaria-like and strengthened, bringing pitiless fevers, for the rest of her life.

In a care home, seventy-two years later, taken hold of yet again, her final hoarse, delirious words would be: 'Fuck. That little git ruined things again. Fuck it all, I could have been happy' – although her children preferred to remember only the word 'happy', the rest being attributed to the combined effects of morphine and dementia.

And the bird was not all that she wanted to talk to her husband about. This ceaseless work had prevented her addressing the growing gap between herself and Paul – but soon she would have time to talk, Christmas gave her four days together with him. Then, there would be time.

Eva did a morning's work before calling her husband; in an office, next to a birdless window, she held a phone and waited for him to answer.

Paul limped back to his car. Blood stained his hands and ran onto his shirt. One of his toes was certainly broken. His thoughts of suicide now became secondary to the pain and the feeling of humiliation. He had to get out of this car park: there could be no more waiting around here. Taking a tissue, he plugged his nose and drove fast to a petrol station. Here he bought a map and filled up the car. He looked shocking, but the cashier didn't seem to care. So, having paid, he pulled his car to the side of the forecourt and tried to decide where to go today, to kill himself tomorrow. One night was all that he needed to recharge and be, once more, strong enough to end this suffering.

Looking across Britain, he felt drawn to several coastal areas. This raised the possibility of drowning. He discounted Wales, but quite liked the idea of Cornwall. Scotland would take ages. After some time he settled on Norfolk, as his drunken grandmother had always said that it was a dead-end kind of a place.

Paul studied the detailed map of the county with care. His eyes moved slowly northwards. When he came to Allingham he stopped. He had been there as a boy, and remembered the long, drab promenade, behind which sat several rows of bungalows looking like an ugly high-tide mark after a storm. In front brooded the North Sea. Clara had said of the place, 'I want to go somewhere sunny next holiday. I'll never come back here.' And she never had. But Paul would return, just the once. With any luck he would arrive in time for dinner, and in the morning he would thank the lady at the Spa shop for selling him all that he would ever need. Paul imagined she had done as much for some of the town's residents before. People in Norfolk were probably killing themselves all the time.

Having re-plugged his unstoppable nosebleed, he drove off.

Paul arrived in Allingham later than expected. The traffic had been heavy, and the motorway had become an A-route early on, leaving miles of narrow roads to be negotiated behind lorries or farm vehicles. By the time that he reached the sea, his toe had swelled to such a size that he was sure that he would be unable to take his shoe off. Swinging his legs out of the car, he aimed a loaded finger at his foot. 'I'm going to kill you tomorrow,' he said.

It was a clear, chill night and stars were everywhere. Fifteen years blinked at him as he struggled along paving he had last walked as a child. Paul stopped and checked left, then right. There were vacancies everywhere. He thought for a moment, before choosing the first guesthouse from a dozen. After limping up some steps, he rang the bell.

The door was answered by a lady of his mother's age who, upon seeing Paul in this bloody state of disarray, appeared suddenly sad.

'You must be looking for a room.'

'Yes, I see you have vacancies.' And he was in.

'No bag,' he confirmed, in answer to her continued silence.

Standing expectantly in the hallway, Paul admired a plastic Christmas tree. Lights glowed in multicolours.

His landlady's professionalism did not desert her on this distressing night.

'Mrs Stone,' she said, before leading the way upstairs and asking if Paul wanted her to wash his shirt.

'I should like that very much,' Paul said, pausing on his step.

'The bathroom's on your left.' She swung the door open. 'It's a whirlpool spa.'

Paul came closer for a polite look and was struck by an image of his body, arm hanging over the side of the avocado bath, wrists ripe with congealing blood, wobbling as the jacuzzi furiously bubbled.

The landlady led him to the front of the house. The room she showed him was small and clean, and boasted a ceramic doorknob.

'Paper in the morning?' she asked.

Paul had already thrown his coat onto the bed, and was unbuttoning his shirt.

'No thanks.'

Sleep brought with it dreams and visions.

There was an abattoir. Bjørn the pig was being hoisted along a line, dangling by his cloven feet, wriggling in terror as the knife approached. He was the only pig in the line for whom stunning hadn't worked. Standing waiting for him, dressed in boots and waterproofs, was Paul. The wailing of metal stained the air.

'Hello, Bjørn,' Paul said, as if to an old friend. 'I'm afraid I'm merely a keen amateur, so you'll have to bear with me.' And the image blurred. On the bedroom wall a radiator murmured.

Waking early from this pain-punctuated sleep, Paul lay still and studied the ceiling – but the sound of a car door closing distracted him: a quietly closed door. It probably hadn't even shut properly.

When he refocused his thoughts, Eva was standing at the end of the room. Her body was not quite in proportion to her feet and head, which were huge and rather menacing. The two stared at each other awhile, before Eva blinked out a tear and was gone. Paul fell off the bed, got quickly to his feet, cursed and flung open the curtains, filling the room with the sanity of daylight. Dizzy, and standing in absolute nakedness, Paul looked out of the window and wondered why there was a police car parked outside.

Paul did not know that his landlady had also endured a restless night. She had taken in guests for many years now, and had seen single men arrive in various states of defeat and bedragglement; some even had bloody noses; but something about Paul's demeanour made her worry. It was his calmness.

'Do you want me to wash that for you?' (That very bloody shirt.)

'Ooh, yes please!' (It's not my own blood, you know. Some landlady or other's. This toilet paper up my nostril's just for show.)

Mrs Stone sat up in bed, in the still-dark morning, frightened. Why had she let him in? She had been weak. Seeing him, so young, yet already forlorn – she had wanted to help. No more. The next boy who turned up like that could stick any thoughts of staying with her right up his bum. From now on she would keep a pot of stones on the shelf by the front door to throw at people like this.

Soon Mrs Stone had worked herself into such a panic that, still wearing only her nightdress, she ran downstairs and out into the street.

Twenty minutes later, a police car pulled up outside Mrs Stone's house. Mrs Stone was with her neighbour, Mrs Bradshaw, who was now more excited than she had been for years. Mrs Stone had been obliged to repeat the story of the killer next door several times. Out of a sense of duty, she added new drama to each rendition.

The policeman, having collected the key, and now convinced that a gangster from London had come to bring terror to his quiet town, silently let himself into Paul's boarding house. Standing in the hallway, he could see into the kitchen, through a window and into the garden, where Paul was now climbing the back fence. The policeman radioed for help, and started running.

With a broken toe and advanced lung disease, Paul was never going to be quick, but the waste ground beyond the fence was scattered with young trees, which concealed him well enough as he stumbled towards the only building he could see: a church.

The morning was still not fully awake, and darkness held on longer in this copse. But the church nearby was illuminated, partly perhaps by floodlights, but also by the figure that Paul now saw beside it – or above it. The figure was God, and God was displeased. He spoke. 'Paul, I'm going to kill you soon, but first you must suffer.'

Paul ran for cover. Thin branches whipped his bare legs. A piece of glass had already cut his good foot. The policeman was nearby, but did not see him until he made a final dash for the church. The entrance was on the far side, and Paul reached it as the policeman emerged from the scrubland. Breathing in coughs and gasps through foam-flecked lips, his eyes wide with madness, Paul knew he could run no further. Blood pooled around his toes. His pursuer was close. Grabbing the door handle in front of him, Paul lurched inside the church, fell over a cleaning lady (who had been on her knees, scrubbing), and cracked his head on the wet stone floor. Sprawled, prostrate, naked, and blind in the darkness, he was ready to die.

The cleaning lady began screaming. From another door a vicar came in.

'Who are you? What do you mean by this?' he demanded of the monster.

The cleaner stood up and widened herself further, like some protective dyke against this flood of unholiness that was upon them. Yet now that Paul lay silently, she could see him clearly, even in the dim light of the church. One arm was lying above his head, so that a broadly hunched shoulder hid half his face. His back was smooth and hairless, reminding her of polished wood. His legs held fat calves that she found so arousing she stared instead at his buttocks. Still-raw blood had been cut from limbs and body alike. At his feet gathered a black wetness.

'This man's hurt,' she said pathetically to the vicar, who had come to kneel beside them. He, too, looked at the horror on his floor. Together, they felt ashamed.

Broken, incontinent, bleeding, Paul truly looked like an escaped martyr: a would-be saint. He had been beaten, certainly – possibly with cudgels. His eyes, when they opened, looked like peeled eggs.

'Forgive me,' whispered the cleaner, and as she stroked Paul's cold, damp hair she recited a prayer. The priest took off his jacket and laid it over Paul. He was about to fetch a bandage, when the distorted conversation of a police radio hurried him outside.

The policeman had caught only glimpses of Paul as he tumbled erratically through the scrubby land. By the time he reached the churchyard, Paul was gone. Sure that he had seen his villain run this way, the policeman vaulted the boundary wall and began to look through the graves. Tombstones stood leaning casually to the side, like accomplices. Jumping between them, the hunter searched.

The constable was at the far end of the churchyard when the sound of someone screaming started him running. As he arrived at the church door, a man came out and ushered him further beyond the porch. The policeman was now bent over, breathing hard.

'Has the bastard run past here?'

There was no answer, so the policeman looked up. Seeing the churchman, he continued more meekly. 'I heard shouting.'

The vicar, shocked, said nothing. Then, looking at his feet, as he always did when he had failed to be truthful, he saw a crimson puddle.

'Yes,' he said, quickly changing tack. 'A man tried to come into the church, but he ran off when Elizabeth screamed.'

The vicar pointed beyond the gate. 'What's he done?' he asked – but the policeman was already hurrying away, leaving the vicar to ponder this question alone.

Inside the church Paul sat on a pew, dressed in the vicar's jacket. He faced the altar in oppressive silence.

Then light and birdsong came into the church with the vicar, who came and sat next to Paul. After some quiet talk the two men stood and walked together towards the vestry. Elizabeth was left alone in her confusion.

Exiting by the side door, the vicar took Elizabeth's saint across the deserted lane and into the church hall. The hall smelled of children. A papier-mâché nativity scene stood, unpainted, on a Formica-topped desk. As they walked, cardboard angels, hanging from cotton, brushed their heads. 'I have some clothes at the back,' the vicar said. 'They're not very suitable I'm afraid.'

He began sorting through a cupboard, as Paul looked on without seeming to see. Out came a pair of pink trousers, a purple shirt, and a large black cardigan. The vicar apologised: 'We put on *Pygmalion* with the Hooten players last spring.'

Paul took the clothes and dressed in the toilet. Yesterday's dried blood washed off with minimal fuss. Still, he looked awful. The vicar had also given him a pair of trainers. Despite these, cold rose in his legs. He wondered how much of him was still alive. When Paul came back into the hall, the vicar, who had been in the kitchen putting on the kettle, smiled approvingly. He gestured that they should sit down, looked through Paul's eyes and said, 'So, tell me who I have lied for.'

There was silence.

'It will go no further than this room.'

Paul moved in his chair.

The vicar gently pressed. 'I'll take back the trousers if you don't.' He smiled, then went on. 'This will remain between you, me and God.'

Paul looked quickly at the door. He had hoped that God had not followed them. He needed to run. Keep on running. He had stopped and now he was trapped. Idiot! Why had he trusted this stranger? This man wanted to catch him every bit as much as the policeman. And why? Was he guilty of something? Had he ever done anything wrong? Priests were people who saw sin everywhere. They were not normal. Cornered, and with the priest trying to undress his soul, Paul became enraged.

'Your God hasn't been around much recently,' he began. 'Until today.'

The vicar was encouraged.

Paul continued. 'He met me on the way here. Having head-butted me, he broke my foot. Whipped me.'

Paul got up from his too-small plastic chair so that he was able to rant with more freedom. His voice rose further. 'He began by promising me death, then screwed my wife. Even took pictures. And now, having taken my clothes, he sits back to admire his work.'

The vicar would have protested, but Paul carried straight on, becoming sweating and hysterical.

'Is he finished with me? Is he satisfied?'

The veins in his neck were writhing. 'I am not a man any more!'

Hanging angels slowly spun as Paul shouted into the empty hall. 'You've pulled out my fucking heart. You have won!'

The blasphemies and swearing, this spitting hate that contorted Paul's face, it all splattered into the room without restraint. Yet the priest was astonished to find that foul residue did not stick to the windows or drip off the ceiling. Instead, the oaths floated into corners and evaporated, leaving in their place only bright winter light and the mild smell of plasticine.

The vicar marvelled at the ways of God. But Paul made murder in the hole where his heart had been.

§ 33

IT WAS ONLY DAYS UNTIL CHRISTMAS, AND PAUL HAD DEATH on his mind: not his own this time, but Bjørn's. This was surely a more logical approach than he had taken thus far. Yes, he had been unbalanced in his actions until now: running naked into the arms of a priest could only be put down to temporary madness brought on by the stress he was under. As for being chased out of bed by a policeman – it was ridiculous, and most undignified. No, things needed to change. He was finally starting to think rationally.

The policeman had obviously been called because someone recognised his description. A search was under way: Stop this young man killing himself! It's our top priority.

Really there was no need for any of that now. He wasn't going to kill himself after all. He was going to kill Bjørn – which was a service to humanity. In any case, quite why Eva had called the police he didn't know. She was off being shafted one day; then (tearfully it was to be hoped) she tried to make everything all right the next. This was a very inconsistent position.

Still, stuff her. Paul had more pressing matters to be thinking about. Bjørn was for the chop, and a plan had yet to be hatched. The priest had been right about one thing, though. Suicide was certainly not the best option. There was, indeed, no way back from that – and it was true that life did have many surprises. Yes, Bjørn would be experiencing one of those unexpected moments soon.

After having left the priest, Paul had, as was only sensible, stopped to phone the Premier Guest House, in order to check that Bjørn was still in residence. Picking coins from a bag in his pocket, Paul stacked enough for his call on the shelf next to the phone. First he called directory enquiries. Whilst repeating out loud the number he had been given, he phoned the hotel. If Bjørn had returned to Norway already, this would be a great inconvenience. Paul nervously tapped his fingers against the cold glass of the phone box.

'Hi, I'm hoping to locate a Bjørn Olsen. Is he staying with you still?'

(Tap tap tap.)

'Oh, splendid. No, I want to give him this message myself.'

Energy, and what he thought might be happiness, filled Paul. Leaving the phone box he felt uplifted and managed an almost brisk walk for a while, thinking all the time how he might dispatch Bjørn without risking a fight, which, in his honesty, Paul imagined he would lose. Perhaps he would make his way up to Bjørn's room, unannounced of course, and knock on his door. Bjørn might open it in a state of total unreadiness – shaving foam all over one part of his face, no top on. How shocked he would be just to see Paul standing there! Let alone if Paul was carrying an axe.

Many places sold axes. There were plenty of legitimate uses for these tools. One such use would be to cleave Bjørn in two. Paul tried to imagine the scene, but frustratingly, although this was his own private fantasy, he did not see himself land one skilled blow on Bjørn's crown. His dream was spoiled by the realisation that he would be unable to swing the axe in such a confined space. The doorframe would get in the way, for a start. Though, if he was to catch Bjørn in the bath, for example, happy carnage would be guaranteed – but this was hardly likely to happen. No, axes were unwieldy things – fine in a proper context, but not suitable here. A knife would be better. It was easily obtained, cheap, small enough to conceal about one's person. Yes, a knife would do nicely. He could probably pick one up at Liverpool Street station.

One small problem with what was otherwise a very simple plan was Paul's lack of money. The priest, fearing what might happen if he let Paul go, helpless and without cash, gave him all that he could quickly find.

'Hang on just a moment longer,' he had said, before diving out of the church hall. Paul, who had been about to leave, was unnerved. He imagined the vicar calling the police. He was already walking out of the hall when the vicar returned and stuffed a small but full bag of coins into Paul's pocket.

'I was collecting these for the lifeboats, but I'll just write them a cheque.'

Paul should have been more grateful, but he feared any delay. He rushed off as quickly as he could, coughing all the time.

The priest worried that he had not given Paul a coat, or even a hot drink. It was as if he had failed a test. He had hoped to effect a life-changing conversion. Instead, Paul had coughed, sworn, coughed some more and hurried off. So, having locked the hall door, the priest walked back through the churchyard alone. His footsteps sounded hollow in the cold air.

Paul marched slowly on. His bag of coins was annoyingly heavy, but the railway station was surely not far now. A dog-walker had pointed and said ten minutes, yet he had been walking twenty already. Paul stopped for a rest. The air promised rain, or snow, so he allowed himself only a little longer before heading on downhill.

The station, when he found it, was almost deserted. Paul had imagined that there would have been at least a guard, and possibly a pair of police officers. If they had tracked him to Mrs Stone's they ought to have been watching the station; but there was no one there. So instead of having to evade uniformed officials, Paul walked straight past the ticket machine and onto a platform that gave the impression that it had been empty for weeks. If there had not been a young mother waiting with her excited daughter far down at the other end of the unnecessarily long platform, Paul would have assumed that this station was disused. The asphalt under his feet was cracked and buckled. The paint peeled from the footbridge. The only sounds were from a bird, and the far-away child singing too-fast Christmas carols.

At a different time Paul's heart might have stopped here, letting him sink to his knees whilst the recently started rain began the long job of dissolving him, eventually washing his residue entirely from the side of the platform and onto the tracks. No one would have noticed, and by the summer all that would have been there to hint at his life would be a particularly vigorous patch of weeds.

Today, however, the worsening pain in Paul's side forbade rest and his quickened heartbeat drove him on to a different end.

§ 34

ON THAT SAME DECEMBER AFTERNOON, BJØRN TOO WAS taking a train. The view from it was mostly grim, but he stared out of the window with a look of calm that had been missing for a long time. His last meeting was over. This was it: the future – and the most exciting thing about it was that Bjørn knew nothing about what might come next. He and Marianne could start afresh. Perhaps they would sell the house? Then the two of them would be carefree youngsters again. That house had brought them no joy.

So what next? He watched South London pass, glad to see the light fade on this last day of his old life, wondering if he felt happy.

The train blundered on and minutes passed. Nothing much was happening; someone took a phone call; Bjørn was still. But if anyone had been watching closely, they would have caught a change in Bjørn's smile. It had been held a little too long. And if that person had wondered – what's up with him, then? – and followed Bjørn's line of sight into the window and off again at an angle, they might have guessed that he had, as the evening darkened, been watching not the sprawl of South London passing, but the reflected image of a small boy standing on a seat and waving a dinosaur about. It is doubtful, though, that if anyone had got this far with their deductions, they would have been able to appreciate what had happened to this life.

And now the train approaches Clapham. People are getting up, there's general bustling and falling about. For some, it's time to leave.

Bjørn was in pain. Brazen yet unseen, a plastic tyrannosaurus had reached over and plucked out his heart. As a result, he was not fully able to see – tears were distorting his vision; but this time these tears

176

contained no memories and no future and he was able to wipe them clear. Then, travelling north from Clapham, and now with more lights outside, Bjørn was able, once again, to look at the passing housing blocks and warehouses.

The train slowed. Anyone watching him now would have no clue that something was wrong. The grisly rupture to Bjørn's chest was hardly visible from most angles. He looked like any other tired commuter; his puffy eyes could have come from fatigue.

Metal squealed as the train lurched. Then, from the middle of his lonely world, Bjørn was brought sharply back to life. He was reading adverts and scrawlings and watching the backs of houses, imagining the lives that went on here, trying to pretend that he could still act normally, grasping at some composure, when he saw that someone had written him a message. On a wall, at the apex of a bend, was written, in two feet high lettering:

'Bjørn, there's no point to life at all.'

But the light outside was not good, and the bend curved quickly enough to ensure that he did not have time to read it twice. Instead, he caught only views of a dark yard.

Unnerved, he got up and stood near the doors, pulling his coat over his wounds, as the train approached the end of the line.

§ 35

TRAINS FROM NORWICH TO LONDON ARE POOR AT THE BEST OF times, so why anyone would feel a moral duty to pay for travelling on one was beyond Paul. Had he the money for a ticket, he would have dodged it anyway – in any event, he thought that he should save all the vicar's coins for unforeseen expenses.

Once safely on board the train, Paul slowly tipped out all these coins onto his seat-side table, then he began to count. The small bag that the vicar had given Paul contained seven even smaller bags. The total had been impressively heavy, but the first smaller bag contained only a pound. Paul began to fear that he would be arriving in the capital as a pauper. He continued counting and found a pound in each bag but one, which was short. This murder was going to have to be done on the cheap – it would require ingenuity. He didn't even have enough cash for a good knife. Not quite seven pounds was unlikely to be enough for much more than a screwdriver.

Then the guard arrived. 'I'm afraid that I have no ticket,' said Paul.

'Any good reason for that?'

'None at all. I've left my wallet at my hotel – which, incidentally, is really starting to bug me – and I think your train is ghastly.'

The guard was startled. 'This will mean a penalty ticket, sir, goodness yes.'

'Fire away.' And Paul provided his address and details with no fuss at all.

Getting around London, Paul imagined, would not be so easy. Realising that his murder attempt might be a shambles brought a new sense of dismay upon Paul. He had no plan.

Confused as to what to do next, Paul abandoned the idea of saving, and instead bought a pastie and tea from the buffet car. He ate it at the wobbly counter opposite the till and, whilst chewing, wondered how many stranger-looking people had sat here recently. He knew it could not be many: he had rarely seen anyone as bizarrely dressed as he was now. This gave him an unexpected glow of pride. Disappointingly, the man who had served him gave not one look in his direction; not even a sideways glance, which Paul was especially looking out for – but being ignored by the world did have advantages. Undisturbed, Paul was able to formulate a plan, or drift away from reality and imagine the future. He had time for both, giving him an air of strange melancholy, and a plan consisting of two stages and a finale.

Once at Liverpool Street, Paul set about finding the knife. The station itself did not have a hardware shop, but a helpful florist pointed him to a nearby ironmonger's. Nearby, once more, turned out to be further than promised, but before the damp and cold of the late afternoon had entirely penetrated his inner organs he was standing before an admirably suitable range of kitchenware. Not only were these knives excellent in quality, the shop itself was just perfect too. Aisles ran in such a way that no one could see him clearly, and pots and bins hung next to ladders, making shoplifting a doddle amongst the distractions. The only consideration was the type of knife. The choice was almost too great, so he asked for assistance. Should he go for a filleting knife or a carving knife? A Chinese cleaver was tempting. The assistant unlocked the protective screen and showed him them all. In the end, Paul chose the one he was looking at when another customer came in and ensured that the assistant's attention was elsewhere. It had an unusually long, thin blade, which fitted well inside his pink trousers (once he had poked most of the blade's length through his pocket). He just had to make sure that he never sat down, which would be nasty. Paul left the hardware shop with a different limp to the one he had come in with.

Now for a taxi. The area around Liverpool Street was crammed with black cabs, and most had their come-and-get-me lights glowing brightly in the murk; but none was willing to stop so near the station – something to do with queuing at taxi ranks, perhaps. As a result, Paul had to walk back to where he had come from and queue up with dozens of other travellers, most of whom looked like they had just finished work.

It was getting always darker and colder. Paul might well have given up and gone home, if he had not lost all feeling already. Even the point of the knife in his trousers had ceased to hurt after a very few steps. He thought that it may have cut a small hole in him, but he had no way of checking easily; and the only clue that it had was the way his trousers stuck to his leg. The evening was dark, though, and there were odd bursts of rain, so it was really impossible to tell.

Five minutes later he was at the front of the queue and telling the cabbie, 'The Albert Hall, please.' Paul had now arranged the knife up one sleeve – he hoped that there would be no sudden braking.

Once they had passed Barbican, he elaborated his directions: 'First, stop for a minute at the Huntston. You know where I mean? It's just off Piccadilly – I need to get some cash at the hotel before going on.' The cabbie huffed, seemed about to say something, but didn't.

When the cab pulled up outside the hotel, Paul got out, smiled at the cabbie, entered through the front door, exited through the back, then walked along Jermyn Street, past where he had been in the taxi some minutes earlier, before heading north to kill Bjørn.

It took Paul more than ten minutes to reach the Premier Guest House, as he had to walk up a hill that had not been there previously. He stopped regularly to look into the windows of shops that any normal person might have paused to admire, so that no one would think him crazy, limping along dead-slow in his comedy clothes, in everyone's way, whilst others rushed to restaurants or plays, or home to houses hung with tinsel.

Finally, Paul could see the place: but he didn't just blunder in, keen though he was to get on with things. Instead, he stopped across the street from the hotel, taking time to watch normal life there, and hoping to pick up some useful trifle or other that might help him in this murder. He found it hard to stand still and concentrate, however, so delighted was he at the rundown nature of the place. What a joy it was to note that the hotel was grotty, indeed seedy. He let himself imagine what sort of businessman would stay at such a place: an absolute oaf, a watery tea maker. Yes, Bjørn was a nothing already, he wouldn't be missed at all. Finishing this chap off was hardly a crime: it was a service. Paul chuckled, composed himself, then walked up three steps and into the hotel lobby.

'Hello,' Paul said to the too-young clerk. 'I wish to surprise a friend, Bjørn Olsen. Could you tell me if he's here, and if so, his room number?'

'I'll call him for you.'

Paul squeaked in consternation. 'No, indeed you won't. This is supposed to be a surprise. Just tell me his room number.'

The clerk looked upset. 'Look, I'd love to – but it's not up to me. I'm not allowed.'

Paul's forehead wrinkled.

The clerk went on. 'It's my manager.' Now he lowered his voice: 'He's a bit of a dick.'

Paul nodded.

The clerk continued. 'Only Tuesday he gave me a talk about "the need for professionalism". So I can't give out room numbers, mate. Not my doing.'

Paul was looking displeased. What was he going to do now? Wait all night on the off chance of some action?

'Perhaps you could surprise your friend down here in the lobby?'

'No, no. That won't do at all! The whole thing would be ruined.'

The clerk wrestled with his wish to help, and lost.

'He's here,' said the clerk. 'I can't give you his room without telling him, but he goes out every night at six, to eat. Nice and regular he is. Back by eight-thirty. No wonder too – he looks knackered, especially this evening. Real grim-looking today. Poor bloke. Too much travelling about. Makes him short-tempered too. But we have our chat every morning. Going home tomorrow – you're lucky you didn't miss him.'

What a bonus. Paul was smiling at his accomplice. 'I'm going to wait outside for him, but remember, this is a surprise!'

'No problem, mate. Not a word. You two have a great time. And, hey, have an umbrella – though I'll have to have it back.'

Paul went out into the street and waited in the rain. The umbrella had obviously been left at the hotel by a past guest. It was missing a spoke and advertised French tuition. What a rotten place to stay: but not even Bjørn was fool enough to eat here, it seemed. Paul wondered how Bjørn had persuaded Eva into one of their beds, but decided that he did not want to think about that further. Instead he concentrated on how Bjørn might look now. Not much changed from the pig photo, he imagined, just a little more haggard. Paul put his free hand in his pocket and held the handle of his knife, and this would have given him a relaxed air, had it not been for his persistent cough. He checked his watch, even though he knew the time. It was five.

Bjørn was upstairs. He had been in his hotel room by four-thirty. A mist had begun to form as he walked fast up from the tube. It combined with the fumes of Regent Street to mask the streetlights. In his room, the gloom was complete. He stood next to the bed with the lights off, still holding his case of shoes, seeing nothing much out of the dirty net curtains – only the pattern of light changing as cars moved. Over the damp, he smelled death.

Bjørn, there's no point to life at all.

He had seen it only once. It could well have said, 'Bob, there's no point to life at all.' Or: But. Or: Bugger.

'Bugger, there's no point to life at all.' A very lucid observation. Quite frankly, since he was having a spot of bother with his chest at the time, he may have misread it entirely.

He stood still, as if waiting for someone, then dropped his case and fell onto the unmade bed. He may have been asleep before the springs stopped bouncing.

§ 36

CHRISTMAS WAS NEAR AND MARIANNE WAS ALONE. HER HOPES had collapsed to reveal a core of despair two days before, yet this morning, in the midst of the rubble, Marianne woke with a feeling of energy that seemed to radiate from her very middle. This surprised her.

So, having risen briskly from her bed (at more or less the same time as Paul was running across an East Anglian wasteland, and Bjørn was readying himself to begin his last day as a shoe salesman), Marianne looked around her house. She turned lights on as she went, regarding each room as a doctor might examine a terminal patient.

'I'm going to sell this house,' she said. 'I must clean.'

Getting dressed in appropriately shabby clothes, Marianne was soon ready for domestic war. She went to the bathroom and put on the light, looking around to find the sort of heavy-duty chemicals that would be needed to erase all traces of Bjørn from her house; but before she got to them, she saw herself in the large mirror beside the basin. Once, she had enjoyed full-scale images of her body. Those days were gone. Recently she had survived by never looking into the mirror in the hallway, and never switching on the light in the bathroom – this bathroom, where she now stood like a brightly lit horror show.

The mirror lasted only long enough to confirm that she wore a holed top and unwashed jeans. She looked at her feet and saw worn socks that she had pulled over grey feet. 'Sod this,' she said, and left. She reappeared only moments later with a large glass vase that had been a wedding gift from Mr Olsen. It was heavy enough to require two hands to lift it above head-height and to smash into the mirror. She did so with all her force, then left, as if she had just removed a spot of dirt that had been annoying her.

In the kitchen, she collected sixty-seven plastic carrier bags – she always knew they would come in useful. Then came the purge. It began in the bedroom. All her unwashed and worn-out clothes were bagged up. So too were armfuls of wire coat-hangers; and everything that Bjørn owned or had given to Marianne, or had expressed a liking for. She donned stout shoes for the bathroom, where she crunched her way towards almost empty shampoo bottles. Handfuls of new hotel soaps went next. Bjørn had brought these back so that he could have something other than the ends of ancient bars to wash with. Then she swept and hoovered. The carpet in the living room, which had never been clean, came out altogether.

In the hallway, Marianne took off her protective shoes and binned them too. Before the end of one frenzied hour, sixty-seven bags were heaped together by the front door in an unruly crowd.

This pogrom of all her things was satisfying in only a very limited sort of way: her house might be feeling liberated, but she was still unkempt and shabby; she still wore her old clothes. Having sat for a while, looking blankly out of the window at her small garden, which itself was not so pretty, she came to her decision: and this was born from the view. She had lived here with it all this time, yet her garden was a sad-looking thing. One day of scattered effort had, if anything, made it appear worse. Some plastic pots, that had looked more like terracotta in the summer sun, were dotted around the tiny patio. One of them had fallen over in the high winds of October, and she hadn't picked it up yet.

When she and Bjørn had come to see the house, before they bought it, she had said: 'Pathetic garden, isn't it?' And she had told Bjørn that he would be amazed by what she would transform the place into. Now she would sell up, and someone else's wife could say the same: 'It's kind of empty here. Do you think they're getting divorced? Still, we'll be able to do things up easily.'

No more of this. Marianne was living the wrong life. Until recently she had been fun and prettyish. She had achieved things. What had become of her hopes? No more would she hang around for Bjørn whilst he seduced his way around Northern Europe. Times had already changed.

Going to the kitchen, Marianne made a list and decided to become, once again, the happy girl who had lived in Florence. If she could bin everything in the house, then surely she could bin the impostor who had been living in her place. She thought seriously about what she needed to help her in this task and scribbled words down in sudden bursts, until her shopping list included French exfoliaters and Swiss moisturisers; perfume, throw-away tights, elegant trousers and roll-neck jumpers; and Chinese-made shoes. This would be only a start, but she wasn't sure that Bjørn had enough money in his account for more – and he would be paying.

The morning had been consumed by cleaning and arranging, so it was well past lunchtime when Marianne took a bus to the shopping district. This use of public transport didn't seem like frugality, because she wanted to make sure that all Bjørn's money was used in the cause of her physical redemption. If there was cash left at the end of the afternoon, she intended to take a cab home.

Darkness arrived in the city, looking unlike that which fell further out. Nowhere sulked or hinted at an early night. Indeed the lights at Hansen's flashed excitedly as she entered and walked towards the ladies' department.

Determined, calculated and well-executed shopping followed. Her worry had been that Bjørn would not have adequate funds to

184

enable her to buy more than that which was totally necessary, as although her name was also on his bank account, she had only a vague idea how much it contained. This made her cross initially, but as she spent her way around Hansen's her mood lifted. She bought lingerie first, then cosmetics – these would be of limited use if she ran out of money now, but the tills still purred when they pulled in Bjørn's card, and she was able to carry on through skirts to jackets, then back to dresses. Next on to nightwear, where the femininity of her choices aroused an acute sense of loss that was only partly offset by the anticipation of a really good haircut. She booked the snip in for the next afternoon. Still the shopping continued, and she was surprised to get as far as nail pre-polish (having returned to the ground floor) without any sign that Bjørn's card was fatigued.

When Marianne had bought everything that she had come for, plus so many other things that she was becoming intoxicated by the ecstasy of it all, she was spotted by someone she knew: Henrietta Dahl. This friend from the past came right up behind Marianne and poked her in the ribs from both sides. Marianne dropped her bags.

'I see that you haven't lost your lust for shopping.' Henrietta was grinning.

'Pinkie! I thought you had moved to Berlin.'

'The locals proved to be less enticing up close.'

A serious expression was shared between them. Marianne nodded sadly.

'I'm sorry things didn't work out, Pinkie. He always was an idiot, though.'

'A fair summary.' (Pause) 'Let's get a coffee.'

They went to a chain café, which served weak coffee and nasty cakes, but did have a pleasing bar counter. Here the two sat, exchanging stories. Marianne spoke as if this last week had not happened: Bjørn was away often, not much to say about that; they had a house, but it was dark. Both girls were happier to talk about earlier times.

'Last month, I saw Ruth,' said Henrietta. 'She's got a kid!'

'Ruth with her child eh?'

There was an unexpected quiet from Marianne. Henrietta, who had been anticipating bubbles of delight, went on with increased gusto, thinking that this might help.

'Yes, a boy. Lovely thing. But the shocker was that he was totally unexpected.'

'This does happen when you're married,' replied Marianne in a new monotone.

'No, I mean absolutely *no* idea. Had a few pains in McDonald's, went to the bog, and next thing she knows, there's Eirik.'

'Surely that's not possible?'

'Well, you'd think that any girl would know, wouldn't you?'

This conversation was giving Marianne a few pains of her own. She was experiencing a disorientating buzzing of confusion in her ears. Had she been standing, she might well have fallen over.

'Are you OK, M?'

'Just not quite right at the moment.'

'You need to go home. You're pale. Go to bed early – you don't want flu for Christmas.'

'No.'

'We'll catch up later.'

Henrietta gave Marianne her card and the two parted.

Marianne arrived home from shopping to find that a Christmas tree had been delivered in her absence. It was a fine-looking thing but she left it outside where it stood, next to the garage – passing it as if Christmas was already over.

Inside the house she turned on several lights, only then putting down all the glossy bags that she had been carrying, whilst keeping hold of the one small plastic bag she had picked up on her way home, at the chemist's.

'You'd think any girl would know,' Pinkie had said; but the impossible is harder to notice. Marianne was shaking. In the taxi, on the way home, she had gone over the last months. (When could she have become pregnant? Had she really not noticed any change?) But by the time she arrived back at her house, walking past her near-perfect Christmas tree to stand here, lost in her own hallway, she didn't want to know the truth any more. She looked at her small white bag, then, having taken a breath, as if she was about to jump from a cliff into the sea, she lunged forward and ran into the bathroom.

Ten minutes later, Marianne was sitting by the living-room window, crying. The tears that fell from her were truly huge, each taking a long time to form in the well of her eyes, gathering themselves as the sounds of sniffing bounced through the emptied rooms.

One enormous tear at a time dropped, and, if she had not been looking straight ahead, Marianne would have seen that within each watery ellipse writhed images of her husband's lovers: their bodies moving in scenes brought back from the past, encouraged to wriggle just once more, before breaking on the newly exposed wooden floor.

So she was to have a child. But where was the father?

Marianne, suddenly so tired, struggled to begin thinking; she seemed about to speak several times before she managed to do so. When sound came it did so as a whisper: 'One more miracle.' The words sounded false. They waited, hovering in the air, as if unsure where to go.

Then, Marianne saw, on the damp patch left by her tears, an insect. She blinked, and when her eyes had focused more strongly she saw that the insect was in fact a butterfly. It must have come from the inside of one of those tears – there could be no other explanation – although she hadn't actually seen it emerge. She watched as it cautiously moved its wings. Having found that they worked, it flapped off into the hallway.

Marianne got up quickly to follow it, tumbling towards the kitchen, where she had seen it go, but in the hall she was passed by the butterfly, which was now off in the other direction. Marianne turned too and ran after it at a speed that suggested she thought this bright thing might be the miracle she had asked for. She almost fell as she plunged to the left and into the bedroom. Here the window was open, to allow fresh air in, and bad out. The butterfly made straight for this gap, as if it had known it was there, and flew outside.

Marianne looked from her window as the escaped miracle fluttered across the snow-covered garden. It was like watching a messenger from a warmer world. That it wouldn't live more than a minute in the cold didn't slow it at all.

When it was gone, Marianne lay down heavily and fell quickly into a dreamless sleep.

§ 37

EVA HAD BEEN VEXED WHEN PAUL HAD NOT ANSWERED THE phone on the day that he ran away. She had imagined him writing at the kitchen table and listening to the ringing: seconds passing. Could be anyone. Could be Eva. Never answer whilst you're writing.

This was a selfish attitude. Not only was he messing up the kitchen, with paper everywhere and no neatly bound end in sight to this book, his second attempt, but he couldn't even be bothered to listen to her telling him about the bird she had seen – the bird that had without doubt been a falcon.

She might have had something even more important to tell him than this. He didn't know otherwise; and he had been behaving unusually for days. They needed a talk, but apparently it wouldn't be now. She left a message on the machine: 'Paul, I'm going to be late. You have dinner without me.' Still he didn't pick up.

But on her way home that evening, Eva's attitude changed. It could simply have been that she was too tired to fight, but, separately, an unusual disquiet came upon her. The tube had emptied a couple of hours earlier, and the calm of the evening was with everyone still left. At Tower Hill she got off and walked upwards into the cold air, then, before really emerging from the ground, she headed down again, under the road, then left past the Tower, through St Katherine's Dock, across a dimly lit car park, over a canal, and down towards home. She walked quickly – at first because it was raining; then, even faster, for no reason she could explain. Her steps rang into the night.

The house was in darkness when she arrived and she saw at once, through those black windows, that everything had changed. Inside it was warm, as if someone was upstairs, asleep. She ran up to check, even though she knew really that it was not so.

Downstairs once more, and the lights are all on. They show the emptiness clearly: everything she knew has disappeared. But there are two additions to her room: one tank, brimful with brine; and an envelope too. She picks it up and looks at the stamp. The letter is gone.

Now she looks at the tank, full of the tears that no one has seen fall from her – she has filled it impressively. Its surface looks to have been mirrored. She comes close and sees that it reflects everything to come – the future, mapped out. Beneath lie the deep waters of the past. Time, it seems, cannot be represented by length or amount – somewhat less than twenty-five years appears now as an eternity. She slips in and is gone.

§ 38

THE EVENING AFTER EVA DROWNED, AS PAUL WAITED ON THE pavement, Bjørn woke in an unlit room near Piccadilly with a headache. This brought with it a welcome air of reality. He had been too tired, too far from home. No wonder he was going bonkers. Had he for a moment there thought seriously about jumping out of the window, head first? Or was that whilst he slept? He had no idea, but with his headache came sanity and hunger. Getting up, he looked at his watch, sniffed, smoothed his hair without putting on a light, then left for dinner, checking his wallet as he came downstairs.

'You're late this evening,' said the clerk as Bjørn came past.

'Perhaps. It's been a strange day.'

'Oh yes?'

Bjørn paused. 'Strange year, in fact. I can't wait to get home tomorrow.'

'Things might pick up this evening, you never know,' said the clerk, deadpan.

Bjørn smiled, nodded once, and left.

Paul had not enjoyed his evening so far. At six-thirty, the clerk had come outside for a smoke, then, seeing Paul, he had come over to try to persuade him in.

'It's freezing out here. And that umbrella's no good against the cold.' He blew out a large cloud.

'I'm fine. There's a right way and a wrong way to go about things – it has nothing to do with comfort.'

The clerk thought about this as he finished his cigarette, but had nothing to add, save, 'Please yourself.' Then he went back inside, leaving Paul as the only person on the street standing still.

Six-forty. Six-fifty. Paul was thinking of making an entirely different plan, possibly involving a late-night fire, when Bjørn came out of the hotel, down three steps, and set off into the night. Paul, recognising him immediately as the head on top of Marianne's bizarre photomontage, took down his umbrella and hid his knife inside it. It was more comfortable, held here, and he was excited that his finale would, after all, work out as he had planned.

Bjørn, though, was almost running. Why would anyone need to move this fast? He was only going to dinner. Paul was making a huge effort just to keep up; his breathing was shallow. He felt sick.

As he fought his feet, Paul tweaked his plan. He had previously imagined following Bjørn for some time, until he was standing in a crowd (Paul had thought that Leicester Square would do well – all squashed with cinema-goers); then, whilst Bjørn was unable to move, Paul would stop next to him and punch his knife through Bjørn's coat and into his stomach. Perhaps he could dig it in further as Bjørn doubled over – he could bend down too, as if his friend was ill. There may even have been time for a cinema moment, in this of all places, when Bjørn looked Paul straight in the eye and realised what was about to become of him.

This, though, might have been expecting too much. A second possibility had been for Paul to be more patient and wait for Bjørn to take some quiet side street (even London has these, whatever the time of day or year). Now alone together, Paul would rush Bjørn from behind and sever his head. His butcher's blade looked up to the job. Yet Bjørn seemed to like the squeeze: he was sticking to the well-used roads. Alleys passed, and with them other endings. Still, a chance would come. Have faith.

The reality was more vexing, though: Bjørn was running away! He had no idea that Paul was behind him, yet he still bounded off like some overactive dog. Paul knew that he would not keep up with this pace for long, so he did his best to continue lifting his feet, decided to kill at the first chance, and hoped for good luck.

They would be stopping soon, yes, not much longer. Keep going a little further. Keep moving . . .

Faith: he was right to have had it, because, as predicted, Bjørn was going to have to slow down. Just a moment more . . .

And, oh yes – here it came! His chance approached. Paul could see what was about to happen – this was the right place, his best opportunity! They were approaching Shaftesbury Avenue. How glorious to butcher Bjørn under the lights of the theatre. Yes, this was better than anything he had imagined – the end of Bjørn demanded an audience.

Having rediscovered a bit of bounce, Bjørn had been heading for Chinatown.

'Where can I get a cheap and tasty meal?' he asked himself.

'Here!' he exclaimed, waving his arms in a circle to let out some of his newfound energy. A woman walking towards him crossed the street.

'You know?' he said to her, raising his voice lest she fail to hear, 'I really should learn to cook. My father did. Then I will be able to serve up feasts for Marianne. I'll start with Chinese – we both like that, and it's colourful. Taste and colour: those are the important things, my girl. Those are the important things.'

Bjørn had almost turned round, during this address, even though his audience had broken into an uneven canter, but he had no reason to notice his would-be killer.

Paul's heart beat faster.

On sprang Bjørn. 'This is it, a new start. I'm going to call M to tell her: Bin the tins, sweetheart. It's the Emperor's lucky menu for you and me from now on!'

(More energetic striding.)

'Ah, here comes Shaftesbury Avenue. I wonder if there's a phone on the other side of Rupert Street.'

Bjørn stopped to wait for a chance to cross.

Whilst Bjørn was waiting, Paul, who had been falling behind, tried to run. Time to get moving – Bjørn must be caught. Yes, wait there. Wait! His heart skipped beats; Bjørn was only yards away.

Quickly drawing the knife, Paul let his umbrella fall. He walked up close behind Bjørn. Here was his moment, his one chance, and he would take it.

§ 39

UNKNOWN TO PAUL, HE HAD BEEN FOLLOWED TO THIS PLACE too. A gang of unlikely-looking thugs had padded along behind him, waiting their chance. Some were dressed as doctors, some as hookers, police, Vikings or clergy: standard fancy dress. None of the other people out that evening seemed to notice this motley band of assassins. Presumably they thought them to be on their way to a party: one more tasteless office night out. The group moved with impunity.

Paul came up behind Bjørn. As he approached, he spoke.

'Wait there, you git!' he wheezed, his voice no louder than a whisper. 'Here I am and I'm going to kill you!'

But Bjørn seemed not to notice – he was already crossing the road and disappearing from view as Paul hissed out these last words, and he certainly never heard them. And as Bjørn moved off,

Paul's voice was dimmed to impotent squeaks by the violence that fell upon him.

The mob was getting stuck in.

Suddenly attacked, vision blurred, Paul staggered around trying to escape these killers. He made every effort to run, to fight, but they were everywhere, even in the sky: God-sent to finish him off. As he flailed wildly around one of the gang grabbed his arm and held it ice-tight, whilst another positioned a garrotte. Some of them embraced him, crushing away until the sound of snapping ribs broke through the Christmas streets. As his heart jumped feebly about inside this collapsed cage, this wreck, Paul sank to the pavement and fell into the wet gutter, where he lay next to his knife like a fallen soldier.

Several people had seen Paul suffer his heart attack. They had watched him collapse. A man in evening dress, carrying an oblong case, came quickly and bent over the body, his own knees now on the pavement. The body was trying to speak and the man leaned close, closer . . .

§ 40

LATE ONE EVENING, SOME DAYS BEFORE CHRISTMAS, A FEW years ago, a man wearing a dinner jacket and carrying a violin headed home, cold. It was raining, but it should have been snow. He had been walking to the tube from an early-evening concert, where he had been sitting amongst the seconds (much interested in a lady's hat in the front row, and the first cellist, who was unusually lovely), when he saw a man fall. The man really might only have been drunk, and wore the clothes of a Christmastime tramp, but the violinist went to him – probably the time of year. The man in the gutter was holding a knife, and was unable to move. Without the obvious immobility, I'm sure it would have been time to run.

'Come close,' the man was saying, and the violinist did just that, ending up with a stranger's stubble rested on his cheek. The stranger seemed to think that he was already dead. The violinist assured him that he wasn't and that help was on the way. Whilst they waited for the ambulance, the stranger talked. He even perked up a bit for a while, finding a little energy before the end – wanted to tell stories about all sorts, this man whom no one there had ever met. Yet the violinist would remember this as if it was just the two of them. Everyone else, I suppose, was standing back thinking that these two were close. Norway, childhood, lovers – it all came out in one brief, fantastic mess. A life.

Later, from across the street, as the dinner-jacketed violinist watched a blanket-covered corpse being stretchered into the ambulance, he wondered who this odd man might have been. The image that remained, after the paramedics had driven off with the body, was of outsized feet. The violinist pondered this as he moved off, speeding up as he saw a gap in the traffic. He continued walking to Embankment – a fair way, but full of things to see at that time of year and better than taking the tube.

Then, at home, whilst undressing next to a running bath, he noticed a fine spray of blood on his white collar. He didn't want to be disrespectful, but he had another concert the next day, so he put it into a sink full of water and added a splash of bleach. Half an hour later it was gone altogether.

§ 41 *The white room*

FAST THROUGH SNOW, BJØRN WALKS HOME. THE AIRPORT CAB driver, this being his last job before Christmas, was keen to finish. And the snow is lying thick in the suburbs. 'I can't risk the next hill,' he said. 'Sorry, but you'll have to walk.'

Bjørn stumbles on, watching his feet disappear and reappear, and over again. And then comes his road, his house, his door. Upon opening this door he is surprised to find that it is snowing inside, too. The place has been gutted but his hallway is filled with white. Nothing is clear. He stands still and looks ahead, confused, as if he's waiting for someone. Meanwhile, the exit is being filled in.

Who knows how much time passes?

Then, through the falling snow, he begins to see past the drifts, to where someone is standing. Beyond the white was nothing, and it is here that she waits. Perhaps she has been there all the time, or has she just come? She wears a long coat, collar raised against this onslaught of remembrance. And pictured thus, it is impossible for Bjørn to tell exactly who she is. 'Marianne?'

There is no answer.

Bjørn sees the flakes fall as inevitably as passing seconds. This is turning out to be the sort of persistent snow that changes plans. If he does not move soon he may never be found. Still he waits. Time is filling the room. It appears that it has come to bury him – and it does not rush, being a seasoned gravedigger.

Yet through this wasteland she moves towards him. She has something to say, leaning closer and doing so as a whisper. But there is no sound, and soon there is no place, just an expanse of white; the couple is now only a remembered blur.

They are gone, but the snow keeps on falling.

Ⓑ *editions*

01 Erik Houston *The White Room*

Love approaches from odd angles; death too. This has something to do with why a failed artist, with a knife in the pocket of his borrowed pink trousers, comes to be waiting outside a second-rate hotel in Piccadilly for a Norwegian shoe salesman to come out.
(ISBN 978–0–9557285–1–8; 124 pp; £6)

02 Jennie Walker *24 for 3*

Do cricketers blush? What happens if the ball hits a seagull? Can the rules be changed? – questions asked by a woman with a lover, a husband and a missing son over the five days of a Test match.
(ISBN 978–0–9557285–0–1; 194 pp; £6)

03 Jack Robinson *Days and Nights in W12*

A book of idle speculation, unlikely stories and occasional history lessons prompted by dull photographs of Shepherds Bush, London W12.
(ISBN 978–0–9557285–2–5; 54 pp; £6)

04 Stefan Grabiński *In Sarah's House*

Translated by Wiesiek Powaga, these tales of the supernatural by Stefan Grabiński (1887–1936) reveal an unrecognised European master whose work is infused with a unique blend of lyricism and horror.
(ISBN 978–0–9557285–3–2; 124 pp; £6)

CB editions publish surprising books. To buy any of the titles above, visit www.cbeditions.com or write to 146 Percy Road, London W12 9QL, enclosing a cheque made out to CB editions (add postage £1.50 for 1 or 2 books, £3 for 3 or 4).